Shonagh Koea was awarded the Fellowship in Literature at the University of Auckland in 1993 and the Buddle Findlay-Sargeson Fellowship in Literature in 1997. She was a finalist in the 1995 New Zealand Book Awards with *Sing To Me, Dreamer*, her third novel. Her fifth novel, *The Lonely Margins of the Sea,* was runner-up for the Deutz Medal for Fiction in the Montana Book Awards in 1999.

Shonagh Koea
yet another ghastly christmas

VINTAGE

National Library of New Zealand Cataloguing-in-Publication Data
Koea, Shonagh.
Yet another ghastly Christmas / Shonagh Koea.
ISBN 1-86941-568-X
I. Title.
NZ823.2—dc 21

A VINTAGE BOOK
published by
Random House New Zealand
18 Poland Road, Glenfield, Auckland, New Zealand
www.randomhouse.co.nz

First published 2003
© 2003 Shonagh Koea
The moral rights of the author have been asserted
ISBN 1 86941 568 X

Text design: Elin Termannsen
Cover photograph: Jan van Huysum, Giraudon Collection, Imagesource
Cover design: Katy Yiakmis
Printed in Australia by Griffin Press

Chapter One

You know you're on the skids when you start using a duster as a bookmark. The novel Evelyn was reading was about a sergeant who killed himself, the volume a fictional but definitive analysis of his reasons for wanting to be dead. She had placed the ripped half of an old tea towel between pages 101 and 102 and set off on foot, already late, for the café at the bottom of the hill.

Yesterday it had seemed a quaintly nonconformist outing to plan: something silly and inconsequential like buying a new sunhat with a pink ribbon, like going to the supermarket and getting the better sort of groceries such as Smyrna figs or French apricot jam. Yesterday it had seemed not entirely invalid to think of what the Clarks had said. He really wants someone shorter than you are, but he's a very nice little man, they said. An ex-headmaster. With a good superannuation scheme, they said. And a double degree. It wouldn't do any harm at all to just say hello, now would it? Just to widen your circle a bit? Particularly with Christmas coming up? And she had said it would probably do no harm at all, and then, that ten o'clock would be fine. Ten o'clock in the morning would be quite an okay time to meet someone for a cup of coffee. She had a cup of coffee then anyway, she said, so she could go down the hill and say hello to him, just say hello to this man they knew, this man who wanted someone shorter, without any harm done at all.

That was what she had said, but today the truth was different. Today she had not wanted to go and say hello to a stranger. But she had no telephone number to ring to cancel the whole thing so there she was, setting off in a light drizzle that showed signs of turning to a downpour, clutching a tartan umbrella and with a fur blazer slung around her shoulders. Today it all seemed undignified, not even vaguely funny. It seemed silly. Perhaps it was merely silly to wish to spend even an hour not thinking her own thoughts, which were suddenly uncomfortably melancholy, to seize at anything to make her forget the stains of green paint she had under her nails and her stencilled bathroom that glistened like the interior of a rare and disastrous shell.

'A fur blazer?' the ex-headmaster had said on the telephone when she answered his question about what she would wear. 'A fur blazer?' We'll give him your number, her friends had said. He said he'll give you a tinkle. A what? she had answered. A tinkle. He'll give you a tinkle. He'll ring to confirm. Oh, she had said, I see — a tinkle. Already, she thought, it was plain that their terminology was entirely different, their language of clothing and words disparate.

'Yes. You'll recognise me,' she had told him when he rang, 'because I'll be wearing a fur blazer.' She listened to her own gritty little voice, wondering if he might be a greenie or just a man who knew nothing about women's clothes, nothing about women at all. Somehow she imagined suddenly that he might be a very conservative sort of man, possibly dull, perhaps mean as well, and she said, 'And my hair tied up with a red ribbon.' She waited for a moment for the small insolent extravagance of that to sink in: a piece of sudden girlish cheek produced out of embarrassment. 'Also,' she said, 'I'm quite tall. Five foot nine at least.' There was a silence. 'Five-eleven,' she said, 'in really high heels.' She waited. 'If Jennifer told you I wasn't five-eleven in high heels I can't imagine what she was thinking of.'

It was, though, quite simple to divine the meaning of it all. Jennifer wanted to get rid of her at Christmas. He rang off without leaving his own number, not even a proper name. 'My name?' he had said when she asked. 'Alan. Didn't the Clarks tell you?' But he had not given a surname, nothing she could look up in the telephone book, nothing at all.

'He'll give you a tinkle,' her friends had said, 'like we said, to make the appointment. We've given him your number and we've made quite sure he's written it down somewhere. Do hope you don't mind. How tall are you?'

'I don't know. Why do you want to know? I'm the same height I've always been. You've seen me. You know how tall I am. I'm however tall I've always been.'

'Never mind. You'd be five nine. He wants five two. As we said, he wants someone short. And you'd be a bit young. He wants someone more his own age group. But time marches on and we're all getting older by the minute, aren't we?'

'Are we?' she had said, suddenly alarmed.

'Yes, definitely. So behave in an older kind of way if you can. Try to remember you're forty-seven.' There was a silence. 'No giggling. Don't tell any funny stories. And don't go teetering along in those high heels, dear, definitely not them. Wear sensible footwear and a nice warm coat — nothing silly. Don't wear the bright pink jersey.' Another silence. 'We worry about you, you know, at Christmas. There's Christmas coming up.' Jennifer's voice chimed out the words as if she had uttered them many times before. 'We think it'd be nice if you had someone to spend Christmas with. We've told him you're five-five so wear flat shoes and sit down a lot. Crunch yourself up somehow. Keep your shoulders kind of rounded and don't sit up straight. And — oh yes — no earrings, dear, definitely no earrings. And another thing, Evelyn — don't mention Fred. Don't say anything about Fred dying and what you used to do before Fred died and all that kind of thing. Don't say anything about that. Nobody wants to know. It's just personal nostalgia, Evelyn, and it's not called for.'

'What?' But Jennifer had gone.

In the morning she had telephoned them again as clouds rolled in from the north and an oily scud broke out over the sea. It would be a rough day, she thought — an excuse not to go out. She coughed, the sound a faint experiment. Perhaps she could say she was ill. Pneumonia. Death. The reading of the will. It all stretched out before her. Hello, you've reached the Clarks' residence but no one is available to speak to you at the mom— She rang off. The answerphone was no use to her at all.

The café was at the bottom of the main street, enclosed in an arcade on a pier with shabby boutiques jostling for space and a junk shop whose owner stacked old suitcases and magazines on the pavement. She went to the post office first and waited in a long queue to buy stamps to place on fluttery airmail letters to places far away, hoping she would be too late, innocently held up so that he would go home. The sergeant in the novel wrote letters. He wrote letters home to his faithless wife and an answer hardly ever came because she was off and away, out with another man.

'We are a distant breed,' Evelyn sometimes said when she was out and the talk drifted to families and what everyone was doing for Christmas. 'Everyone has gone a long way away for some reason or another. They don't seem to be letter-writers, though I find it very easy to scribble a note. It seems a strange thing that years ago, at the beginning of it all, I was the brightest and the best and the one destined to succeed and go away and be famous but somehow I have been the one who stayed at home and looked after things.' Sometimes she did not even get that far before someone interrupted.

'Why do you have to talk about the past?' Jennifer Clark had said last week. 'I've known you for years so I feel I can tell you that you're sometimes a bore, and I mean that with all the affection in the world. Someone has to tell you, and we all think it's best coming from a loving old friend. We've talked about it, and that's what we've decided.' Or was it the week before? Time had become slightly blurred since 'Silent Night' started to be played over the intercom at the supermarket again and her thoughts had become blurred as well, as she contemplated the arrival of kind invitations, the caring telephone calls, the cards in the post that said *Our thoughts are with you even though we will be far away on holiday and cannot phone on the magic day.* Not Christmas again, she had thought. Not so soon, surely?

'I talk about the past,' she had said, 'because I don't see that I have a present.'

'Nonsense. There's always something under the tree for you, you know that, and we mostly don't ask you to dinner on the day because of all the noise and the children and so on. It's always such a fuss. I've always said you're much better to come later on, a day or so later or even as far on as New Year and then we can sit quietly and just have something cold and there's not the fuss. There's usually tons of turkey left over. We've all got more time, and it's much, much nicer. We're all more carefree then.' Jennifer tick-tacked away over the parquet floor in her Bruno Magli mules. She had become very brisk and businesslike since her second marriage to a wealthy property developer five years ago. Before that she had lived in a flatette with a shared bathroom, cried a lot and seemed more friendly.

'Yes,' Evelyn had said. 'Of course.'

'Anyway, maybe you'd better hurry off home, hadn't you?'

When she had stood up, suddenly startled, Jennifer had said, 'Well, you'll have to think about your hair, won't you, and a few things like that? Like what you're going to wear, for instance. I don't,' she said, 'think the jeans again, do you, dear?' So she had said no, definitely not the jeans and not the high-heeled shoes and not the earrings, and had gone home. In the bathroom mirror her face was palely reflected, featureless, bleached of expression and the hair thinner than she remembered it used to be.

'Perhaps a different style?' Jennifer had said. 'Give Chanteuse a call.' She had pressed a card into Evelyn's hand. 'There's her number.

She's an absolute marvel. She's done my hair for years. I think something shorter and snappier, don't you? Have a talk to Chanteuse and see what she thinks. And maybe a colour rinse, something to give you a bit of pizazz. Tell her I sent you. You could trust her with your life.'

Stanley, her Chinese hairdresser, had managed to fit her in yesterday.

'Just a trim?' He had combed her long hair over his hands before picking up the scissors. Evelyn's hair had once been the exact shade of vintage champagne but had darkened during the last decade to a colour she thought sadly was now merely pale brown. Her natural curls and ringlets, though, were exactly the same as they had always been. She found this cheering. 'Just ends trimmed up? Very good hair. Very nice hair. Good condition.'

She sat in the black plastic chair and held the clips Stanley sometimes handed to her. He ran the salon all on his own, had only one client at a time these days.

'Can't cope with pressure any more,' Stanley used to say. 'Nerves shot. Another clip? Thank you. Good.'

'We're getting along fine, aren't we, Stanley?' she would say. 'My hair's going to be okay, isn't it, Stanley? What I mean is, Stanley, things aren't so bad, are they, and my hair's in reasonable condition and it's not the worst hair you're going to cut today or anything like that, is it, Stanley?'

'Hair very good. Everything fine.' He used to gaze deeply at her reflection in the mirror as she held out another clip.

'Thank you, Stanley. I feel better now. Do you know the other day I read in a magazine that in Beijing, even now, quite ordinary people dig up pieces of Ming porcelain when they're working on the roads. There's a market somewhere on the outskirts of the city where you can buy them sometimes. People have stalls and have bits of Ming for sale quite cheaply. Wouldn't that be marvellous, Stanley, to go and buy some Ming for hardly anything? To find something really precious amongst the ordinariness?'

Stanley nodded and snipped carefully under her left ear.

'Trouble is,' he said, 'not going to Beijing.' He held a lock of hair against the line of her jaw for a long moment. 'Right length,' he said and began to cut again, and when he had all her hair clipped up on top of her head and was cutting the back, a few strands at a time, he said, 'I miss Fred. I trim Fred's beard every week for how many years? Seven years? Eight? Fred has beautiful hair. Fred is very good customer. Tears are good,' he said, watching her in the mirror. 'Tears clean eyes. Tears clean skin. Tears are good.'

Outside the café a small man was waiting. He was wearing a tracksuit vividly striped in scarlet and the short sleeves of the top showed muscular and heavily tanned arms, even though the day was freezing. A maverick cold front had brought unseasonable snow to some parts of the country in the past three days and the temperatures had suddenly rivalled those of midwinter.

'You must be Evelyn,' he said as he stepped forward. The street seemed deserted, except for the two of them. 'You're number five,' he said with terrifying clarity, 'and I've got another three to look at, one a day for the next three days. I think it's best to be honest, don't you? I don't drink tea or coffee but let's go and find something, shall we? Usually I just have a glass of water.' He ushered her through the swing doors of the arcade. 'But I'd better have something just to be sociable.'

'A glass of water? Isn't that a bit kind of cold?' The soles of her Spanish riding boots tapped desperately on the linoleum floor of the arcade like the tiny hooves of an elk fleeing before a storm. 'On a day like this?' Outside, the sea was blowing up against the seawall and a fine mist of stinging spray clouded the windows of the passage to the shops. 'Do you drink Milo perhaps? Or Ovaltine?' For heaven's sake make an effort, Jennifer had said. Don't talk about the past. Don't talk about bloody Fred and how you miss him. Been there, done that. We're all sick of hearing about bloody Fred. Fred's dead. Face it. Talk about other people's interests, not your own. You can be terribly selfish and boring. Someone has to tell you. We love you, but it doesn't blind us to the fact that you can be a bore. You have become, Evelyn, a bore.

'Ovaltine is supposed to be a healthy drink and lots of people say it's delicious.' She was pacing herself beside him now, taking slightly longer strides so she sank down further with each step and looked shorter, her knees faintly bent. Taking slow, deep breaths to a count of four, breathing out to a count of four — anything to stop the rising sense of panic and horror. It is only coffee, she thought. Only an hour, perhaps only half an hour, each word separate in her thinking like pills taken from a bottle, nothing slurred about the actions or the thoughts. It would be exactly the same, she thought, if she had decided to buy a cup of coffee in a crowded restaurant and had to share a table with a stranger. Nice place, isn't it? Yes, quite good really. Do you come here often? No, I just nipped in for a moment, in rather a hurry. How strange, so did I and, speaking of being in a hurry, I must rush.

No, he did not drink Ovaltine, he said. He never had a hot drink at all. Just the water. It was his Auntie Flo who put him off tea all those years ago when he was just a student and she had him to stay in the holidays. Have a cuppa, my dear boy, said dear old Auntie Flo, and dished up liquid brown Nugget, or something similar, in a battered teacup, and it had put him off for life.

'How interesting. Sometimes things do that,' she said as they passed the magazines and the suitcases all higgledy-piggledy by the door of the junk shop. The café was only two doors away now. 'Something happens and it puts you right off something for life. That was obviously how you got put off tea. What a sad thing. You've probably got a very sensitive nature, haven't you? Your Auntie Flo, you say? Florence is such a pretty name, isn't it? Was her full name Florence? How pretty. Have you ever been to Florence? To Italy? Are you, perhaps, a traveller? Was your Aunt Florence your father's sister or your mother's? What did she look like, your Auntie Flo?' She had tried to talk about his interests, and bought her own cup of coffee.

'I'm sorry,' she said at the counter. 'I've become very independent in recent years. I always buy my own, if you don't mind.' And he had looked perfectly happy as he waited for a little tap on an automatic drinks machine to fill a paper cup with his own lemonade.

'Small,' he said to the Chinese man behind the counter, who cocked an enquiring face. He handed over a one dollar coin. 'You have to watch them,' Alan said to her, 'or they'll charge you for a large.'

'Will they? Oh, really? Are you sure?' She was waiting while her own coffee was poured, the Chinese man's eyes dark and unfathomable. They contained, she thought, the incomparable withdrawal and isolation of another exile. 'Thank you,' she said, and gave him the money.

'He'd be five-six, five-seven — tall for a Chinese.' The ex-headmaster nodded his head back towards the counter. 'Shall we sit over here?' She let herself be led over to some round tables beside a slightly open outside door, through which rain had seeped and now lay in puddles on the floor. The view of the sea over one of his shoulders was grim and grey. 'My wife,' he said as he went, 'died sixteen years ago.'

'Perhaps she couldn't help it,' she said. She sat down on a little chair that looked lower than the others by a millimetre or two. 'Perhaps she didn't want to die but she just couldn't help it.'

'Well, I've been on my own, anyway, for sixteen years.' He sat down, faintly aggrieved, and sipped the lemonade like a bird. 'She was five-four, my wife. Maybe,' he said, the voice tentative and experimental as if he had only just had the thought, 'she might have lost an inch or two as she got older, if she'd lived. Women do, I've been told. She might have ended up five-three, five-two. Who knows.'

'Who indeed.' She watched him and thought he might be waiting for her to ask how his wife had died. Cancer, she thought, or a car accident. The silence lengthened.

'People have all sorts of interests,' she said at last, her voice very careful, as tentative as that of the café proprietor. 'Some people are very interested, for instance, in cars.' She darted a look at him. He sipped his lemonade again.

'Not me. I'm not a car nut. Not a good investment, cars.'

So, she thought, it was cancer and not a car accident.

Outside, the waves lapped against the seawall, the water oily with debris after an intermittent storm that had raged for three or four days. There had been warnings over the radio about sewage pollution.

'I went out to dinner last night,' she said, speaking suddenly, like a person jumping out of her skin. 'To quite a New Yorky restaurant. One of those long thin ones that go back a long way from the street, only one table wide. The tablecloths were all white, most wonderfully starched. It was very stylish, really. I quite enjoyed it. The food was nice, too.' Don't talk about yourself, Jennifer Clark had said. Don't be selfish. Ask him about his interests. Think of others, Evelyn. Don't talk about Fred. Say something bright and sparkling. Make yourself pleasant. Be a nice companion.

The sergeant in the novel had often gone out with others in his platoon. He got drunk with them and sang all the way back to the army post, and when he got put on a charge he charmed his way out of it. When they found him dead it had been a mystery to them all why he did it. Such a gift of the gab, the CO said. He seemed so bright until towards the end. He seldom mentioned personal matters. Someone said he had possibly taken up with a barmaid in the town where the unit was stationed but this may not have been correct.

'When did your husband die?' The ex-headmaster was unde-terred, his small hand firm upon the beaker of lemonade, his gaze cool and clear. Outside, the waves began to beat against the seawall suddenly. Perhaps a turning of the tide, she thought, a sudden swirl of water beneath the surface of the dirty sea. 'Was he a big man? Was he tall?'

'I've forgotten,' she said. 'I don't ever think about it.' You have to move on, Jennifer Clark had said. Fred is dead, Evelyn. Forget it. It's a long time ago. I can hardly remember what Fred looked like, actually, if I'm to be honest. And actually, if I'm to be very honest again, Evelyn, I'd have to tell you that Marky never really liked Fred. Marky's a mover and shaker, Evelyn, and that's why I'm where I am today. I've got a beautiful home. I can have a face-lift, a new car, a holiday any time I like. You've got to move on, dear. Move on.

'It was a long time ago,' she said. 'You have to move on, people say. People die, and you move on. You learn new skills. That's what people say.' There was another silence. 'He would have been six-two,' she said. 'Perhaps six-three. It's a long time ago. I've forgotten. He might have been only five-eleven. Perhaps I just imagine he was six-two. It could be my imagination playing tricks on me because it was such a long time ago.' She waited. 'And I've forgotten,' she said. 'I've forgotten.'

He took another little sip of his drink.

'I cook a mean pasta,' he said. 'I went to cooking classes. You get sick of eating burnt food, don't you, sick of eating carbon? I cook a mean pasta.'

'I'm sure you do.' There was a long silence. 'So there's a wonderful skill,' she said, rousing herself. Perhaps I was a little rude to say you're boring, Jennifer had said. You're just dull, that's all. Dull, dear. 'How clever of you. How marvellous. At the restaurant last night some of them ordered pasta, various pasta dishes. I'm not sure what they were but they looked very nice. I had fish,' she said. 'That was nice, too. Do you, perhaps, go out to dinner sometimes? Where did you last go out to dinner? Was it nice? Was it a nice place?' Talk about what he's been doing, Jennifer had said. Ask him about where he's been and what he's been doing. You talk all the wrong way, Evelyn. You put people off. You've got to draw them out of their shells. Right, she had said. Okay then. I'll try to talk differently.

'There's a place I go to where you can get a lovely roast dinner for nine dollars.' He took another little sip of his drink. 'It's not worth cooking it for that, not with the dish to wash and the gravy and the mess.'

'How wonderful. How clever of you.' You've got to tell them they're marvellous, Jennifer had said. You've really got no idea at all, have you? Someone has to tell you and, sadly, it's got to be me. 'I think this dinner last night might have cost more than nine dollars, but it was a business thing. I just went with various clients and associates. It was a business dinner so I didn't pay but I'm sure your roast dinner's a much better buy, this roast dinner you have sometimes. This roast dinner you have regularly,' she corrected herself to make him out to be glamorous, darting out all the time, an habitué of nightspots where magnificent sauces were served in silver jugs. She put her finger through the handle of the coffee cup and felt no warmth at all. Perhaps, by now, it would be cold, she thought. 'A much, much more brilliant buy, just brilliant. And probably much more nourishing and better all round. In those New Yorky kinds of places, well, they don't give you many vegetables, do they? They're always rather short on the greens.'

In the officers' mess there had been complaints about the food, before the cuckolded sergeant killed himself. There had been complaints about green vegetables and about an insolent waiter who was later sent to work in an army laundry in Singapore. He had died there, of starvation and maltreatment, in a POW camp. But that was quite a long time after the sergeant died, perhaps two or three years. The relief of Singapore had come too late for the insolent waiter-turned-laundryman.

'Can you cook?' He looked at her thoughtfully.

'Yes,' she said. 'I can cook.'

'I've got two children and they're both just great in the kitchen. They're both earning. My son's been living at home but he's qualified now. My daughter's just bought,' he said proudly, 'her own home. Both of them are bringing in a wage.'

'My goodness me, how splendid.' She watched him, and he seemed to be waiting for something.

'Have you got any children?' He was peering into the beaker that had held the lemonade. 'I think there's a bit of something in the bottom of this. I think there's an insect or something.'

'Don't even think about it,' she said. 'That's the best way, and then you won't upset yourself. Don't even look at it or think about it for an instant. And, oh yes, of course — you asked me about children. They're all grown up.' In a peculiar way he had embarrassed her by asking about children so she retreated, like a thrush into a thicket, into plurals. She made her only child — Edward — a plural. It seemed, somehow, easier to say they. 'And earning,' she said. 'They're earning.' Try not to talk in that silly way you've got, Jennifer had said. Try to talk in a more modern way, like other people. Nobody knows what you're talking about half the time. 'My son is six-four and he's earning. He's bringing in a wage. They're all bringing in a wage.' She sat very straight in the little chair and looked at the ceiling. A seaside café is a melancholy place on a windy day, particularly so in very early summer when the weather has turned to ice, she thought. 'And they've got a friend who's so tall that when you open the front door you're looking at his shirt buttons and you can't even see his head.'

The ex-headmaster stared at the sea.

'And he's earning too,' she said. 'Not that it really matters because he's just a friend. But I'm sure his mother's pleased.'

'I've looked at four,' he said as if she had not spoken. 'And then the Clarks gave me your name so that makes five. I thought it was only good manners to meet everyone and say hello, you know how you do?'

'Of course, of course.'

'I've been all over the place.' He named far-flung suburbs, many kilometres apart, some of them extremely hilly and perched on razor-backs.

'My,' she said, 'haven't you had a time of it.'

'I thought it was only good manners to do it,' he said again.

'And it was, it was.' She was doubling up on everything now, trying to provide an expansiveness of conversation. 'Thank you.' And when there was another of those silences she said quickly, 'Do they give you horseradish with the beef?'

'Beef?' he said. 'What beef?'

'With the roast dinners. Do they give you horseradish with the beef, and mint jelly with the lamb? At this restaurant you like — the one where you have the lovely roast dinners.'

'I don't like anything like that. Horseradish?' he said. 'Horse-radish? I don't think I've ever had horseradish. You can have mint sauce if you like, but I never ask for it. I'm not very fond of sauces. I don't like gravy. I only make it myself if my son's home. He likes gravy. But I don't bother much now, not since I found this nine dollar place. There's some kind of notice over the counter about a wine sauce if you want it, but I've never asked for it.' He coughed faintly, a little hacking sound like a tomahawk on boxwood. 'I don't drink. And I don't usually have the extras. I don't like extras.'

'How very wise,' she said. 'You're probably very wise. I think the thing I most admire in life is wisdom.'

'It's an extra two dollars.'

'Wisdom? Is it?' For the first time in the last hour she felt a faint sense of rising hilarity.

'No — the wine sauce.'

'Oh,' she said.

'The Clarks said you said "Oh" a lot. They warned me about it. They said, "She says Oh a lot but she's very good-hearted and a good little worker."'

'Oh,' she said.

'Goodbye,' he said at the doors of the arcade five minutes later. 'I've got another one to look at tomorrow.' He mentioned a bay further north. 'It's an hour's drive at least,' he said. 'I'm going through the petrol like nobody's business. I'm doing one a day so after tomorrow I've got another two. I'm not really sticking to consecutive order. You were, as I said earlier, number five.'

'Well, good luck. Take care.' It was raining by then so she snapped the umbrella up. *Bonne chance* with the pasta,' and when he gave her a little sideways glance she said, 'I mean, good luck. Just good luck, ordinarily.' The ex-headmaster tilted his head slightly sideways, birdlike and enquiring. 'I mean good luck with everything,' she said, 'not just the cooking. Just general good luck.' You and Fred, Jennifer had said, always with your heads poked in books, both of you talking away in that odd style of yours — all about books, nothing real. Get real, Evelyn, get real.

Behind them the proprietor of the café was mopping the wet floor, sopping up the puddles of rain with wide and generous movements that were as rhythmic as a dance. The handle of the mop was firmly held in his beautiful hands as an oar of a quinquereme might have been grasped on a great journey over distant oceans a thousand years ago.

'Goodbye,' she called to him, turning her back to the street outside and the ex-headmaster as well. 'The coffee was very nice. I hope business picks up for the rest of the day. Thank you.'

'They're everywhere,' said the ex-headmaster.

'Oh, I know,' she said. 'We're all everywhere, all of us, just everywhere.'

'He didn't like you.' That was Jennifer Clark ringing that evening. The day had deteriorated into a continuing storm, thunder rolling away to the north and the sky parched by lightning. 'He's just given us a bell and I thought you'd better be told. Just in case you were waiting. He said you were gushy. He said you were more gushy than he wanted.'

'Gushy?'

'Yes — gushy. He said you gushed.'

'Gushed? I did not. All I said was that a few of the things he mentioned were marvellous. You told me to say things were marvellous.'

'Not all the time, though.'

'I don't think I said things were marvellous all the time. I just used the word occasionally, just now and again.'

'He didn't like you, anyway. That's an old-fashioned way of putting it. I'm sorry, Evelyn, I don't mean to be negative, but he didn't readily identify with you. He wasn't all that impressed. You were far too tall and he wanted someone older, more his own age group, and he didn't take kindly to the clothes you wore — he said you looked unusual. His exact words to me just now were, "Is she a bit odd?" Just like that. "Is she a bit odd? I haven't seen anyone dressed like that before. She wore a fur blazer. Is she a bit arty?" His exact words.'

At the enquiry into the sergeant's death someone had stepped forward — was it one of the NCOs? Someone in the camp, anyway. I thought he seemed odd, sir, he said to the commanding officer. He seemed to have bad dreams in the night, sir. We used to hear him shouting. He seemed a bit odd, sir, that's all.

'He thought I was odd? I thought he was odd.'

'You thought he was odd?' Jennifer's voice was rising now, getting an edge to it. 'Why, pray, did you think he was odd? Why, pray, would an ex-headmaster be, as you say, odd?'

'Oh,' she said, sitting down at the foot of the stairs beside the little telephone, 'wearing a tracksuit on an outing when you didn't know the other person and it might have been nice to be tidier, having short sleeves on such a cold day, bunging on at great length about his stupid drinks and how he never drinks tea, noticing how tall everyone was and commenting on it. Being unkind to Chinese people.' There was another silence, during which she could hear Jennifer's breathing become heavier. 'And so on,' she said, 'ad infinitum.'

'He wasn't at all impressed by the fact that you hadn't gone to meet him dressed how you said you'd be. You'd said something about a red ribbon in your hair and that's what he was looking out for but when you arrived you didn't have one.'

'Oh that,' she said. 'I forgot.'

'You forgot? And I wasn't going to mention this, Evelyn, but I've checked with Chanteuse and she says she's never heard of you, that you never rang about your hair, so what am I doing wasting time like this on someone who's so ungrateful? It isn't a small thing, you know, to have a good word put in for you with a hairdresser of the calibre of Chanteuse. I know people who would kill to get an appointment with

Chanteuse at short notice. Chanteuse is ever one to be highly placed at the hairdressing champs, and that's putting it mildly, dear.'

'I don't think there's any need to shout like that, Jennifer. I went to Stanley. He trimmed up my ends. Stanley,' she said, 'understands me. I've been going to Stanley for years.'

'In the hairdressing world' — Jennifer's voice contained a harsh note now — 'nobody has ever heard of Stanley, Evelyn. As an example of your oddity your choice of Stanley, and not Chanteuse, is insane.' There was a long silence. 'You are definitely,' she said, 'becoming quite odd. For instance, you've never adequately explained why you didn't turn up to my garden party lunch that weekend back heaven knows when, or why you suddenly redecorated your bathroom and in such a silly way, too. I would have thought you'd confide in me of all people.'

'Oh that,' she said. 'That was absolutely nothing. It was of no importance. I did it all myself, just quietly on my own.' She stared at her right hand, again imagining she could still see the faint stains of green paint beneath the fingernails. 'Painting the bathroom was just a sudden whim, that's all. It was nothing.'

'Precisely my point.' Jennifer was exultant now. 'You're odd.'

In the night the thunder still rumbled from time to time, but without conviction, the storm slowly working its way over the hills and losing strength on the way. The lightning was now just an unconvincing little snap of brilliance here and there. There was nothing virulent about the weather any more. It had exhausted itself and Evelyn, exhausted as well, slept in pale silk pyjamas between white linen sheets, the bed itself covered with another piece of old white linen embroidered in white silk thread. Leaves and flowers. A mythical beast. A garland or two. Sometime in the night, perhaps in the deepest and darkest part when dreams become reality for a moment, when fancies walk, she found herself in the restaurant again. The New Yorky tables were still in their little rank, marching one at a time towards the back wall, the maitre d' more talkative than he really had been, the other guests quieter. It was more subdued, almost aqueous, and she found herself gliding forward with no worries of tripping or sitting in the wrong place.

'You've become very clumsy,' Jennifer had said. 'It's because you don't stop to think. Try to be less clumsy.' But in the dream she danced forward like a ballerina, her feet skimming the bare boards of the floor, the other diners respectful and kind, their heads bowed like acolytes as they consulted the menu, all music distant. The seat opposite hers at the table was empty this time. The dumpy little woman who had talked earnestly of men she had known and those she had slept with and what her father thought of it all — well, that woman had gone and taken her stained brown eyes with her, eyes that had seemed to have no whites, darting little dark buttons of eyes whose glances flickered here and there.

The door out to the street swung open again and a man entered. Frederick. He walked quietly through the door in his best checked overcoat, which he had bought in London, his very best coat that disappeared after the funeral from the cupboard under the stairs and people said they had never even seen it there ever, not even once. Liars, she had thought. Liars. And his suede gloves. He was wearing his best suede gloves. They had gone at the same time as the coat. Perhaps, she thought now, they had been in a pocket? Perhaps the thief with the coat also had the gloves? He came straight up to the table to sit in the empty place opposite hers, as if he had received an invitation too and had been told over the telephone exactly where to come and what to do. His eyes were dark and fine and he gave her one of those sideways glances, half smiling, that meant they would stay only as long as politeness required and then they would go away up the street, laughing, hand in hand, and about their own business. Perhaps they would go to a library or a bookshop. But she was already standing, already leaning over the narrow table to place her arms over his shoulders, her cheek against his.

'Oh, Frederico,' she said. 'Frederico. Wherever have you been? I've looked and looked for you everywhere. I've hunted everywhere for you. Where have you been? I've been waiting so long, Frederico.' And she heard her own cry echo in the night like that of the sergeant.

Chapter Two

A lot of people often waited on the pier where the café sits with its empty tables and its Chinese proprietor with the exiled and watchful expression. The timetable for sailings was clearly painted on a large wooden board where the ferry docked, but still some people never knew when the boats went. They just wandered along to the pier to wait for the next one, and it was an accommodating place, with shops, the café where Evelyn had met the ex-headmaster, an ice-cream parlour, an oriental acupuncturist whose notice in the window read, 'All consultations taken sitting upright in a chair. All massages accomplished fully clothed.'

The pier, in its brightly painted way, had an aura of innocence. Perhaps the acupuncturist with his needles and his whispered secrets of worrying ills was anxious to foster this idea, eager to preserve the childish innocence of the place, although he would know who had a rash beneath the right breast, a swollen knee with a pustule on the left-hand cartilage, a redness of the eye that would not abate even with the strongest antibiotics, a worrying and secret wart that could be shown to no one. The acupuncturist must have known all this, even though the consultations were done sitting upright in a chair and clothes were kept on, allegedly, at all times. This was what Evelyn thought.

Couples with ice-creams from the parlour walked with an air of childish guilelessness along to the end of the wharf, where the boat arrived and left, the ice-creams in the wafer cornets often in astonishing colours and held like luminous small lanterns in the hands of the brave — the vivid green of lime, boysenberry's royal purple, brilliant pink to denote raspberry, paler for strawberry. Other varieties were nearly black with melted chocolate and rum, or a rainbow of mixed jellybeans set like gems in redolent vanilla. The couples, some of them elderly and with walking sticks, inspected each other's faces for traces of cream, for dabs of chocolate, as if they were children again and needed to be clean for the short journey over the harbour to the city.

There was a childishness about the pier. Come on, Edna. Hurry up, John. Coming, Gran. Where's Auntie June? You heard the voices clearly, like a choir singing with absolute clarity, each name like a drop of water, and far below, where the piles that held the pier met the sea, the waves sucked and roared while tracts of dark water swirled. There the channels had been dredged deeper than could be imagined.

In a guidebook published the year before last there was a story of a giant stingray that was caught, but only by underwater camera, beneath the pier. In recent times, it said. Well, when was this? What did the term 'recent times' mean exactly? The guidebook said: In recent times a giant stingray of a type found only in the deepest and most distant oceans was discovered basking on the floor of the sea beneath our very own ferry wharf. This remarkable occurrence, and in the inner harbour too, was noticed only because a deep-sea diver went what is called below to check barnacle encrustations on the struts holding the wharf and noticed the giant in the course of his inspection. After eyeing the diver for some moments the stingray flapped delicately away in its deliciously frilly fashion.

This last sentence did not appear in the guidebook, whose language was prosaic. The cover said it was written by someone with a very plain name, a name unheard of in literary circles. It may have been a nom-de-plume for someone who, rightly, decided to remain anonymous.

The sentence about the stingray flapping delicately away in its deliciously frilly fashion was an invention from the fevered brain of Evelyn because the assembly of words in the guidebook saying the stingray went away was so dull. The exact words in the book were: 'After some moments of eye contact the denizen of the deep swam away.' What did a dull sentence like this mean? There was no romance there, no charm, no vividness of thought. Evelyn liked charm and vividness. The sentence was like a lump of un-aged cheese dumped on a plastic plate. There were also three clichés: Some moments. Eye contact. Denizen of the deep. They were unbecoming in a description of such a rare and wonderful creature, with its fins like an angel's wings, deciding to rest upon the floor of the sea beneath the pier where dull couples with mortgages regularly ate green or purple ice-creams, shouted at their children, waited for Gran outside the toilets and stared at souvenir tee-shirts in one of the small shops dotted along the pier's length.

The pier was destined, when rebuilt, to be a shopping Mecca, a kind of mall, but the customers proved sparse even though the opening ceremony was performed by a VIP whose speech and appearance had probably been completely forgotten. In an obscure corner of the building there was a bronze plaque to commemorate the occasion. Its lettering was so sharp and clear that it looked untouched by everything, including glances.

Most people went to the wharf to catch the ferry or to rush home after crossing the harbour from the city, a first step to going somewhere else. Their minds were probably fixed on another spot. When we get to the zoo, they might have been thinking. When we get to town. When we get to the cinema. When I get home from work. They were not thinking of the actual realities of the pier, so the shops selling real things did not do so well. The emporiums trafficking in ephemera fared better. Magazines to read on the short journey, newspapers, ice-creams to eat while waiting for the next boat — these were the big sellers on the pier.

If someone saw a sunhat that looked pretty in the little shop that sold hats the next thought to occur could be that in town there may be a better one, certainly a larger selection of hats in a bigger shop. We'll leave it till later. We'll see. You could hear the idle promise distinctly in the vague voices. We'll see about it when we come home. We might come back later. The shopkeeper turned away, disappointed, knowing they would not buy the hat later because by then they would have either bought another one elsewhere or forgotten about sunhats completely. Those for the ferry, ice-creams in hand, rushed towards the boat with joyful expressions. It was a minute early today so the tides must be good. It would be a nice journey.

In other places piers may have offered larger entertainments, bigger shops. On a pier right across the other side of the world, for instance, you could walk down the middle of the structure under a kind of ornamental veranda that was open at either side. There were seats where you could sit to take in the marine views. At the end of that pier there was a big wheel, for that was where all the big rides were to be found. There was a second pier nearby that was equally antique and much restored, officially designated an historic place. There were even theatres on these piers where you could be made to laugh by comics or cry by dramatic actors, depending on what you required. Most people chose the laughter because they were on holiday and they wanted to do something out of the ordinary. They wanted a change.

But the pier where Evelyn wore the fur blazer but forgot to tie up her hair with a red ribbon to meet the little ex-headmaster who had stoically bare arms on a freezing day and a psychological fetish about the height of other people and possibly also his own — that pier was far away from the historical associations of these other famous northern piers with their atmosphere of alleged or possible holiday debaucheries encompassing overeating, staying up late and flagrant infidelity to one's spouse.

The pier where Evelyn bought her own coffee from the exiled Chinese café proprietor was thousands and thousands of kilometres away from them. The little pier with rain leaking under a door to form a pool near the table where the ex-headmaster perched and found Evelyn too gushy — that pier was in the Southern Hemisphere where the oceans possessed warm currents, and curious sea creatures sometimes basked secretly on the floor of a harbour. The shops on that little pier were of a desultory and sporadic sort and there were no big rides, no big dipper or big wheel. Occasionally, in the holidays, a hopeful entrepreneur might place a large plastic duck, or elephant, at the end of the pier, some creature large enough for a small child to sit on and be jiggled about for a minute or two after a fifty cent coin was put in the money slot. A ride, if it were to be called a ride, of the very tiniest kind.

Sometimes some of the shops were there for only a week or two and then they were gone. According to the newspapers there was supposed to be a recession hitting the retail trade. Shops came and went from that pier at a pace that was almost hysterical.

A few of the garden seats along the pier had been damaged by vandals. People hurried to the pier for the ferries, or away from it to go home. Hardly anyone sat there to regard marine views, and if you had asked them what they thought of such things as marine views in general they may not have understood the question. Such things as marine views, on that pier, did not seem to have a great relevance.

In the Northern Hemisphere again, the marine views were thought to be excellent from the historic piers where people went to laugh or cry. The sands there, as they were called in guidebooks, were extensive, there were excellent promenades, winter gardens, an aquarium, splendid bathing, magnificent accommodation and a tower — anything anyone might require. An eight-foot shark would even gaze at you through armoured glass in an aquarium underneath the theatres if you wanted to see a shark before you ate too much ice-cream or were unfaithful to your husband, or wife. None of this bore any resemblance to what was on offer near where Evelyn lived.

A kitchen designer took premises for two weeks on the pier where Evelyn had coffee with the ex-headmaster. Then the emporium, on the second Friday after the opening, was seen to be suddenly empty, with signs of a hasty departure such as an ill-written notice placed upon the door, a cardboard carton lying on its side at the back of the shop, smaller pieces of detritus left lying on the carpet.

The shop selling baby clothes went elsewhere. One dealing in crystals and other New Age merchandise remained, but had a lot of specials on a wobbly and shabby table by its door. One or two of the junk dealers moved larger pieces of furniture into empty shops opposite their own, perhaps by arrangement with the lessors. It was difficult to tell exactly what was going on in the retail trade on Evelyn's pier. A small antique shop continued to do quite good business in the less expensive lines of old jewellery, much of it real, though the stones were small and some may have been doublets — just slices of the real gem over glass of the same colour — but they were all correctly labelled because the proprietor was meticulously honest. Quite a lot of costume jewellery from the 1930s changed hands readily there. Girls in boots bought it and decked themselves out in Art Deco cluster earrings made of silver and black bugle beads, wore their grand-mothers' lock-knit petticoats on top of each other two or three at a time and preferably of different lengths, and had imitation, or real, tattoos of roses and snakes up their forearms and thighs.

A tiny beach to the left of the pier attracted a few swimmers on fine days but it was early in the season and the cold spell as Christmas was approaching ensured the beach was empty. The other little beach, on the right-hand side of the pier, was always more popular because it was larger and sandier and the water did not become frighteningly deep so suddenly. Neither of them was ever, even at the hottest and most populated times of year, even vaguely like the sands by the antique piers that had theatres and actors and rides and comics. The stingray that once basked on the bottom of the sea under Evelyn's pier was the nearest thing it had to match any of these delights and, at the time Evelyn had coffee with the small ex-headmaster, even the guide-book that mentioned the huge creature had yellowing edges and civic authorities had decided not to order a reprint.

About a week and a half after the ex-headmaster with the short bare arms had a small-size paper cup full of lemonade with a spider on the bottom in Evelyn's reluctant company, the Chinese café proprietor branched out into a slightly wider range of food. In letters carefully formed in red chalk on his blackboard menu he wrote that chilli con carne was now available at five minutes' notice, and also lemon cheese-cake with or without extra cream, only three dollars fifty per large wedge and fresh every day, also pasta and coffee for only seven dollars per large serving (sauce unspecified), kumara chips three dollars ninety and Thai fried rice with pork six dollars fifty.

At the shore end of the pier, which was slightly like a long oriental toenail extending out into the sea from a stubby foot of land, the hills rose steeply. Along the sides and crests of these spines of quite valuable real estate, rows of Victorian (and later) cottages teetered in an untidy fashion, some much larger than others, a few even as big as merchants' houses, with large return verandas and towers from which the wives of sea captains must once have viewed the return of the fleet.

Evelyn lived in one of the smallest cottages, tucked secretly into a corner slightly below the crest of a gentle hill. After two or three days of rain the door of her old letterbox usually jammed and was almost impossible to open because of the wood swelling, but as she received little personal mail this was not a great inconvenience. The bills were always readable even if they were damp, and unfailingly required paying regardless of the weather.

As Christmas approached, this pattern of mail changed markedly and she would receive perhaps twelve or thirteen Christmas cards from people she had once known or still knew vaguely, some of the greet-ings printed on excellent paper and containing messages that were well intentioned, though brief. Once there had even been just such a card, from someone she hardly knew, purchased in New York at Tiffany's — by, possibly, a careful character who stockpiled stationery and liked it to have trademarks that made his importance plain. She had kept this, carefully wrapped in tissue paper, in a drawer of the hall table. Until it was finally lost in some kind of violent house-cleaning episode, or maybe a house move (she had moved house twice in the last few years), she sometimes looked at it in a mystified kind of way. The name written below the printed message of greeting was not a familiar one. Perhaps, she would think, it was from that friend of a friend of Jennifer's whom Jennifer had once brought to lunch unexpectedly and at the very last moment, really without an invitation. The lunch had been all right because there was enough fish pie that day to go around. She thought she remembered it, and imagined the lunch must have been reasonably okay — hence, possibly, the card purchased at Tiffany's. There had also never been another, so, again, she imagined that her own appearance anxiously dishing out that fish pie from the old pottery container and hoping it would be enough had been a brief and unimpressive thing and had been, perhaps like the pie, quickly forgotten. Was that unexpected guest with the fine taste in Christmas cards yet another short little man? she wondered now. Was the world full of the little bastards?

On the day of her meeting with the ex-headmaster a Christmas card, though not from such a notable shop as Tiffany's or made of quality paper, was waiting in the letterbox when she returned from having the cup of completely unremarkable and virtually tasteless coffee. There was still no sign of a parcel from Edward, who always meticulously sent her a gift that was both extravagant and delightful from some obscure part of the world where the postal system was sporadic and unreliable. The gifts arrived as if Christmas might be not a day but a lengthy period covering October through to May the following year. This year nothing had come, so far.

'When is Edward coming home?' Jennifer would enquire through pursed lips.

'Probably never, Jennifer. There's not much opening for his type of work here, really.'

'Musicians.' Jennifer made music sound like a crime. 'Who wants them?'

'He's not exactly a musician, Jennifer. He's a musicologist. He studies the music of obscure tribes. He works for the BBC. He makes documentaries.'

'My Jared's doing marvellously well. He sells the better sort of used car. Why doesn't Edward do something useful like that?' Another reprimand. Jared was the only result of Jennifer's first marriage, apart from a few black eyes that had now long healed and masses of bills, most of which the senders had probably had to write off.

'I don't think Teddy wants to sell cars.'

'Hmmph.' Jennifer could make her mouth look very thin. 'And how many times has he been divorced now?'

'Only once. I did really like that French girl he married but she got very lonely with him away so much. I think the marriage just sort of lapsed. I think they're still friends.'

'Hmmph.' Jennifer seemed to be waiting. 'Has he still got all that silly hair?'

'What silly hair?'

'All that long hair.'

'I think he's got a ponytail now. From the odd photo he sends I think he's got a ponytail.'

'Hmmph.'

Today's new card also had an aura of possible reprimand, as if somehow her absence from places to which she was now not invited required punishment. The card read: 'Evelyn! How are you?!?! We don't seem to have seen you for ages!! And ages!!! I must give you a ring sometime!!' (signature indecipherable).

Chapter Three

Evelyn's cottage, neat and precise when viewed from the street, possessed a wealth of curious architectural features that were not readily discernible. They were like secrets, known only by the owner or occupant. For instance, when she was upstairs, in what must originally have been just a loft, her distance from the front door was so great that she could not hear the brass door knocker, no matter how vigorously it was rapped upon the stout old navy-blue door. Yet the cottage was extremely small.

A very long, thin hall, too narrow for two people to walk side by side, led from the front door to the staircase at the back of the house. The staircase itself, more like a ladder and made of thick bare wooden planks, was extremely simple and also very narrow. Like an artery, it led to the one large upstairs room where Evelyn mostly lived, and it was through this artery that sound had to penetrate, and failed. When she was in the house most of her spare time was spent in that one room because it offered everything she needed. There was a large and very comfortable bed where the linen was always crisp and the blankets inviting. The linen was old, but had been of good quality and some of it had been hemstitched by hand with small looping threads of red cotton, and on those sheets a set of initials, much faded due to washing, was still faintly discernible in the top right-hand corner. These had belonged, she thought, to a distant relative. Apart from being far-flung her family all had a taste for good bed linen and even left it to one another when they died. The contents of linen cupboards were sometimes mentioned in wills or codicils when aunts and great-aunts, cousins and second cousins or grandmothers died.

To my great-niece, Evelyn, I leave the contents of my linen cupboard.

They knew, she often thought, that she would look after things and could be trusted with quaint valuables or even items that possessed no monetary value but had been esteemed by their owners for their quality and charm. Thus Evelyn slept in this upper room in bedding of the best quality, though extremely worn, while having nightmares about the power bill and the approach of yet another ghastly Christmas.

There was also a window seat upstairs. This ran beneath a small bay window and on this she had placed various cushions made of old silk and linen, so she could sleep there as well in hot weather. In the summer the air was full of humidity. Faint breezes from the sea, which was very close, just down the bottom of the road, did not seem to reach as far as Evelyn's cottage, tucked into a tiny and irregularly shaped section with several small rocky outcrops and topsoil so sparse and hard it was like mean icing on a stale cake. On nights when there was no breeze and the heat was so intense it was difficult to breathe, Evelyn curled up on the cushions of this window seat with the case-ments wide open. Surrounded by the scent of the night she slept as delicately as a bird. Towards morning the weather would sometimes change. A coolness would come into the air and there would be a drop in temperature; a wind might spring up, so she would awaken cold and cramped, and glad of it. Then she would creep over to the big bed to curl up again beneath a blanket and sleep once more.

Apart from the bed and the window seat the room contained

a large armchair with old velvet upholstery that felt like the skin of a seal, many books, a large chest of drawers in which she kept her clothes, and an old wooden filing cabinet with large brass handles. In this she kept her life. There were old photographs, receipts, invitations, bills, letters and some pairs of kid gloves in mauve, blue, pink, ecru. A long time ago she had worn them, but no longer did so.

Last Christmas she had found among her presents a large pot of hand cream whose label said: *Le Jardinier Crème Adoucissante pour les Mains, Protège et Adoucit les Mains Desséchées. Idéale après le Jardinage.* The prettiness of the French language, written in flowing script upon the flowery label, took away the sting of the words until she re-read them, translating them as she went. The hand cream was for work-worn hands, the hands of a gardener who toiled in the soil and had work-roughened skin in need of nourishment. So she sat on her hands or put them in her pockets as much as possible now, secretly embarrassed that her need to work in the garden to grow vegetables and fruit to eat and flowers to make her life prettier had been noted. She wished she could wear the old kid gloves in the drawer when she went out because they would have covered her clean but broken fingernails, her knuckles that often bore gashes from rose thorns, palms that were always slightly wrinkled from hard work, for she attacked the work around the cottage with a quiet frenzy. She scrubbed the steps and the small front path, washed out the mossy letterbox with household bleach, shampooed the carpets, scraped the moss and grime from the windows, painted the walls, washed the ceilings.

In the garden she dug the thin soil and made compost from any cuttings or trimmings and this she spread over the small tract of land until, slowly, it did begin to bloom. She had to admit that fact sometimes, just quietly in her own mind, perhaps on a Sunday afternoon when she had been out planting and digging all day. The section had begun to bloom. There were signs of success around the place. The house smelt of soap. The garden smelt of flowers. Most things were clean. She had sewed curtains from old velvet until her fingers were so worn they bled. She had dug and planted so much and so often out on the tiny hillside that, sometimes, she thought she might vomit if she had to lift the spade again to start work.

In the mirror her face looked back at her as it always did now, neatly oval, always pale because she did not tan easily, a faintly bewildered look about the eyes, the mouth carefully expressionless. But there were old photographs up in the filing cabinet that showed her laughing in careless mode, looking up at Frederick and laughing, turning around to smile at someone in the row behind hers at a concert interval. Dancing. Meeting people. Being met. Climbing into limousines. Wearing a pink sunhat to match a pink dress, ditto blue and beige, sometimes mauve, often black. Italian sandals. Gold chain bracelet around the left ankle. Standing beside a new car. Walking in the gate of a large house. In an evening dress with a couple of prime ministers. There were photographs showing all those things hidden away in the filing cabinet upstairs and in none of those pictures was her expression as careful and circumspect as it was now.

The person who had given her the hand cream last Christmas was a man she thought she had known well, and Jennifer had said at the time, 'Has he given you a present, Evelyn? Well, isn't that lovely — he must like you. But aren't you a funny little fish opening your presents before Christmas instead of waiting for the magic day.' She had looked at Evelyn in that hopeful and expectant way Jennifer always had, like a person waiting for confidences. Jennifer always called Christmas a magic time and a magic day. 'And professionally wrapped, too,' Jennifer had said. 'Well, my, my, Evelyn — you're a dark horse. Aren't you lucky.'

Evelyn had sat with the unwrapped and translated gift in her worn and battered hands and said, 'No, I'm not, and he doesn't like me. He doesn't like me at all. This gift — well, it's only a politeness, that's all, just a matter of business. He possibly sent his secretary out to buy a whole lot of stuff for various clients. He may have got a discount for a bulk order. And as for opening my presents early — I'm just getting one or two of them out of the way so I don't have to think about them. You know what it's like, Jennifer — the business gifts? The ones that are meaningless?'

He now slept, she knew, with the extremely plump owner of an immensely successful fashion shop that specialised in larger sizes. The woman had long red fingernails, and perhaps, seeing these daily, he might have remembered Evelyn's own worn hands when she had signed something or talked to him on matters of business quite a while ago, that was all. Or as she handed him one of those glasses of wine or a little sandwich when he had begun to visit her at home instead of dealing with her small bits of business at the bank.

In the beginning he had always brought gifts — bottles of better wine than she usually had in the cupboard under the stairs, small but specialised boxes of gourmet chocolates often in two or three colours, pâté and foreign crackers done up in cellophane and tied with a red bow. He may have a personal social system, she thought when the hand cream arrived, whereby former passing favourites were sent a last simple, and suitable, gift the following Christmas.

Perhaps her worn hands had become a familiar sight to him as she plumped up the cushions on the white linen sofa in her small sitting room, as she took a damp linen dinner napkin off a little tray of sandwiches and said, 'You can't have a drink, Charles, without having something to eat, you know. You must have one of these. I made them myself and they're only tiny. If you have one you'd hardly know you'd eaten anything at all.' And, as she followed his gaze out of the little window — she always sat him where the view was best — she would say, 'Yes, it's a pretty little place. I do think, Charles, it will be quite nice when I've finished with it,' as if, somehow, she was a confident and charming creature who often did up old properties and knew what she was doing and was not a person with broken nails, nightmares and a lurking sense of nameless horror about the electricity bill, the telephone bill and much else.

She had kept various unpresentable aspects of the place a secret from him at that time: such things as the rats that infested the kitchen walls and all the ceilings when she moved there the year before last and which had now been poisoned, the sewer line that ran beneath the top part of the garden in the upper northern corner, the broken wall along the side boundary and all the problems with drains, rising damp and the fact that the shelves in most of the kitchen cupboards sagged so markedly it was impossible to store anything on them until she called a builder in to renew them.

'When I've attended to one or two little things and done a bit of redecorating and so on, Charles, it'll all be just fine, you'll see. I should make money on it,' she would say airily, the lightness of her tone a lie in itself. He was an investment banker and that was how he talked himself. He would not really want, she thought, to hear about the rats and the other difficulties, so she would hand him a sandwich and pour him a glass of what was really his own wine, probably brought to her the visit before last, telling him some pretty but vague anecdote about how she was making Austrian shades for the upstairs windows out of gingham. She would say something like that, but nothing about the rat poison, the rot the builder had found right through to the floor joists under the kitchen when he tried to fix the shelves, or the gas leak in the bathroom that could have been serious if it had not been found in time. Nothing about any of that. Just nice pretty things, and then she would sit down in the other chair, with her pretty knees showing below the hem of her frock and her hands neatly hidden as much as possible, the thumbs turned in because they were always the most battered, those thumbs.

Everything always pretty, that was what she had attempted. She kept a pair of clean gardening gloves beside the fireplace so she could put them on to throw wood on the fire, thus protecting her fragile and battered flesh as much as possible. And even the firewood was like a series of little lies cut to length because she saved the best pieces for his visits and burned broken ends of timber and bits of rotted stumps when she was alone.

'It's a good wine,' she would say, lightly again. 'Don't you remember? You brought it to me — was it last time you came to see me? — and I promised I'd keep it for you. See? I wrote your initials on the label to be sure it wasn't used for anyone else.' And there she would be, smiling shyly and faintly in that tentative way she had, perhaps

40

wearing one of those little black dresses she still had hanging upstairs in the wardrobe: timeless garments, she always told herself. They would make her look chic, not pinched and peaky with fright about everything.

'How amazing,' he would say as he read the label on the bottle. 'An honourable woman who keeps her promises. Odd,' he would say, 'I'd completely forgotten all about it. Did I really give you this?' He would read the label doubtfully. 'Well, I suppose I must have. It's not a label I really know very well.' It was only later that she recalled his forgetfulness on these minor but telling points and wondered if he took wine and gifts to a lot of female clients who were single and not entirely uncomely if he turned the light off and grasped their scented flesh, his eyes firmly shut. The size of Frederick's estate would not have been sufficient to catch his interest for a moment so perhaps he had been resting between richer forays or even doing something he mentioned once idly in conversation.

'In my line of business,' he had said, 'you need to know how the other half lives.' Perhaps, she often thought now, that was what he had been doing, and perhaps he had given her wine of a cheaper and more ordinary sort because she was of so little real interest.

Now she merely telephoned the bank if she needed to check on anything, and asked to speak to someone else. And there were no more of her pretty notes addressed to Charles on postcards purchased from art galleries showing beauties of bygone ages wearing sumptuous garments and expressions as tentative as her own. The receptionist had very quickly grown accustomed to her change of modus and no longer said, 'Hello, Mrs Jarrold — shall I switch you straight through to Charles?'

These days the receptionist just said, 'Who are you with now? I see — I've got it here on the computer. Sharlene's looking after you now, isn't she? I'll just switch you through.' And there would be Sharlene, whom Evelyn had never met but who sounded sensible and middle-aged, talking kindly about interest rates and what she might possibly expect in the way of income from Frederick's estate for the next quarter, and, more important, when she might expect the lodgement of it in her cheque account. The news was never good. Interest rates, as always, were falling.

Even her faint attempts at catering — the little sandwiches, for instance — had perhaps been too tentative. Possibly, with regard to catering, the rich fat shopkeeper with red fingernails just emptied a packet of crackers, not even small ones, into a dish and shouted, 'Help yourself,' in a bold, loud voice that emanated from a huge mouth richly encrusted with carmine lipstick running slightly at the corners. And then, 'I've got to get back to the shop by two so you'd better hurry,' and she was already lifting up her frock to take off her size eighteen black satin knickers. Perhaps that was what Charles really liked. Perhaps it was not Evelyn's worn hands and her worn nature and her pale hair and pale face, her reticence and hesitation, that were at fault at all. Perhaps he hated sandwiches and also pale, sandwich-making, well-mannered women who secretly imagined someone may yet love them.

'He doesn't like me at all,' she had said to Jennifer last Christmas as the festive wrapping, golden holly leaves patterned on red shiny paper, from the hand cream, got caught by the wind and was whipped away across the patio. 'Not in the way you mean, Jennifer.' She had gone outside to play with the children in the garden. Jennifer said as she went, probably imagining the remark was inaudible, 'She's got to be a funny moody thing, our Evelyn, these days. She needs to make an effort.' But the effort she had made had been so foolish, so badly judged, such a terrible secret, that it seemed best to hide herself in a crowd of small children who could not even catch a ball reliably, were too young to explain clearly what the colour blue meant, or what an elephant or an ass looked like in real life.

Chapter Four

At night she would think about the sergeant. He occupied her mind long after she put the book down and placed the duster in between the last two pages she had read, put the light out and waited to go to sleep. She would be filled with a creeping weariness from the day, as kind and reassuring as one of her own blankets, but it was a sort of nocturnal foolery to trick her into thinking she could sleep through the night. There would, she knew, always be the sudden awakening at two in the morning and it was then that she would lie quietly thinking about the sergeant.

At first when he received the news that his wife had run off he was distraught. He became so distraught so quickly that his distress become immediately public; also the reasons for it. By nightfall on the day the letter arrived, everyone in the platoon knew that his wife had had an affair with another man. Whether it was written by the wife herself or a member of her — or his — family was a mystery. The novel never quite explained that. She would lie there in the darkness, the fluff of her own fine old blankets under her chin, and she would ponder this, trying to remember the exact sequence of events. Perhaps a neighbour wrote the letter: the neighbour who may have been looking after the children, allegedly for just an afternoon or an evening, while the sergeant's wife went out somewhere. But the sergeant's wife had not gone where she said she was going. She did not return. She had run off with someone, maybe an American officer who had given her nylon stockings and chocolates and much else, or maybe with the actual neighbour's husband. So perhaps the neighbour's wife had become, innocently, as much a cuckold as the sergeant. Was that how it went?

The details of the fiction were written in a blurred and very academic manner, the words sometimes very long, the language convoluted, the social psychologies arcane. Perhaps its writer wished the reader to imagine anything within a framed repertoire of betrayal. Would it really matter whether the wife had run off with a neighbour or someone else? She had run off. That was all that needed to be known, just as all Evelyn needed to know now was that the banking consultant had been attentive and kind for a while and had seemed to think she was special, but that none of that was true. He had even asked her to his office quite a while before last Christmas so he could introduce her to other people on the staff and they had had coffee and cake brought in by his secretary, as if Evelyn had been a special visitor or a very, very special friend. The staff regarded her kindly and carefully. She imagined at the time that this was because they sensed she was special to him. She wondered now if all they had thought was, 'Oh, God — not another one.'

The details of the incident — like the fat shopkeeper who may or may not wear size eighteen black satin knickers, the obscure brands of cheaper wine, her little sandwiches — were not important. Even the time was not important. It had happened before last Christmas, in the two or three months leading up to last Christmas. Now it was this Christmas — a year later. A long time. Time for someone to live and die or travel around the world several times, get married and decide on a divorce, or be picked up and then put down again. Time for anything.

But in the novel the waiter in the officers' mess knew all about the whole thing by dinnertime that night, so by then the wife's elopement must have been common knowledge even in the kitchen. Perhaps the cook had told the waiter about it as he stirred the soup. The waiter himself got into trouble over the serving of that soup. The CO said he had served it insolently, whatever that might mean, and someone else claimed that the waiter had slipped slightly on a mat and spilt a drop or two of the soup. Perhaps, they said, the insolent waiter was drunk.

The waiter remained quite detached from all this melodrama. He answered questions coolly. His voice was clipped and beautiful, his vowels perfect. Possibly it may have been jealousy about his aura of social awareness, his atmosphere of having come gradually down in the world, that caused tongues to be loosened against him. When he was transferred to another unit and went off somewhere else to be killed by the Japanese he went quietly and without a fuss, in a state of perfect dignity and restraint, all his syllables still beautifully modulated. Hardly anyone spoke of him again. He might never have existed at all. One of the officers always remembered him because they had been to school together. That was all.

Evelyn would lie in the big comfortable bed upstairs listening to the clock strike two, then three, then four, and she would think about all this. Perhaps she could go and hide where the waiter went, she would think. Could she go there? But where was it? Where exactly had he been killed? Singapore, she thought. And how could she possibly rely on someone to kill her, quickly and mercifully, when she got there? Could she hide herself in that lost place for people who know unspeakable secrets, decades after the fictional wartime banishment of the insolent waiter? And yet, in a curious parallel with the knowledge the waiter must have possessed about the officers in the mess, the only people who could possibly have the faintest knowledge of what had occurred to her would be waiters, waitresses, the girls on supermarket checkouts, taxi drivers and the staff on the door of a theatre.

Sometimes Charles had taken her to plays. Someone must have collected their tickets as they had gone in, and might remember her.

She still had one programme in a box downstairs on her desk. A line from that play had been printed on its cover, in white letters on black paper like a startled and shocked eye flashing in the darkness. *Here in this house, you lay next to me in bed and contemplated betrayal.* That is what it said and she thought of that sometimes as the clock was striking through the night and the novel about the sergeant who killed himself lay beside her with the duster thrust between the pages.

The people taking tickets at the doors of theatres must see many people, hundreds of couples, hundreds of parties, dozens of groups, she would think. Her own sudden appearance at theatres and then her equally sudden absence from the same locations for later plays would not be a shameful and noted omission. One tall man in a silk blazer with the easy air of someone fortunate and seldom disobeyed, a man with the commanding air of having spending-power — there were many such men in theatres, restaurants, bars, cafés at any given time. One more or one fewer would not be noted either, yet he probably still did the rounds of them all with the overweight shopkeeper with the long red fingernails. A fat woman. A thin woman. A big raw-boned woman who had difficulty perching on a New Yorky-type bar stool because her legs were short. A slim, pale, long-legged woman wearing a little black dress sliding delicately onto the same type of bar stool. There was not much difference, really. Staff in bars saw such things all the time. They were trained not to notice. They were trained not to say things like, 'Good evening, sir — your usual again, is it? And what would the lady like? The other lady always had a small glass of champagne but' — pause, one two three — 'what would we like this evening?' They were trained not to say things like that because remarks of that sort caused fights. The duplicity of people was laid bare by such observations and no owner of a bar wanted his real estate to turn into a battle zone. The staff were judiciously and deeply trained. They went to bar school. Thinking bar owners got psychologists in to lecture them about how to handle drunken or insulting customers, those who would not pay and the wide periphery of those who may have been up to no good in some way or another but were reasonably well tailored and were using current credit cards that did not make a red light flash when secretly checked. The secrets of her brief escorted foray out into the nightlife of the city would be safe, she thought, shut away behind the impassive faces of bartenders and waiters.

About the girls on the supermarket checkouts she was slightly less certain. She would always get a small supper ready for when she and Charles came home — perhaps little smoked salmon sandwiches or, once, she prepared lightly poached asparagus to eat before the play, a play so lengthy and enervating, so dramatic and full of horrors that it did not end until nearly midnight, a fact that was thrashed out vitriolically in the Letters to the Editor column of the local newspaper and hacked into vigorously by the same newspaper's theatre critic. He said Act Four could have been completely expunged. Parts of her own life, she thought later, needed similar treatment but that was a while later, after the telephone calls from Charles had ceased and gifts of wine and boxes of chocolates were a memory.

She had quickly cooked asparagus in an old French pan in the early evening that night, and served it — as twilight came deeply down upon the cottage — with the very best ham and thinly sliced homemade bread and butter on china plates with worn blue gilded borders. She had flitted about the kitchen in her cream satin robe and she and Charles sat quite companionably in the old kitchen, still faintly sleepy from a siesta, like children having a nursery tea before a Punch and Judy show. The play, she remembered now, had simmered with hidden violence, but they had sat in the kitchen with their asparagus and ham and with the pretty sound of silver cutlery upon porcelain as if the evening would be happy. It had seemed happy at the time. The play, though violent and sad, had finally ended. The restaurant where dessert had been booked for midnight was still shiny with silver and crisp with starched napkins at that time. The bouquet of white orchids on long languorous stems in a vase at the reception desk was undimmed by the night. If anyone had become ill, or died, in that place that evening the body had been taken away without any sign of fuss, and the architecture and decoration remained beautifully untouched by any trauma.

But there had not been another visit to the theatre after that night, nor another nursery tea at the old kitchen table. She had not had to go to the supermarket again to wander along the aisles looking for some dainty and delicious item of food, something of marvellous simplicity to give him.

The local supermarket was quite small; so small that the manager often walked along the aisles and said hello to people. There were only five checkouts and although there were different shifts of operators during the day and into each evening the faces had become quite familiar to her, as hers possibly had to them. Might there be one, she wondered now, who might have noticed how her shopping changed, might have seen that she went through a brief phase of buying ham off the bone especially sliced by the assistant at the delicatessen counter while she waited? Vol-au-vent cases plus a bag of choice mushrooms and six slices of best Italian salami? Asparagus? Peaches?

'Would you like a peach?' she had said, and he had glanced at them idly and said, 'No.' But she did not have peaches very often and they looked, to her, so delicious in their pink splendour in a pottery bowl that she said, 'Are you sure? Are you really sure you won't have a peach?' If anyone had offered her a peach she would have eaten it immediately because she had a peach so seldom.

And croissants too. She had bought croissants to have for breakfast out on the little terrace. 'I have bought croissants,' she had said, as if it might be an important thing, something special. 'No, thanks.' He was already turning away and looking at his watch.

Even Teddy had asked her about it once. Perhaps it was the time he telephoned briefly from the airport in Munich back about last May.

'Are you still having dinner with that friend of yours?' he had asked. In the background she could hear the clatter of an airport — people, voices, announcements, crowds.

'What friend, darling?'

'That chap you've mentioned once or twice. I think you said he was called Charles.'

'Oh, him,' she had said. 'No, darling, that was just something to do with the bank. It was a sort of a bank thing, a business thing. It was because of the trust funds in the bank but someone else looks after them now, someone called Sharlene. She sounds very nice.'

'Oh, good.' He had caught her trick, early on, of saying 'oh', she thought. 'That's all right then. Look, I'll have to go now. I've got my call. I'll ring you from Istanbul if I can. I'll be there for two weeks and then I'm going to Mongolia. Don't do anything I wouldn't do.' He rang off, laughing.

'Mongolia?' But he had gone. They must sing in Istanbul and Mongolia, she thought as she replaced the receiver, and there must be lost tribes of forgotten people there. Singing thinly to herself she went out to dig the garden.

Chapter Five

The garden around the cottage was on a steeply sloping lot that may, when it was originally surveyed and sold, have been the least popular in the area. Other houses sat on larger and more commodious pieces of land, mostly flat. Some might have a slight upward slope outside the back doors of the trim bungalows and villas that had been built on them but there was always space for a little greenhouse, a small gazebo, even a swimming pool here and there.

Through the large and enveloping trees she sometimes heard faint shouts of laughter, sounds of distant music from further down the road where there may have been a party around one of those pools. There was room to spread out in the other gardens and, over the years, people had planted large trees, sentinel oaks at gateways, even an avenue of birches. That led to a large villa on a slight rise in the land on the next street. Its veranda probably contained more architectural space than Evelyn's tiny cottage. Its windows, when she walked past, seemed to glimmer like the better sort of teeth in a widely opened and carnivorous mouth. The people from that house did not say hello because they flashed out their gateway, through their own avenue of trees, in a large black car that looked like a bruise against the springing green growth of the birches. That was, of course, in summer. In the winter when the birches lost their leaves the visual effect of the car against the trees was like that of a wound.

Other people in that street and her own were more friendly and gave her plants for the rocky little garden that had always been full of docks and thistles, so defeating and unprepossessing a site that no previous owner had even bothered to plant a lemon tree. Outside her back door the land rose steeply in a series of small rocky crags, everything in miniature like a bonsai garden, the cottage planted squarely only a metre or two from the street. The rest of her land, if it had not been so steep, might have been as large as a tennis court. But there were daisy bushes now, growing slowly but tenaciously among the rocky outcrops, and red geraniums struggling around the edge on the lower parts.

One or two seedling trees, of mysterious origins, had appeared near the garden shed and at the time the suppers and visits from Charles ceased they were about as high as Evelyn's once smooth and pale thighs, now much scratched by thistles and bruised by her constant clambering over the site to plant more cuttings gleaned at random from over other people's fences on her walks around the area. Whether any of these plants would grow, or for any length of time, she did not know, but she continued to tramp over even the steepest and rockiest parts of the tract of land putting them in the ground because the alternative was to sit reading the novel about the tragedy of the sergeant or to make unsatisfactory telephone calls to Jennifer whose superior air in conversation now seemed linked to Marky's meteoric rise in the business world.

Evelyn no longer truly perceived Jennifer as a friend so it was undiminishing, though very dull, to be so sternly exposed by her. There was simply no more face, no more status, for her to lose in front of Jennifer, and to converse with her was merely like pressing a cut.

Perhaps conversing with Jennifer, and thus constantly irritating her, was like running a small nail down the side of the dark limousine in the next street, the face of whose driver was only faintly discernible behind the tinted windows.

'I've only got a moment,' Jennifer would say to Evelyn, voice faintly muffled as if she might be already turning away from the telephone, 'because I've got to get a full leg wax before I meet Marky for lunch in town.' She would name some restaurant or another with a grand name. Evelyn, standing on the cottage's stony old kitchen floor with her gardening shoes left outside the back door, pulled a few thistle leaves off her jersey.

'I was out in the garden and I just thought I'd ring to say hello.' That was what she might have said. It sounded ineffectual even in her own mind before she uttered the words. And yet once, a long time ago, when Jennifer was between marriages, she had often stayed with Evelyn and Frederick and sobbed most bitterly every night, as Frederick handed her a large martini from the sterling silver shaker, now sold, that no one loved her, even her own father was a bastard and had walked out on her when she was three and she was also dramatically overdrawn at the bank and had nothing to wear. Fred would discreetly hand her a cheque in an envelope and they would already have ratted secretly around through some of the cupboards and drawers in the big house they lived in then so they could send Jennifer back home to her flatette with a good winter coat that had hardly been worn, a woollen jersey or two, some pots of homemade marmalade, a few hilariously worldly and cynical but cheeringly irreverent novels still in their own dust-jackets, and maybe a leg of export-quality lamb and a large assortment of fresh vegetables from Frederick's garden, all packed up nicely in a large basket which they would say she could keep. Plus a bottle of Bombay Gin, a few silver bangles, some spare sheets and towels and a ten-visit season ticket to the cinema. But that was then, and this was now.

'Have you rung about anything special?' Jennifer would say. 'It's just that I'm running late and I've got this appointment to have my legs done — by Michelle, you know, and she's so hard to get, you have to book in weeks ahead — before I meet Marky for lunch at Trocadero's. You haven't been there? Evelyn, you're just going to have to make some sort of effort to get out, aren't you, because if you want to shut yourself away people will just let you. Someone has to tell you. You're not getting any younger or any prettier, you know. Why don't you ring a friend, or something, and go out to lunch somewhere nice? And now I've just simply got to rush, my dear. Cheery-bye.'

There was always house-cleaning to do in the cottage. It produced dirt, she thought, automatically. Yet again she would get the scrubbing brush out ready to clean the old stone and wooden floors and to send sweet-smelling tides of soapy water into the farthest corners of cupboards and wardrobes.

'Whatever are you going to do with it?' Marky and Jennifer had said when they called briefly and unexpectedly, carrying a huge potted white cyclamen in full flower, on her first day there. The luxuriance of the plant and the desolation of the scene created a peculiar juxtaposition, Evelyn had thought. A grocery voucher might have been a more suitable gift, or even a pie. The removal truck was still down the street. There had been a problem of access to the little place up such a narrow road and the truck could not come right to the door.

'I'm going to clean it,' she had said, stalwart with exhaustion and ashen with apprehension. Whatever have I done? she had thought all day because the cottage looked even dirtier than she remembered when she bought it, and nine leaks, hitherto unsuspected, had begun to drip water in various parts of the bathroom before the day's rain had even become well established. The room was now virtually awash.

'You're going to have to do something urgently about these leaks, Evelyn, I hope you know,' said Marky as he stared at the bathroom ceiling. 'And I suggest kitchen designers immediately for all the service areas — you're just not going to be able to manage, you know, Evelyn. If only you'd asked me for my opinion I'd have told you to go straight for one of those Tuscan-style townhouses with just a patio where you could have a parsley plant in a pot and not have to bother ever soiling your hands. Central vacuum system, lock-up garage, built-in barbie, the lot, and only half a million. I could have had a word in their ear and got the developer down to four-fifty, no sweat. Maybe you might have had to go to four-seventy-five. If only you'd discussed the matter with me.' It was useless telling him she did not have that sort of money.

Jennifer had by now opened the back door onto the devastation of dock and thistle.

'Just come and take a look at this, Marky. What an appalling mess.' She was looking up at the garden. 'Evelyn, you'll have to get landscapers in, and the sooner the better.'

'Oh, Evelyn,' said Marky. 'Evelyn, Evelyn.' He was shaking his head wearily in exasperation, and also to dislodge droplets of water that had fallen onto it from the leaks in the roof. Jennifer snapped her umbrella up, indoors. There was nothing more to say. They had been silenced that day by the silhouettes of rocks and vigorous weeds viewed through rain, which had suddenly become torrential. The day had become so dark that it was necessary to put lights on in the cottage. The removal men thumped about disconsolately placing furniture against the walls and asking where her bed was to be put. 'Upstairs,' she had said. Their expressions became even more bleak and they began to drag it, in pieces, up the little stairway. The mattress jammed on the bend.

A faint light had also come from the narrow windows of a dark tumbledown villa on the rise at the back of her garden. The occupants there must also have put their lights on. In her own little kitchen the single electric bulb dangling from a cord in the middle of the ceiling showed a drift of dirt across the floor.

'Evelyn, it's so dirty.' Jennifer was brushing her coat nervously.

'It's not dirt.' Marky had been very grim. 'It's rat shit, Evelyn.' He was peering closely at the floor with his reading glasses on the end of his nose. 'Come along, Jennifer. We must go home.'

Before she had been living in the cottage a week the owner of the dark house on the rise had been bludgeoned to death. But elsewhere, she always averred stoutly, not exactly there, not over her back wall.

Certainly it was indeed the man from over the back wall who had been killed, but he had been killed at least ten blocks up the road, she had told Jennifer and Marky so many times that the words slipped out like a cliché or a childhood rhyme known off by heart. But notwithstanding the forthcoming homicide, and the rat droppings, the sight of the little house on that first day was not beguiling.

'Oh, Evelyn,' said Marky again. This was his first, and only, visit. 'Evelyn.'

'It's going to be beautiful,' she had lied bravely. 'It's like a hillside in Greece. I'll plant it in olives. In no time at all I'll be living in the dearest little cottage in the middle of an olive grove. In Greece olives grow wild on the rockiest hillsides no trouble at all. Olives will grow anywhere.' But this could have been another innocent lie because she had never been to Greece and had read such a sentence once in a magazine, remembering it now with a vivacity so desperate she even managed to smile, or bare her teeth, as she said it.

The rocky hillside had slowly responded to her care. At first the ground was so hard she found it difficult to dig holes deep enough to plant anything, even a daisy cutting or geranium slip, but she altered her gardening technique after that, whether in cunning or defeat she did not know. Now she strode carefully over the site, always wearing stout old shoes because the area was full of broken glass and old shards, and she merely made deep slits in the inhospitable clay soil with a shovel and poked plants into these cuts to survive as best they could. And, strangely, many of them did. The stalwart roots of old rose cuttings and ragged slips of daisies she snatched from over the fences of strangers did what her own tools had failed to do. They gently and inexorably wormed their way through the harsh soil, and sometimes — quite often — even flowered. So the little hillside had slowly become dotted with odd growths of this and that and between them the docks and thistles rioted in drifts and dandelions grew as big as dinner plates. To this horticultural mayhem she went forth most days with an old paring knife in her hand and a small paintbrush soaked in weedkiller in the other and slowly stabbed or murdered this vigorous growth of unwanted stuff, and equally slowly the small geranium bushes, the drifts of old daisy plants and the roses spread and grew larger in the space provided. Some of them seemed to even like the place, or become desperately accustomed to it after a few months, and one of the roses threw out huge new branches the height of a tall man, all the flowers upon them a cheerful and vigorous red. She felt this was a good sign.

'How's that garden of yours?' Sometimes Marky might be home when she visited Jennifer and would appear from his study to say hello. 'I do wish you'd said something to me, you know, Evelyn, before you jumped in there. I feel I could have advised you better. I see you in a nice neat little townhouse in an upmarket suburb, with just a court-yard, or even a balcony. At your age I feel it would have been much more sensible. As I told you at the time, for four-fifty, maybe four-seventy-five, I could have swung a good deal for you. I would have made sure my own cut would have been absolutely minimal, my dear, absolutely minimal.'

'I'm managing just fine,' she would say, stoically bland. 'Things are growing. I have a rose that's higher than a person now. It takes me a whole week of gardening to fill a bucket with broken glass. In the beginning I used to fill a bucket a day. I've sent photographs to Teddy and he says it's beginning to look like a cottage in Simla.'

'Teddy's mad, and so are you. Be it on your own head.' He would be turning away, but might perhaps turn back a little just for a moment. 'By the way, Jen told me you'd invited us to dinner but she no doubt explained, did she, that we're under very great stress at the moment with the business and various things and we're not really dining out much for the next few months. Maybe next year. Or the year after.'

'Of course,' she had said. 'I understand perfectly.' And the thing was that she did. She did understand perfectly that Marky, in the privacy of Jennifer's pink dressing room or when he had collected her in the Mercedes from the manicurist or the beautician or the hair-dresser who was the only person in the world to be qualified sufficiently to get the colour of Jennifer's hair exactly right in a totally natural manner so the grey would never be suspected, well, he had probably said to Jennifer that Evelyn was just a pain in the neck and not worth knowing and not to say they would go to dinner with her even for old time's sake because she was no use at all any more and there was never anyone there worth meeting. There was never anyone else there at all. It was all perfectly true, and there was a kind of relief in knowing it, so she put the kilogram of best blade steak in the freezer and placed the recipe for beef in red wine away in the kitchen drawer.

The docks and thistles, even the dandelions, were becoming fewer but there was still a rough growth of coarse grass that sometimes nearly smothered her new plants, so she would go out with the old hedge-clippers to cut it down. Parts of the garden, after she had done this, looked like a curiously foreign individually cut little series of lawns, possibly of a sort that could be found in India, where someone was paid ten rupees an hour to trim a lawn with nail scissors. In the midst of this secret foreignness she grew faintly pleased and sometimes, when the clippers became too blunt to cut the grass swiftly or sweetly enough, she would take them two suburbs up the road to where there was a large business with a red sign that said you could get tools sharpened. To this place she regularly took the hedgeclippers, handing them over the counter with an apologetic air because mostly the orders seemed larger, the customers more full scale.

Garden contractors were often there with their trucks and vans, running into the front office with consignments of skillsaws, hacksaws, lawnmowers and electric hedge-cutters to be attended to before midday. The stories she heard drifts of while she waited always involved urgency of an extreme sort and many customers waiting, perhaps angrily, for the hedges and lawns to be done before sunset that very day. So she would position herself at the end of the queue with the clippers tucked under her arm and would wait quietly for her turn.

The man behind the counter was usually expressionless. He listened, with equanimity, to angry stories involving abuse, huge financial loss and violence on a daily basis.

'My clients are going to kill me if I don't turn up today.'

Quite often she heard remarks of that sort.

'We'll do the best we can,' he would say, or something like that. 'Come back after lunch. I'll see what I can do.'

When it was finally her turn at the counter, intimidated by these other urgencies, she would tell him that her clippers were a very small order, she knew that, but if they could just be sharpened sometime or another that would be fine.

'Got a bit of ryegrass, have you?' he asked once as he inspected the blade, so she told him about the steep little section and how she had to cut the grass between the struggling plants so they might have room to grow. He was not a man whose appearance was easy to remember. He had darkish eyes, she thought. Medium height, perhaps. Possibly vaguely tallish. Darkish hair. Medium age. Medium everything. He seldom spoke. He just tied coded and numbered labels on the tools and, in an undertone, told the people when to collect them. Come back next Thursday. Maybe Wednesday — give me a call before you come, just to make sure. Definitely not till late next week. Those were the sorts of things he said.

But sometimes, if there were not many customers, he would ask her about the ryegrass, whose stringy growth blunted the blades of the clippers more tellingly than anything else, and she would tell him about the dandelions that were as big as plates or saucepan lids and had roots like carrots. Once, when one of the roses had a flower, she told him how the colour was brilliant pink on the first day and it slowly faded to cream until, at last, the petals dropped and lay on the stony ground like some kind of currency, a taxation paid to the soil to ensure it bloomed again. And she told him, too, about how she went out with the old paring knife in the evenings sometimes and cut off dandelions, the dried husks of the plants lying on the slope like the hoofprints of a spry little deer with poisoned feet.

The day after the meeting with the little ex-headmaster she set off again for the sharpening shop, driving gently through the back streets with the clippers wrapped up in an old newspaper on the seat beside her. The garden was a dirty place to work in. It was not a clean, dainty garden, not a courtyard garden into which one could issue in the evening in one's best clothes before going out to dinner, stainless steel trowel in one manicured hand, to dig out a tiny weed or two. It was filthy with hard-packed clay, rank weeds full of prickles, and debris that lay in drifts on the surface and beneath. Under the ground, within a spade's depth, lay smashed bottles, badly opened rusty tins, jagged shards of old china. The garden was a filthy place and everything in it became filthy as well.

She washed the clippers after each usage and then covered them with a special oil so no rust could form, but they were not dainty or sociable clippers — not French clippers like Jennifer's that could lie prettily on a car seat and not cause any damage. Jennifer's clippers had handles hand-painted with scrolls of roses, and she had matching French garden gloves embroidered with flowers and made of kid. In this rig-out she sometimes greeted guests with some remark like, 'I was just tending my wee roses and violets.' A landscape gardener who came weekly kept a few things growing quaintly in little pots near their barbecue and Jennifer occasionally put on the gloves and grasped the clippers, possibly because they had been a gift from a well-heeled client of Marky's, and stood there saying, 'I hardly know where to begin,' before taking the gloves off again.

Evelyn's clippers were real. They were large and plain, the handles worn from years of use. She drove north through the mid-morning traffic to get them sharpened again, ready for Christmas, which she planned to spend silently and alone in the garden.

The sharpening shop seemed peculiarly empty.

'Christmas rush,' said the man over his shoulder. He was sorting through things on the shelves. The place, apart from doing the servicing of tools, stocked a few lines in secateurs, garden forks from England, at high prices but, according to their labels, made of tempered steel that would last for generations and with handles of the best oak. There was sometimes a wheelbarrow or two and lawn-mowers that were nearly new and had been, perhaps, traded in on larger or better ones. 'Everyone's tearing round doing their Christmas shopping,' he said. 'They're not thinking about tools. I'm having a bit of a clean-up here. I've got a bit of time today to do things.'

Evelyn placed the clippers on the counter.

'Sharpened again?' he said, and reached for one of the coded labels, then changed his mind. 'Name?' he asked, and grasped a small piece of cardboard with string attached from a basket on the counter. He tied this to the clippers and waited, pen in hand.

'I'm usually 14A or something like that.' Evelyn stood like a child at school, hands on the counter. 'Just some kind of number and letter of the alphabet.' Perhaps, like a prisoner, she had become accustomed to being nameless, just a number, she thought. 'You don't usually put my name on the label.'

'Oh well,' he said, 'it's Christmas. We put names on labels at Christmas around here.'

'Jarrold,' said Evelyn. 'My name's Jarrold.'

'Christian name?' He had written nothing yet.

'Evelyn. Evelyn Jarrold.'

She saw him look at her worn hands with the ragged nails planted squarely upon the edge of the counter like those of a felon in a dock. I am guilty of the crime. I am not guilty of the crime. Sometimes, she would say to Jennifer, I wonder if I killed Frederick without knowing it. Did I not notice he was going to have a heart attack and should I have seen it? But I just thought he was working too hard and needed a rest. I just thought he'd suddenly got very tired and it would be rude to say something about it. I thought he'd just got tired. I tried to help him more without his knowing. I killed Frederick, Jennifer. I killed him. And Jennifer would say, Get a grip, Evelyn. Have a manicure or something. Get a grip on yourself.

'Are you the gardener in the family?' The man was inscribing her name in neat capitals on the label. 'No one else interested in gardening?

Husband not a gardener, then?'

No,' she said, 'there's only me. I'm the only one there.' Her solitary confinement, the imprisonment of work, was self-imposed. Cut by glass, scratched by tins and beaten down upon by the fierce sun, she worked indefatigably in the garden.

'So you're on your own then?'

'Yes.' He smiled, she noticed.

'Address?'

'You don't usually take an address.' Her hands were still planted on the counter. 'Usually I just come back in three or four days and they're done.' There was a silence. 'They're the only clippers I've got and I really need them so I'd never just leave them here. I'd never not collect them, if you see what I mean.'

'That's fine,' he said, 'but sometimes towards Christmas we do the odd delivery. I'm not promising anything, but we may be able to deliver. It just depends on whether we stay as quiet as we are now.' So she told him where the cottage was, spelt the name of the street and went away out to the car again with her shabby hands in her pockets.

'Will there be someone there?' he had asked. 'If we deliver the clippers will there be someone home? We don't like leaving things on a doorstep.'

'Oh yes.' She had turned back from the doorway, hands in those pockets now and her left thumb beginning to throb. The skin on her hands had become so worn it sometimes spontaneously split in ragged little tears on the ends of her fingers or the balls of her thumbs. 'I'm usually there. I'm usually at home working at something or another. If I'm not outside I'm inside, if you see what I mean. There's so much work to be done I have to be there doing it. There's only me to do it all.'

'Ah,' he said, and smiled again. 'I see. Maybe I should just take a telephone number,' he said, 'just in case.'

Back at the cottage she found a message from Jennifer, slightly breathless, on the answerphone. Please ring urgently, I've got something wonderful to tell you, Evelyn. She stood looking out the kitchen windows contemplating this remark as she put sticking plaster on her thumb. Whatever could Jennifer have to tell her that was so urgent? And why did she sound less contemptuous than usual? She sounded quite pleased, almost happy, even somewhat respectful.

Chapter Six

'Evelyn, Evelyn, this is so exciting!' Here was Jennifer on the telephone, summoned by Evelyn's ripped and stained right index finger upon the telephone's buttons. 'You're just —'

'Jennifer, I rang you to tell you that —'

' — never going to believe this.' She continued as if Evelyn had not begun to speak. 'It's absolutely marvellous news, just marvellous. Please don't interrupt, Evelyn. You're going to be so thrilled I don't know how to break it to you.' There was the sound of muffled footsteps, some faint laughter. 'But hang on a minute will you, dear — I'm just saying goodbye to someone.'

'Shall I ring back later?' Evelyn stood in the little stone-flagged kitchen looking out the open back door. 'I rang to tell you I've made arrangements for Christmas. There's no need to think of me at Christmas at all, thanks.' Liar, she thought, waiting. 'And I don't want to meet any more people you think I should meet. Please don't try to jack me up with people any more, Jennifer, because I hate it.'

A few yards away the garden spade stood propped against the garden wall beside two new olive trees that had to be planted. Perhaps, while Jennifer said a lengthy goodbye to her visitor, it would be possible to start digging a hole for one of the trees. Rampant growth on a small clump of evening primrose plants, undeterred by her mendacity, obscured the view further up the garden where red geraniums were still flowering and seedling hollyhocks had taken root ready for next summer. Things were not looking too bad.

'Evelyn, I simply don't know what you're talking about and I'm not even going to listen to a word of it. I'll be with you in a moment. You just hang on.' Jennifer seldom sounded so enthusiastic these days, so pleased. 'It's just Madame Magnolia Sharma Singh — I have to give her a cheque. She's that beautician I told you about, Evelyn, that one who does jasmine massages in your own home together with holistic beauty therapies to lighten the soul and illuminate the complexion. You really ought to try it, Evelyn. It would do you the world of good, particularly considering what I have to tell you. You're going to be so excited.'

'Am I? But, Jennifer —' But Jennifer had gone, the sound of a distant foreign voice coming faintly and mellifluously from the telephone receiver, followed by retreating footsteps and the sound of Jennifer's front door slamming. It was bound with beaten copper and had been made by an emerging artist four years ago. He now seemed to have fallen into obscurity but his hand-chased and signed front door remained in Jennifer's house. It closed, as always, with a metallic clang like the gate of a luxurious penitentiary. Maybe dealing with Jennifer had killed him or his career, Evelyn thought — or both.

'Back again.' Here was Jennifer once more, slightly breathless. 'What a marvellous day I've had, Evelyn. I feel totally rejuvenated. But what I've got to tell you is even better. Evelyn, sit down. I don't want you to get too much of a shock, pleasant though it may be. Evelyn, Alan has rung again and he says he's going to give you another chance. Isn't that wonderful? Say something, dear. Please speak.' The silence lengthened.

'Alan who?' said Evelyn at last.

'Alan who you had that lovely cup of coffee with the other day. He's told me all about it. He rang a little earlier. We had more time to talk than when he telephoned last time. He was in rather a hurry then and had a cold coming on — he's prone to sinusitis, but you can cope with that — and he thinks he may have given a wrong impression.'

Evelyn sank wordlessly down into a foetal position in a corner of her own kitchen. The ex-headmaster, she thought. The one with superannuation and the two children who were both earning. The one who drank only cold water winter and summer and who had been put off tea by his auntie.

'Evelyn, please say something. Are you there? He feels now he may have been a little hasty in his previous assessments. One or two of the other women he met seemed marvellous at first sight and he was rather taken with someone up in one of the northern bays somewhere — I'm not exactly sure where. I don't know whether it was an expensive bay or one of the cheaper ones, but never mind about all that. Further investigation has uncovered a can of worms, Evelyn, a can of emotional worms. As I said to him, "Alan," I said, "Evelyn is beyond reproach. There's absolutely no problem with gender specificity there, Alan," I said, "Evelyn is all woman. And nor would you have any burden of debt from accumulated traffic fines." One of them was an undischarged bankrupt, Evelyn, and the other one he really liked turned out to be a cross-dresser who danced all night and had an enormous number of bills to pay for traffic infringements. Instant fines, Evelyn, instant fines — he said it was totally ghastly. Evelyn? Evelyn? Are you there?'

Evelyn stared out her kitchen window. On the inland side of the little property it had proved difficult to get any plants to take root at all. The ground sloped up there extremely steeply and the soil, oddly marshy in winter, set like stone in the summer when the sun beat down on the clay. But even there she had succeeded in getting things to grow at last. A small cascade of late polyanthus made its way down the slope from the stump of a tree, long felled. She had often wondered, ever since she came to live there, at the stupidity of anyone who had cut down any tree that would grow in such an inhospitable place. Even if it had been an undistinguished thing, just some kind of unnamed and unspecific trunk with branches and leaves of the most ordinary sort, something that would cast a shade in which someone could sit, it would have been preferable to the nothingness of the site. What moron had cut it down? But flowers were growing and further up the slope, by the garden wall, there was ivy and some lilies that had green trumpet-shaped flowers, and an old hydrangea whose blooms had improved markedly in the past year. There was also a seedling tree, possibly an apple, she thought, about knee high.

'Evelyn? Have we been cut off?' Jennifer's voice in her ear had a piercing quality that was very unattractive. Evelyn wondered why, these days, she seemed to know people whom she did not like any more. She had quite liked them once, or had been indifferent to them when things were different and when she was different, but now she no longer cared at all for most of them. Sometimes, when invited out, she would look around a room at a throng of tall, bold women called Mimi, Patty, Merridee and Jane — they all seemed to have names of that sort — and she would think secretly that she disliked them all and could not even think why she had gone there or been asked at all. But she knew that when she went home someone, perhaps Mimi or Jane because they were slightly less unkind than the others, would watch her go and would sigh and say that she was not what she was. 'Did you see her hands?' they might ask, and Jennifer would spring in then. 'Those hands of hers are quite disgusting. I mean — look at mine. I've got three granite bathrooms and I have my cleaning woman only in the mornings on weekdays when Marky's at the office so I do housework sometimes and you don't see me worn away to the bone like that. It's a form of ostentation, really, the way Evelyn goes on. She just plays to the gallery. What she needs is a new hairstyle and a whole new image and she needs to take a bit of care of herself but I can't get her to listen. Evelyn is just the limit, really. One wonders why one bothers. I've been the soul of kindness to Evelyn. I've given her no end of advice and has she taken any notice of it? No.' That is the sort of thing Jennifer would say.

'Evelyn? Have we been cut off?' There was the sound of banging. Jennifer was probably bashing the telephone receiver on the hall table to make it work. 'Are you there?' Her voice was raised now.

'Yes,' said Evelyn. 'I'm here.'

'I think you could sound a bit more pleased, Evelyn, after all I've done for you.' Jennifer was into moral blackmail now. 'I've gone to such a lot of trouble for you. Had it not been for me you might never have met Alan at all, and now what we need to do is set up another meeting and get you ready for it. The first thing we have to think about is that awful hair. Now — have you ever thought of having a little colour rinse put through it? Maybe red, I thought. What you need, Evelyn, is something bright.'

Awful hair? She lifted a handful of curls with her left hand and drew it in front of her eyes. 'I think my hair's all right. Stanley says my hair's fine.' She waited for a moment. 'Frederick liked my hair,' she said, her voice suddenly authoritative like that of a general ordering the big guns to the front. 'And as for being bright — I am bright. I have an IQ of 130.'

'That's not what I mean. I mean your hair needs brightening up, Evelyn, and you need a manicure regularly and you need regular leg-waxing. That thing you use, that kind of thing like a razor but it isn't and it pulls the hairs out of your legs — well, that sort of thing came out of the ark, Evelyn. No one does that any more.'

'Does it? Did it? Don't they?' She stood on one slim and hairless leg like a shy heron.

'And it must be agony, Evelyn, having the hairs pulled out of your legs individually like that, just one at a time.'

'It pulls out several at once, Jennifer, and it's not so bad. There aren't a lot.' In her own voice she heard a faint defence for herself.

'Rubbish. Face it, Evelyn, you're in the Stone Age with beauty treatments. I'll speak to Madame Magnolia. If you're suddenly so very shy she'll come to your own home. She comes to mine but that's because I'm so terribly busy. I'm absolutely inundated with work. I simply do not have the time in a day to front up at her little salon. And there's no parking, anyway. I'll have a word with her and see if I can arrange for her to come to you. I've told Alan just the teeniest fib. I've said you're busy earlier this week with an out-of-town guest but you can meet him in two or three days. That gives us a bit of time to get you ready. We want to have you properly presented this time so he gets the right impression. And, I've saved this for the last, Evelyn — I know you're going to be delighted. He says he wants to take you to lunch at his favourite restaurant.'

'Not a roast dinner? Not in the middle of the day?'

'How did you know?' Jennifer gave a fruity chuckle. 'I just know things are going to get off on a better foot this time. You must be intellectually in tune already.' She rang off with what sounded like a faint scream but Evelyn wondered if it might have been the preliminary whine of Marky and Jennifer's fax machine on a separate line, spewing forth some message or another, possibly about one of Marky's business deals or Jennifer's charity committees or the restaurant they jointly owned in partnership with an octogenarian Greek with a drink problem. Evelyn placed the receiver back on its cradle and it rang again immediately.

'I forgot to tell you' — it was Jennifer again — 'that he didn't say a thing about how tall you are, Evelyn, so you must have done the walk right and taken longer strides so you looked shorter, just like I said. I'm absolutely thrilled to bits for you.' She paused for a moment to take a deep breath. 'And I've suddenly had another thought, Evelyn. Something needs to be done about your eyebrows.'

'My eyebrows?'

'They're far too definite, Evelyn. They need styling.'

'But I tidy them, Jennifer. My eyebrows are perfectly tidy.'

'Thinner eyebrows are in this year. I'll ask Madame Magnolia to style them for you too. I want you to be a knockout for Alan. You need a completely new image. This is your last opportunity, Evelyn, to make a really good impression and we're going to pull out all the stops.'

'But I didn't like him,' Evelyn began to say. 'What about how he looked? How he looks?' But sometime during the last few moments Jennifer had hung up again.

Chapter Seven

'So,' said Andrea as she gazed in unblinking concentration at her television screen, which was so large it was called a home cinema, 'what kind of erection could he sustain, Evelyn, and how was it?'

'Who do you mean?'

'You know who I mean. Stop being evasive, Evie.'

'Oh,' said Evelyn. 'Well, yes. Charles.' She sat silently for a few moments.

'I'm waiting.' Andrea took another mouthful of wine. From outside the windows the sound of Saturday night traffic seemed suddenly hushed. 'I'm not remotely interested in whether you thought he might be like Frederick. We've been through all that, Evelyn, dozens of times.'

'Only about six.' Defensive now, Evelyn swallowed an olive whole.

'Six,' said Andrea, 'is enough. Now, what sort of an erection did he have?'

'I'll have to sit here for a minute and think.'

Andrea was Evelyn's best friend and Jennifer disapproved of her strongly because she was a socialist with leanings to Marxism, wore rimless spectacles and vastly expensive couture clothes from such arcane establishments that the garments looked like hastily assembled dishcloths with the threads coming undone. She was a divorcee who had had a communist lover for several years, but had now given him up because he never sat with his back to a door and always slept with the bedroom light on. Andrea wore pure cotton pyjamas in mud colours, handwoven by Third World villagers who were trying to help themselves, which she purchased from boutiques so exclusive they were painted black from floor to ceiling and had no window displays.

'I mean,' Jennifer would say, 'if she's going to spend all that money why not buy something pretty?'

'That stupid bourgeois bitch,' Andrea would say of Jennifer.

'I think you mean bourgeoise, don't you?'

'Just shut up, Evelyn, and stop being so pedantic. Have another glass of wine. And what about one of these olives?'

'Righto,' Evelyn would say to all three remarks. Andrea was warm-hearted and kind, though snappy on the surface, and meant no harm. Revealing remarks involving thoughts of suicide, feelings of nameless horror, worries about money, flingettes, absences of orgasms and much else left Andrea reassuringly unshocked. Nothing startled her.

Andrea's sitting room was minimally Art Deco with a large sofa on which Andrea and Evelyn were now sitting and eating pizza out of a box from the Italian takeaway down the road. In the middle of the bare floor was a handwoven rug reputed to be a later copy, somewhat suspect, of an Eileen Gray original. Above the sofa hung a large painting almost as big as the entire wall. A brief but telling outline of a hammer, it loomed above the two women like a hoarding advertising a film about violent death. Scribbled in one lower corner of this work was a notable signature. Out in the hall was another large work, in acrylics this time, which merely consisted of a four-letter word painted in black on a yellow ground, with embellishments.

Evelyn sat with her head tilted back and gazed at the lower edge of the artwork showing the hammer. It was odd, she thought, that the two women she saw the most of were so wildly different. Her now non-friend Jennifer had such an alarmingly predictable lack of taste, the walls of her house scattered lightly with dabby watercolours of the French countryside in gilded frames, or of Montmartre, but these were mainly hung in the cloakrooms and lavatories. Jennifer did not seem to revere Montmartre. Andrea's house did not contain a single article, even a teaspoon, that was not a significant design of the twentieth century. Her entire residence, though not large, was dynamically sculptural, and often profane, in its architectural significance. More smaller acrylics upstairs also showed four-letter words. Andrea was often photographed for art magazines, her house even more so, and she lectured at two notable educational establishments on the upsurge of various political schools of thought in the twentieth century.

Jennifer often called her a cow. That cow Andrea. And Andrea said that Jennifer was a cow as well as a bourgeoise bitch. That cow Jennifer. They loathed each other from a distance, Evelyn transversing the intel-lectual, decorative and physical space between them like a messenger, mostly wearily.

When Evelyn, talkative from drinking wine with Andrea on Saturday nights, began to describe Jennifer's faux French gilded sofas and her faux marble side tables Andrea would sit with her head in her hands saying, 'Whatever can you do with a person like that? Why on earth do you know her, Evelyn?' and Evelyn would say she knew Jennifer out of habit.

'I've known her for so long,' she would say. 'She used to be nicer once. I can't think how not to know her — I've tried, and it seems too difficult. If you don't return her calls she just comes and bangs on the door. If you're very rude she doesn't even hear. She doesn't listen to anything I say. I'm not sure she actually listens to anything anyone says any more. If you slam the door on her she just thinks the wind's caught it and made it close suddenly and she tells you that you need to buy a doorstop.'

Andrea's favourite anecdote about Jennifer was the one where Jennifer's neurotic pedigree cat had been extensively sick on the pale blue carpet — something bile-ridden, black and containing fragments of cicadas — and Jennifer had rung the most expensive carpet shampooing firm in the city on her colour-coordinated cellphone before fainting. The worst thing Jennifer could find to say about Andrea was about how Andrea had no garage in which to put her car so it was left out on the street.

'I mean,' Jennifer would say, 'how disgusting can anyone get? And why doesn't she get herself a man? Why doesn't she get herself some kind of boyfriend or whatever?'

'She did have one.' Evelyn would pipe up bravely. 'She had some kind of a lover or boyfriend or something for ages, for years. But it just didn't really work out because he put politics first, second and third and if there was anything left over it was politics again and —'

'Do be quiet, Evelyn.' Jennifer would sigh loudly. 'I've heard it all before so many times. Couldn't she have compromised?'

'I don't think Andrea's one to com—'

'I'm going to have to hurry you along, dear, because Marky's due home any minute now and you know he doesn't feel comfortable when you're lolling about in that old fur coat with your jeans rolled up to the knee.'

'Mid-calf.'

'Mid-calf, then. He's just not comfortable with that little look, Evelyn, so I'm going to have to hurry you along. It's just not his scene. And what's that in your hand? Olive pips? How disgusting. Just put them here in this little Ming bowl and I'll get Mrs Thing to clear them away when she comes. And for heaven's sake, give me that glass. You look as if you're going to take it home with you, clutching it like that.'

'Andrea just wanted to be loved,' she would say at the door, but by then it was already slamming. 'That's why she got that communist boyfriend and hoped everything would be all right but it wasn't. She wanted to be loved.'

On Saturday nights Evelyn usually went around to Andrea's house to watch television. They ate bought pizza, drank a bottle of wine between them and analysed any recent horrors which usually pertained to men, sex, money, tradesmen, bills, leaking tiles on the roof and problems with the plumbing. Going to Andrea's house was far more interesting than going to Jennifer's, from which Evelyn usually returned home deeply depressed after an hour or two of being told what she needed to improve about herself. Sometimes she wept secretly on the journey back to the cottage. Just about everything she did was wrong, according to Jennifer — general attitude, psychological stance, expression, clothes, legs, hair, et cetera. From Andrea's she returned home laughing and intoxicated.

This evening Andrea and Evelyn were back into detailed scrutiny of Evelyn's unexpected fling — or flingette, as Andrea called it, because it had been so brief — with the investment analyst called Charles for whom she had stencilled her hall and bathroom ready for his second overnight visit, which never came. Andrea was the only person in whom Evelyn had confided.

Evelyn took another bite of pizza and continued to stare up at the painting of the hammer. Everything, she thought, was so very complex.

'Going up all the time.' That was Andrea again. 'I didn't know you liked it that much, Evelyn.'

It was sometimes difficult to keep up with the speed of conversation at Andrea's place, thought Evelyn as she continued to stare up at the picture.

'What's going up all the time?' she said at last.

'That.' Andrea waved a hand towards the hammer. 'It lingered around the ten thousand dollar mark for quite a few years but it's whizzing up again now since he died. Paintings are always worth a lot more once the artist dies. But I didn't know you were interested. I thought you mainly liked that kind of older stuff.' She took another slice of pizza. 'Like landscapes and portraits and watercolours of cows and that sort of shit.'

'Um,' said Evelyn and ate some more pizza. Andrea had such a nimble and volatile mind it was often best just to listen and say as little as possible.

'And you still haven't said what Charles was like. I've asked you repeatedly.' Andrea was never tactful. 'I think you're definitely being evasive.' She flicked the remote control for the television. They were watching a video of a family party of some kind, something involving Andrea's ex-husband's second family. 'We don't need to see that bit,' she said. 'You don't want to hear them singing "Happy Birthday" do you, Evelyn? Oh, God — there's Granny.' A tall, thin, elderly lady with a narrow face smiled grimly from the screen. Andrea pressed the Mute button. 'We can miss all that and fast-forward to a later bit. I want you to see Stinkerbell.' That seemed to be the name Andrea had given the second wife. 'Maybe we'll get to the part soon where she sings.' Andrea fell backwards in a mock faint. In the background of the video the trees looked extremely tropical and the sky was a vivid and electric blue.

'Which island do they live on again?' Evelyn sat staring at this silenced drama. Twenty or thirty people of all ages seemed to be milling around a large garden and there were white plastic tables under palm trees where food was being served from large brilliantly coloured dishes. As she watched, a small boy came closer and closer and finally must have pressed his face against the lens of the video camera. There was a brief and silent tussle of some kind and he ran off with his thin arms extended. He had a pale, marble-like complexion. His head was narrow and hairless.

'Just look at the little shit,' said Andrea. 'He's had all his hair shaved because he got nits. And I've already told you lots of times, Evelyn, that they live in Fiji but I can understand how you'd forget because who wants to remember?' Andrea did another of her mock fainting attacks, crumpling up momentarily in a corner of the sofa. 'So, anyway,' she said when she had recovered, 'what was the illustrious Charles like? You still haven't said, Evelyn. What sort of an erection did he have and was it okay? I mean, Evelyn, was he big or little or medium-sized or what?'

'He was so-so.' Evelyn took another piece of pizza from the box and sat with it in her hand, trying to think what everything really had been like. Andrea was always so frank, so open, yet esoteric, about everything. Her own attitude, she thought, had been very different. She had been afraid she would look ugly with her clothes off but she had managed to toss them off and away into various corners of her bedroom with an air of nonchalance that she remembered now with secret pride. Her camisole top had fallen on one of the bedposts and had, afterwards, been easy to rescue but her chiffon knickers had been sucked up the vacuum cleaner the following day by accident. They had blocked the hose and she had had to pull them out using a bent wire coat-hanger. They would not, she thought, ever be the same again. She had thought they must have completely and magically disappeared but they had fallen into a dark corner of the bedroom behind a large chair where the shadows were deepest. The resolution of this small mystery occurred only after Charles had gone off to the airport on some business trip or another. He had gone dashing out of the house with a croissant held reluctantly in one hand and his coffee left half drunk on the kitchen table because he was already late for his flight, he said, and the car he had arrived in was, at that exact moment, half an hour overdue at the car-hire firm near the airport.

He had kissed her goodbye briefly at the gate and waved frantically and, she thought wrongly, enthusiastically out of the car window as he drove around the corner, and she had never seen him again. His subsequent letters — just notes, really — were about only business, were very short and had been dictated to his secretary. There had been a brief message on her answerphone after the weekend in which he merely said, 'Thank you, Evelyn, how very nice to see you,' which could have been about anything, she thought later. He was a careful man, circumspect in his dealings, and careful and circumspect with himself, though secretly profligate, she sometimes thought now. The weekend seemed to have disappeared as if she had merely imagined it.

'Perhaps medium,' she said. 'Perhaps a faintly ungenerous

medium.' She thought for a moment or two. 'Or a larger small. But then, I haven't ever had anything much to make a comparison with. What, for instance, does the word small mean? Or large, for that matter?'

'And is it really true,' said Andrea, still fiercely pressing the Mute button, 'that he hasn't even written to you properly or anything since and that you've just had two notes about your fixed deposit from his secretary? Not even flowers or anything? Just some tiddy little message on your answerphone and that's it?'

Evelyn nodded, pizza in hand.

'Disgusting. What a bastard.' Andrea pressed another button or two and the sound returned, the picture giving an impression of greater enlargement and brightness. 'Now here we are, Evelyn. Here's where Stinkerbell sings.' The screen was suddenly filled with a large figure in black draperies. 'Hopeless clothes,' said Andrea. While they watched, the singing started. 'The voice of a crow,' she said. 'Listen to it. And a below-average IQ, do you believe it?'

'Has she got warts?' Evelyn leaned forward to stare at the television screen more closely.

'No, but thank you, Evelyn. I wish she had.' Andrea pressed a few more buttons and the screen darkened permanently. 'I don't think we need to make ourselves vomit any more, do we?' The silence was sudden and delightful. From far away Evelyn could hear a blackbird singing in a tree down the street. Perhaps a passing car had awakened it.

'Is she rich?' There appeared to be no other explanation.

Andrea nodded. 'Extremely,' she said. She picked up a nearly empty bottle from beside the sofa and dribbled the remainder of the wine into their glasses. 'This isn't bad really. Shame how the bottles run out so quickly. You've hardly got the wretched thing open and it's empty.' She put her spectacles on the end of her nose and stared at the label. 'Where did you get it?' They took turns to buy the pizza and wine.

'At the supermarket. On special.' Evelyn took a gulp from her glass. 'I never pay more than nine ninety-five.' The sharp taste of a somewhat acid and youthful semillon sauvignon blanc combined piercingly with the pizza's olives and anchovies.

'Have you choked?' Andrea gave her a few sharp slaps on the back. 'And you still haven't really said, Evelyn, what it was like. What sort of erection did he have?'

'I haven't the faintest idea.'

'Don't be ridiculous, Evelyn. You must have some idea what it was like?'

'Well,' said Evelyn, 'it was kind of okay, I suppose. It was not exactly stiff and yet not exactly not stiff either.' She took a deep breath. 'Maybe it was bendily stiff.' She thought for a moment. 'Or stiffly bendy. I haven't really got much to compare it with, like I said. I'm not used to anything any more. I've never known many people. Or men, really. I've never known many men. I've never known any men, really, except for Frederick.' She sat deeply in thought again. 'It was okay, I suppose. I can't say it was marvellous and I can't say it was bad. It went off okay, that's all I can say. It wasn't as embarrassing and dreadful as I expected it might be. He was quite kind. He spoke to me quite nicely. I slept quite well. I was surprised, really. Early in the morning I woke up and went downstairs. I made a pot of tea and took it upstairs on a tray with two pretty china cups and saucers. I imagined he thought it was an odd thing to do. He seemed surprised. He said, 'My God, I haven't had a cup of tea in bed for years.' I tied my hair up with a satin ribbon and I wore my pink silk robe that I keep for best. I'd painted my toenails the same pink and I thought they looked pretty but perhaps they didn't. I don't really know, Andrea. That's about the whole story.'

'Did you have an orgasm?' Andrea was relentless. She had once lectured for four terms on medical socialism at an avant garde polytechnic just before the then head had a nervous breakdown. Medical exactness had never left her.

'No.' In a way it was a relief to finally tell the tale of that now-distant weekend. 'But it was okay. It was not unpleasurable,' she said. 'It was quite nice. Perhaps that's going a bit far. It wasn't exactly quite nice, but it was not un-nice. It wasn't hideous. I thought maybe it would improve another time. You know, Andrea — with the ice broken it might be better next time? That's what I thought. And I was rather disappointed, really, about the whole thing.'

'About the orgasm?'

'No, no,' said Evelyn, impatient now. 'I was rather disappointed because I made such a nice batch of marmalade especially because I thought he might like some on his croissants when I got his breakfast in the morning and he didn't want any. He said he didn't like marmalade. I usually just have a piece of toast. I never have croissants. They're too expensive and they've got too many calories, but I bought some at the supermarket and had them ready to heat up. So he could have croissants and homemade marmalade. You know, Andrea — I wanted it to be a treat and really nice.'

'Evelyn, Evelyn, whatever are we going to do with you?' Andrea did some more fainting and eye-rolling. 'You're completely hopeless. And you haven't even said if his eyes were open or shut? Whether they have their eyes open or shut is a very telling thing. Didn't you know that?'

Evelyn began to feel a delicious lassitude as she drank the last of her wine.

'In the morning they were open. When he was asleep I suppose they were shut.'

'You know what I mean, Evelyn. Stop trying to fob me off. You know I don't mean were his eyes shut when he was asleep because people's eyes are shut when they're asleep and people's eyes are open in the morning. We all know that.'

'Shut,' said Evelyn at last. The numbing effect of the wine was creeping down her arms now. 'When . . . well, you know, Andrea . . . um . . . his eyes were shut.'

'That's a very bad sign,' said Andrea. 'You've always got to beware of men who make love to you with their eyes shut. You're just a baby, aren't you? Didn't you know it's inevitable that they're thinking of someone else? Maybe an ex-wife, maybe a current wife they're cheating on, maybe someone they've got their eye on somewhere and she doesn't give a toss. He was thinking about someone else. Maybe,' — Andrea had a habit of using the word 'maybe' and she was very brisk now — 'at that very moment in time he was already lusting after the fat shopkeeper and he was pretending it was her. Maybe there was something he really liked about her big fat legs and her great big fat back and her big thick arms and her big thick feet. Men,' she said, 'are really peculiar. Men are not at all like women. Sadly.' She sighed and looked thoughtful for a moment. 'I mean,' she said, 'just think of Thingummy' — Andrea sometimes called her ex-husband Thingummy — 'and that singing and the IQ and everything.' She sighed deeply again, then brightened. 'At least you've got the hall painted and you've sorted through all your nail varnish and thrown out all the stuff that's gone gooey. You've collected the dry-cleaning, shampooed the carpet in the front hall with Wondersoap and bought an Yves St Laurent deodorant instead of that Mitchum stuff from the supermarket. Did you have your bikini-line done? No? Never mind — another time.' Andrea was a pragmatist. 'You've done a lot, Evelyn. You've travelled on. Emotionally speaking you've been on a very long learning curve and you've reached a psychological destination.'

'Have I?' Evelyn sat on the Art Deco sofa, the empty glass in one hand, a piece of pizza in the other and the television screen dead in front of her. 'I just thought —' And she stopped there. She had thought Charles might be like Frederick. She had thought that someone might love her, that is what she had imagined, and it was a simplistic idea that was so absurd it was best left unuttered, particularly in Andrea's house. She had thought that someone might not only like her but love her, and it had been a ridiculous idea.

'How long had you known him?' Andrea had turned off the video of the family birthday party after the woman in black sang 'None but the Brave'. Now she clumped out to the kitchen to make coffee. Andrea's shoes always came from a bespoke shoemaker and thick soles were in this year. 'And what was the foreplay like?' From the back of the house her voice came thinly. 'Or need I ask?'

'There wasn't a lot,' shouted Evelyn. 'And twenty-five years. I've known him sort of vaguely for twenty-five years. Just at the bank — you know how it is — when Frederick was alive.'

'What?' Andrea was using the electric coffee grinder now and its noise drowned out all sound. Evelyn walked through the house and stood in the kitchen doorway.

'I've known him for twenty-five years,' she shouted, 'and there wasn't a lot of foreplay. In fact there was hardly any at all. There was kind of like none.' At Andrea's place it took only about thirty seconds to pick up the jargon and speak it authoritatively. 'It was just, you know Andrea, the whole thing sort of immediately with no preliminaries. There was no foreplay at all.' At that exact moment of utterance Andrea suddenly switched off the coffee grinder. The outcry echoed around the suddenly silent house, up the staircase, out onto the back veranda and out through the trees of the garden where spinach and herbs grew in profusion. Another house had been built next door, almost on the boundary, and from it came the sound of a window slamming shut.

Andrea had another mock fainting attack. 'That's just Wendy,' she said. 'She's like that. She'll just be having a little tantrumette about the noise from my place.'

I thought the hall looked shabby when you were here. I had not properly regarded it before then but, when I walked around the house after you had gone, everything seemed distressingly silent, and the hall was shabby, I thought. So I have painted the walls with a flat cream paint that looks like old-fashioned distemper and the old boards now have a curious charm, the roughness of the wood giving the paint a faint bloom. And I have painted a kind of mural on one wall — a great spreading tree of mythical form and proportion whose branches seem to embrace the entire house, and around the skirting boards of the downstairs area and also the bathroom I have painted leaves and flowers in French green and grey. I have gilded some of the leaves but

have left the flowers plain. What kind of blooms they are I do not really know because I invented them myself. Perhaps they are a cross between a tulip and a rose but I wanted them to be of compelling charm. The little house now looks like a forgotten wing in a foreign palace, used perhaps by servants or concubines who are not favourites.

That is what she had written to him on fine grey notepaper and at the time she had inscribed the words their hideous truth had escaped her.

This sweet message provoked no reply from Charles. After a while she ceased to wait for one.

Chapter Eight

In the morning the mist sometimes lingered over the sea, the skyscrapers of the city rising mysteriously from this as if they floated on clouds and did not actually touch the earth at all. The trees in gardens on either side of Evelyn's property dripped moisture from rain that often fell before dawn, the sound of the water on the roof like that from small fountains so at this time she sometimes dreamt of Florence where she and Frederick had once been for a holiday.

On such a morning, quite early before she had even awakened properly or had gone downstairs, the telephone rang. Christmas was now just a week or so away.

'Evelyn.' It was almost an exclamation. 'You sound odd.' There was no hello or any greeting. 'Mark here. I'm just giving you a tiny call on my cellphone.' There was a long silence. 'Evelyn? Are you there?'

'It's quite all right.' She was putting one arm through the sleeve of her satin robe. 'Yes, I'm here. I'm just waking up.'

'Waking up, Evelyn? Why aren't you up? It's nearly seven o'clock.

I've done quite a bit of business already. Made a few calls. Moved and shaken a bit. You know how it is.'

'No,' said Evelyn. 'I was dreaming of Florence.'

'Evelyn, dreaming of Florence isn't going to get you anywhere, you know. It's time to face reality. Now, I'm just giving you this little call while Jennifer's otherwise occupied. She seems to spend more and more time in the bathroom these days, but let's not go into that here. I don't want her to know I've rung so this is just between you and me and the gatepost, if you get my drift.'

'Is it?' she said. Drift? Gatepost? Whatever could he want? she wondered. It must be a long time since Marky had actually had a conversation with her except to say, 'Things going okay, are they, Evelyn? Oh, great,' even before she had time to reply. 'Shame you didn't consult me about real estate, Evelyn.'

'Evelyn, I know Jennifer's very set on the idea of you and Alan being some kind of item,' he said now, 'but just going about the city in my own little way I've come upon someone else I'd like you to meet.' The silence lengthened yet again. Sometimes, thought Evelyn, she wondered whether Mark and Jennifer ever noticed that their monologues with her provoked so few replies. Possibly they did not want a response or they imagined none was necessary. 'Maybe we could arrange this discreetly without Jennifer knowing, do you think?' He seemed to be waiting. 'Hmmm? Evelyn? Are you there?'

'Yes, but —'

'I'll just give you a few facts and figures about this guy. He happens to be a client of mine. Tallish. Fifty-five-ish. Not a bean because his partner absconded with the lot, Evelyn, and by the lot I mean the lot. He's very involved at the moment with a frightful court case trying to get some of the money back — no doubt you've read about it in the papers.'

'No, I haven't, but —'

'Evelyn, please don't interrupt when I'm talking. Interrupting is a very un-Feng Shui thing to do. Now, getting back to this man who, just for the sake of convenience, I'm going to call Paul. Well, Paul's having a very bad time of it as we speak, but he's a lawyer, Evelyn, a real live professional man with actual genuine qualifications, Evelyn, so I think that's something that could be considered. Evelyn? Are you there? I've told him I know this woman who could scrub up quite nicely if she made an effort. What you need, Evelyn, is someone to get the old juices flowing. Pop into one of those boutiques in High Street and buy the odd little outfit. Maybe something in an animal print, but this is just the vaguest suggestion. You haven't got bad legs — don't think I haven't noticed. Maybe black tights, I think, or fishnets — they're very in this year, according to all these magazines around the house that Jen spends hours gazing at. Never reads any of the articles, I might add — just looks at the bloody pictures. If you got one of those new haircuts like Jen thinks you should have, and had a colour rinse put through — she thinks more auburn but I feel maybe go the whole way, Evelyn, go blonde. Really take the bull by the horns and begin to live. Anyway, what I've been thinking is that when Paul gets free of this huge court case I'll put on a little business lunch to introduce you. If I have it at the club it should be tax deductible; we can put you down as a partner's wife or something, worry not. That's my game plan. I could even say you were someone's secretary, I suppose, but that's just a minor detail and we can settle that later, more towards the time.'

The silence seemed endless. Outside the windows of the cottage the mist had cleared and the skyscrapers now looked firmly rooted in the ground. There was even the sound of distant traffic.

'Did his wife take all his money?' When Evelyn finally spoke her voice sounded unused, even to her. In the years she had lived alone it seemed to her that she had heard the sad tale of men whose wives had taken all their money so many times it made her want to scream.

'No, no, Evelyn, you've got it all wrong. His partner took all his money — his business partner, some bastard in a snappy suit who went to all the right schools and now he's done a bunk. Wore the right ties. Drove a BMW. We all thought he was kosher. Not so, sadly. There's this huge court case Paul's working on at the moment trying to get some back but the poor chap's gone environmental, Evelyn. We think it's the strain. He's started caring about the world. He's gone to live in the country on a patch of mud he's bought with what he's got left. There's some kind of shack on it — the roof's shot, the floor's shot, but he's happy there and he says he loves it. No, Evelyn — he's never been married. No children, no ex-wives, no child support: ideal for you, Evelyn, I would have thought, and a lawyer too. The problem with him — as I see it — is that he takes on all these greenie cases about pollution so he really doesn't earn the big buck. Sometimes he doesn't even charge them and I've said to him, "Paul," I've said, "do not go down this track, I beg of you." He really cares about the world, Evelyn, and I've said to him, "Please, Paul, do not do this. The world can look after itself, Paul," I've said. "What you need to do is look after Numero Uno." What he needs is a good sensible wife — someone who can live in the country, doesn't want much, won't cause any trouble, can cook and keep quiet and won't have men hanging around causing any fights or bother or breaking his heart or wanting to give cocktail parties or anything like that because, Evelyn, I'm telling you straight here — this is a man right at the end of his rope. He's begun to care passionately about ducks. I feel it's a very bad sign, Evelyn. Are you listening? When I thought about it the name that came immediately into my mind was yours, Evelyn. Evelyn, I thought. Ideal. Just get yourself tizzied up a bit for starters to get the ball rolling and maybe when you go to live in the country you can let it all hang out. No need to bother then, Evelyn. You could even buy those Indian muslin guru frocks from op-shops to wear on the farm — no one would notice, Evelyn. You'd be quite free. I'm just suggesting the blonde bit to get him interested.'

'Oh,' said Evelyn.

'And another thing, Evelyn — he grows potatoes. He's got a couple of paddocks in spuds around the shack, and when I say shack what I really mean is one of those little old country cottages that could be quite nice if it had money spent on it. Now, you're as fit as a fiddle. You could easily whiz around, no sweat, and dig the potatoes and all sorts of things like that while he's away dealing with the Greens. You could sell that place of yours and spend the money fixing up Paul's place. You're a dab hand with a paintbrush, so Jennifer tells me. You could even paint it in your spare time. Just the life for you, Evelyn — the great outdoors, fresh air, a professional man, what more could you want? We could come out every Christmas and you could chuck half a lamb on the barbie. Maybe you could even grow a few grapes and make your own wine and have a cow for your own milk and cream. What fun, Evelyn. You'd love it.'

Wordless, Evelyn clutched the telephone receiver. From the other end of the line came the sound of distant water running, a door slamming, strangely slow approaching footsteps. Jennifer usually had a very quick tread. How odd, thought Evelyn.

'I'll have to go soon.' Mark's voice lowered to a whisper. 'Jennifer's showing signs of coming out of the bathroom. Now, not a word about this to anyone. It can just be between the two of us. Jennifer's mad on the idea of getting you all coupled up with that little wimp Alan who doesn't even drink tea but what I say is — Paul's your man and don't forget it. You'd be marvellous out in the country. Just what he needs. I'll put in a good word for you. I'll say you're a good little worker and you can make a meal out of nothing. Oh, and by the way, I think I owe you a sort of apology about that son of yours. I know I'm always saying he's a no-good hippie bastard with long hair who goes around the world listening to illiterate nongs with no clothes on tooting on nose flutes or whatever, but Jennifer says he's got a doctorate in music and it isn't exactly like that. But if he's got a doctorate in music couldn't he change over somehow and get a doctorate in something there'd be more money in? Cosmetic surgery's all the thing at the moment. A friend of a friend of mine's making mega-money on Botox. Just a suggestion, my dear, from a good friend. Please do believe me when I say I have your best interests at heart.' He rang off quickly.

Evelyn stood holding the telephone and staring out the window. It looked like being a hell of a Christmas.

Chapter Nine

If the insoluble horror of how Christmas could be managed were turned into a piece of architecture it would be a bathroom, Evelyn decided. Even the noises of the plumbing in such a room could encapsulate her own quiet anguish. Mysterious gurgling, distant cataracts, dripping, groaning sounds coming from the old cistern, sepulchral bubblings from the water tank inside the roof — these would cover the emotional territory of it all, she thought.

She was lying in bed early the following morning studying the ceiling as if it may contain some clue — even a map — of how to command her days until Christmas, and maybe even until long after the festive season was over. It was the days after Christmas — Christmas itself having used up all her energies — that usually provided the true test. Some years, since Frederick died, the actual day of Christmas had been managed not too badly, but after Christmas she would feel a sense of nameless and rising desolation that was almost insupportable.

The ceiling of her bedroom contained no true clue about the

management of all this, but there was something faintly alarming about the soaring roof beams, surely needlessly extravagant in a house so small and perhaps a sign that she should not even contemplate having Christmas at all? The idea of Christmas was possibly as luxuriant as that use of timber in the ceiling, and as unnecessary.

The area of plaster between each beam was stained by indeterminate household emergencies such as minor leaks when the wind came from a peculiar quarter or when small storms loosened less important sheets of roofing iron, curious shifts in diverse and unusual winds that just once or twice may have driven a cupful of rain onto the plaster. Some of the marks could even have been caused by previous owners of the property trying desperately to clean them with unsuitable scouring cloths or detergents, possibly even as other distant Christmases approached during which they would be condescended to by their friends, or enemies, for living in a habitation so small and stained. In these faint markings Evelyn believed there was indeed a vague map of her past, present and future — unreadable, unheralded, unutterable and obscure.

Sometimes Jennifer made the odd remark, interspersed into the ordinary conversation, so that any obscurities or obfuscations from Evelyn could be agreeably hidden within the framework of the remarks of other people whom she thought more interesting and could thus be happily forgotten. Like the small stains on the plaster of her ceilings, they remained indelibly marked in Evelyn's mind. Jennifer usually set up a kind of hierarchy at her parties, so if she spoke to Evelyn it was always while she awaited words from someone she thought was more important, her glances flickering over Evelyn's shoulder to see if anyone better might be coming along at that moment. So the secrets of the previous Christmas did in fact remain something that only Evelyn was able to contemplate. This she did regularly and painfully. Even Andrea, in whom she had semi-confided, had no idea of the extent of her anguish. Perhaps it was shame, not anguish at all.

Jennifer's casual remarks were easily deflected.

'What about that man you have dinner with?' she would say.

'Could you have Christmas with him?'

'What man?'

'That man — that one you sometimes have dinner with? Didn't you say you sometimes have dinner with someone, Evelyn? Wasn't it your accountant or somebody?' Jennifer waited. 'No, I've got it wrong. Wasn't it someone from your bank? A name with one syllable, I think. Was it Charles?'

'I have dinner with all sorts of people. I can't actually think exactly who you might mean, really.' And she would put on her air of abstraction, which became more and more genuine for anarchic reasons as time passed. Jennifer would never have understood. 'There's that man I know who's gay — do you mean him? I have dinner with him sometimes. And there are the Wilkinsons — they're a sweet couple I sometimes have dinner with. Digby's really super, but of course he's married to Imelda and absolutely devoted to her and —' Blah blah blah. It was inwardly amusing to rabbit on.

'For heaven's sake.' Jennifer snapped a lot these days. 'I do sometimes wonder if you're all there, Evelyn, the way you chatter. And,' she would say triumphantly, 'you seem to be getting worse.'

And then there would be the homecoming to the little cottage. As there was only one bathroom it was impossible to close and seal the door against the sight of the brilliant stencils she had done so blithely. They were, mercifully, not so comprehensive as the stencilled and spreading tree that enveloped the hall. There were just a few rows and wreaths of leaves and a couple of mythical flowers on a door, that was all. So she would lie in the bath contemplating those and all that they had meant. There were a lot of colours in the quiet nightmare of it all, she often thought as, prescient and watchful, she lay in the cooling water — Jennifer's lipstick always so blazingly red against the porcelain prettiness of her cosmetic complexion, the grey of the sky which is how it usually seemed to look now, her own pale and featureless face as it gazed stonily back at her from her little mirror, the green of the painting she had done in the bathroom, the multi-colours, some gilded, in the hall.

'You need to brighten up,' Jennifer had said, was it yesterday? Or the day before?

'Yes,' replied Evelyn, but without conviction and went slowly home through the darkening streets.

'We're having just a very few people in for drinkies and you could stay if you'd like? Just a few people from the motor industry that Marky brushes up against in his work? There's quite a nice man called — oh, what is his name? — who's between marriages at the moment.' Jennifer had not been altogether welcoming.

'No, thank you,' said Evelyn. 'I'd better go home.'

'Perhaps that might be for the best.' Jennifer's expression was cheerfully rueful. 'He's having quite a bad time of it at the moment over the settlement. The wife's playing up about money and all sorts of nasty things like that and there's been an incident with his secretary that's causing a bit of bother for the lawyers. Better, perhaps, to leave it, don't you think?' It almost seemed as if it had been Evelyn's idea to meet him, and not one of Jennifer's sudden non-brilliant notions about how to get rid of her at Christmas. 'As I understand it' — Jennifer sounded very cheery — 'he's planning to go to Fiji for Christmas anyway, so that's not much use to you, is it? He's going deep-sea fishing with his son. The son still speaks to him but the daughter doesn't.' Jennifer's front door slammed. From behind it Evelyn heard her shout, 'Goodbye.'

So she had driven back to the cottage, the red rear lights of cars in front of her like eyes that were not too friendly. At the traffic lights at Powerscourt Road she wound down the window of the car for a moment and heard, from far away, the sound of violin music, a melancholy air being played slowly and lovingly, the notes clear and sharp like cold fingers on someone's warm arm. The busker, she thought. He would be playing outside the supermarket again, catching the last-minute shoppers dashing in to grab something to eat on their way home from work, small coins tinkling in his violin case. It would not do to tell Jennifer about the business of the busker, just as news of Charles and the consequences of knowing him had to remain a secret from her. Andrea understood, but Jennifer never would.

The busker often sat outside the supermarket in Powerscourt Road and also the one nearer Evelyn's cottage. There the tang of the salt air cast a bloom over the windows of the delicatessen department and seagulls strutted outside on the tarmac where the cars were parked. They searched indefatigably for crusts or chocolate peanuts dropped by children, and hurled themselves screeching, in gangs, on dropped ice-creams, while the children who had loosened their grip on the cone for just a moment screamed in their mothers' arms. The busker often played there, sitting on his amplifier box with an air of nonchalant ease, greeting people, particularly women, as they passed.

'You are beautiful,' Evelyn heard him say yesterday to a woman with 'I Come From New York' written in sequins across her tee-shirt.

'Say — thanks,' said the woman, and put a twenty-dollar note in the violin case. The busker smiled enticingly. A tour bus full of American tourists was in the area that day. He played something else then with an air of trembling tragedy, perhaps a bit of a Bach partita, and Evelyn later saw him having coffee with the woman at one of the pavement cafés. Toothlessly smiling, he had spread himself out in an anorak worn to an anonymous khaki and was sipping a cappuccino with a liberal froth of milk and chocolate dust on the top. 'Would you like a pastry as well? Or maybe a sandwich? Or something cooked?' the woman was asking. The café owner hovered.

'I'll be back in Queens by Christmas,' the woman said a moment later. 'What do you imagine you'll be doing?' The busker's reply was lost in the foam of the coffee and the sun glinted on his bald head, which was turning pink. Everyone, thought Evelyn, was flushed with plans about Christmas.

Back in the cottage the telephone began to ring as she stepped in the door.

'Have you heard from Alan?' It was Jennifer again. 'He was going to ring.'

'Not yet.' She waited, almost breathless.

'That's very odd. He did say he was going to. He's kind of

rethought various strategies and due to other things being not quite what he thought they were — as I think I told you — he said he'd definitely be considering you again. He most definitely said he was going to ring and give you another chance, Evelyn. He mentioned lunch. He sounded really enthusiastic.'

'I'm not sure I want another chance.' Evelyn let the silence lengthen. 'Or lunch.' Not that roast, she thought, with no wine sauce? Surely not that?

'Don't be silly, Evelyn.' Jennifer's voice suddenly took on a reedy note. 'Oh dear. Oh dear, oh dear.'

'Whatever's the matter, Jennifer?'

'I can't explain. I'll have to rush. I'll have to dash off.' She had gone. The call ended abruptly, with a crash, as if the telephone receiver had been thrown on to its cradle.

Evelyn went to the window and stared out at the empty street. The little road was completely empty. Whatever could be the matter with Jennifer? On various occasions lately she had had to rush off suddenly. Jennifer spent half her life at the beautician's having her fingernails done or her hair tinted or her face massaged. Only last year she had had major work to revitalise her skin. Last August there had been a small cosmetic operation on the neck area more or less under the chin, to tighten things up a bit. Her hair was regularly rinsed with semi-permanent colour especially mixed by a hair therapist and she had fortnightly appointments with an exclusive podiatrist who gave her an in-depth pedicure. Her teeth had been capped in an operation that cost eleven thousand dollars and her fingernails were actually artificial, made of something that had been formulated during the US space programme. With such polishings and constant refurbishments of Jennifer's body whatever could go wrong with it?

Puzzled, Evelyn stared out the window. Not even a cat or a dog or a sparrow moved in the landscape beyond her cottage, though far away a seagull screamed over a grey and gloomy ocean. Everyone was out shopping, she supposed, buying things for Christmas, their houses empty and un-tenanted and artificial Christmas trees sparkling in corners of festively decked sitting rooms. Jennifer would be getting the decorators in to do her house in some kind of theme any day now. It was odd, she thought, that Jennifer had not mentioned it at all, but she had seemed to be so preoccupied. Perhaps, mentioning her decorations had just slipped her mind.

Last year Jennifer's leitmotif had been red apples. Everything was covered with bright red artificial apples — the tree, the festoons of greenery roped around the sitting room and out onto the patio to form, as Jennifer said, a continuous decorative mood, roped up the banisters of the stairs and hanging in festoons from the chandeliers. The year before that what had it been? Perhaps gauzy golden angels in various sizes hanging from golden cords all over the house — or was that another year? She could not quite remember. Marky had got the edge of a wing in his eye and had to be taken to Accident and Emergency one evening after a pre-Christmas cocktail party, but the retina, the doctor said, had not been detached. Another year the whole house was done out in silver bows made of tinsel ribbon when tinsel ribbon with wire edging to keep it stiff was really just the newest thing. There had also been a tartan Christmas one year, and an all-white Christmas with large whitewashed branches, bare of bark, propped up in every corner and covered with white satin bows. In this bleached interior skeletal landscape nearly everyone had looked ill.

The busker, perhaps, just needed women as decorations at Christmas, she thought. Maybe they were all the festive decoration he required at Christmas or any time. The woman who had given him twenty dollars, the one from Queens, had worn a tee-shirt trimmed with red sequinned motifs, possibly all the seasonal glitter he wanted. Perhaps, once, he had been a stage star and had been able to mow a swathe through girls who clustered for his autograph, to make passes at women who came to his concerts. Only a couple of days ago she had found a punnet of strawberries on her own doorstep together with a scrawled note with a signature she could not read.

'Did you get my strawberries?' The busker had stopped playing 'Danny Boy' when she came out of the supermarket with her carrier bag full of groceries the following day. Toothpaste, parsnips, a packet of manila envelopes, bath cleaner, wholemeal bread. It had been a motley collection and not one to hint at romantic entanglements. Towards last Christmas she might have been buying a few provisions in case Charles called in — rice crackers flavoured with Japanese seaweed, salmon pâté and a bottle of one of the cheaper sauvignon blancs that was not too much like battery water. Already then, though, if she had thought about it, Charles was occupying himself elsewhere because he had ceased to bring her vintage wine for what he grandly called her cellar. With a little shrug and a small demurring glance she used to stow these away in a dusty cupboard under the staircase. And that was hardly a staircase at all, just more or less a stalwart ladder on not too great a slope. Everything was an illusion, she thought now.

'Thank you, Charles, how good of you,' she would say in that light little way of hers, unaware that the tiny, slowly perceived horror of the hand cream for worn hands was to be delivered by the postman. Definitely, she thought now, he would have given a bulk order to his secretary for all the women with worn hands whom he had plundered and then discarded during the year, herself the last of them.

'Did you get my strawberries?' The busker had been determinedly attentive. He had stopped playing the melancholy rising scales of 'Danny Boy' and sounded a few notes of a partita.

'I've noticed you like that one,' he said. 'You always smile when I play that one.' He regarded her triumphantly, grinning. 'And you'll stop walking and listen.' She wondered how he had lost his teeth. 'I put some strawberries on your doorstep.' A child wandered nearer and stood gazing into the open violin case with the coins glittering at the bottom. The busker gazed fixedly at Evelyn.

'Not a bad day,' she had said, pointing at the money and hoping to deflect him from the subject of the strawberries. She had taken the strawberries inside, thinking perhaps Charles might have called in, prompted by a fit of nostalgia or conscience — or anything — and left them there as a surprise. But there had been no proper note, nothing in the letterbox to explain the gift, just the scribble of something wavering in pencil on a rough piece of paper tucked under the punnet of fruit. Not Charles at all, she had decided, but ate the berries after her dinner that night, biting into each luscious fruit slowly to feel the texture of the flesh. It had been a wonderful year for strawberries and they were everywhere, mounds of them spilling over pavements outside fruiterers, stacked up higher than a person at the supermarket, for sale at stalls on the roadside once you got out of town.

'I didn't leave the cream,' said the busker. 'I thought it might go off. Shoo, shoo.' He was shooing the child away now from the coins in the case. 'I didn't know how long you'd be so I didn't leave the cream. I thought I'd come in and we'd have strawberries and cream together. I knocked and knocked but there was no answer so I just left the strawberries. I waited around for quite a while.'

'Did you?' So that was who it was, she thought. She delved around in her purse and thought that if she put a coin in his case he would start to play again.

He waved a munificent hand.

'For you,' he said, 'I play free.' He played another few bars. Something Spanish this time. 'I left a note,' he said, 'but perhaps you couldn't read it.'

'I did find a piece of paper but I wasn't sure what it said.'

'I can't write,' he said. 'I just scribbled something.' He grinned at her toothlessly again and she regarded him carefully. Perhaps, she thought, she could teach him how to write.

BUSKER LEARNS TO WRITE. FORMER BUSKER PLAYS FOR ITZHAK PERLMAN. THIS MAN IS A GENIUS, CRIES GREAT MAN. FORMERLY ILLITERATE BUSKER SENSATION OF MUSICAL WORLD. BUSKER TESTED BY MENSA — IQ 190. SELL-OUT CONCERT AT ALBERT HALL FOR FORMER BUSKER. FORMER BUSKER WEDS RECLUSIVE BEAUTY WHO TAUGHT HIM TO WRITE. SHE GAVE ME A LIFE, SAYS EX-BUSKER. LUCKY EX-BUSKER WINS LOTTO. EXCLUSIVE COVERAGE — SEE EX-BUSKER AND BRIDE'S FRENCH CHÂTEAU IN OUR NEXT ISSUE.

A series of invented headlines rushed through her mind, possibly in *Hello* magazine, which Jennifer read avidly. Jennifer would probably insist on being in all the photographs wearing a large gauzy hat and a Patrick Steele suit with bead embroidery. The busker chewed his tongue tentatively and gummily, and watched her. 'I never learnt at school,' he said.

'I'm sorry,' said Evelyn, 'I was thinking of something else just for a moment.'

'I never learnt to write at school,' he said, 'or read.' There was a long silence. 'Or count.'

'I see,' she said. 'There are adult learning classes you could go to. People would teach you how to read,' she said. But not me, she thought, definitely not me.

'I'll come back another day with more strawberries and cream and we can sit and have strawberries and cream together while I play to you. I've always thought you looked a lovely lady.' His eyes looked small and round and very bright and he regarded her experimentally. He did not seem anxious to discuss reading and writing. 'Your house looked very nice,' he said. There was something calculating about him now, she thought.

'It is.' Immediately she knew this was an error. 'But it's extremely small, absolutely tiny, hardly big enough even for one person let alone two.' She waited for a moment or two. 'Even if they're just eating strawberries and cream. And mould grows in the kitchen cupboards. I have to neutralise it with household bleach at least once a month.'

'Where I live there's no room at all. I can fit in anywhere. And everything's covered with mould.' He waited. 'Do you know the Robinsons?'

'The Robinsons?' Everything was becoming more bewildering by the moment, thought Evelyn. 'I don't think so.' Her voice was very careful. Two or three children holding ice-creams on sticks were waiting in a gaggle slightly to the left and an elderly lady stepped forward briskly and placed a twenty-cent coin in the violin case. '"Happy Birthday", please,' she said, and waited as well.

'You seem to be busy,' said Evelyn.

'Never too busy to talk to a lovely lady.' He smiled again and Evelyn wondered again exactly how he had lost his teeth. Had they been punched out in a bar-room brawl over women when he perhaps did gigs in pubs before he took to the streets? Or had they just slowly rotted away from lack of care? 'You seem to be looking at me very hard,' he said, and smiled again.

'Sorry. I was just wondering about something.'

'The Robinsons said they knew you.' He was oddly persistent.

The elderly lady gave a little gesture of impatience and walked away. 'Well, really,' she said as she went.

'They said they knew you by sight,' he said. 'I told them what you looked like and the Robinsons said you lived in that house by the big tree that had the red flowers in summer. That's how I knew where to find you. The Robinsons are friends of mine. I spent last Christmas with the Robinsons.' He waited again. 'But they're going away this year.'

'I see,' said Evelyn. So that was it. 'I don't think I know them, really. I don't think I know people called Robinson.'

'They know you all right.' He played a few notes and the children brightened. The lady was turning around now, looking back towards the portico of the supermarket where the busker usually perched. 'They said they see you working in your garden and they say hello when they walk by.'

The Robinsons must be just one of the many couples who walked past her cottage wearing running shoes and tracksuits on the keep-fit route, thought Evelyn. The street was quite steep and walking or running up it increased the heart rate.

The busker began to play 'Happy Birthday' and Evelyn wandered away across the carpark. Through a few cracks in the asphalt small flowers struggled — mostly weeds but there was a stalwart stunted daffodil, late for the season. Perhaps, like her, bewildered by the darkness and unsuitability of its living conditions, it had found it diffi- cult to find a way up to the light and air. The music stopped for a moment and when she looked back the busker was waving wildly.

'Cheerio,' he called. 'See you later.'

Back home in the cottage the telephone was ringing again as she stepped in the door.

'Hello? Is that you Evelyn?' It was Jennifer. 'Evelyn, I was a bit abrupt last time we talked but I don't seem to be terribly well somehow. I just had to go. I don't want to explain.'

'Of course not.' Evelyn thought her own voice sounded very reassuring, though she was inwardly bewildered yet again. Whatever could be the matter with Jennifer to cause these constant sudden disappearances?

'Anyway, getting back to what I was talking about, Evelyn, we're quite worried about you. We're only trying to help.' Jennifer seemed to take a breath or two and be almost hesitant. 'I could even come over and stay with you for a night or two if you'd like me to — you know, Evelyn, just for the company?'

'No, no.' She almost shouted the words. 'Please — no, no. Good heavens, no.' Having Jennifer to stay would be just a litany of endless complaints about the size of the cottage interspersed with anecdotes about her beautician, her hairdresser, Marky and money; also gold bangles, Bruno Magli shoes, Louis Vuitton luggage or handbags, even smaller items such as Louis Vuitton keyrings and wallets would be discussed in detail.

'Well, we worry about you, Evelyn. If only you could meet someone you like. And' — she seemed suddenly hesitant — 'I'd really love to be away from home even just for one night so I could go into the bathroom and not have people ask me about it. Marky keeps making remarks.'

'Bathroom?' said Evelyn, 'But you know you hate my bathroom. You've often said so. You've always said my bathroom's completely inadequate and you hate the shower. You told me once that my shower's the worst shower in the world. You'd hate being here, you know you would. And as for people — I like lots of people.'

'You know what I mean, Evelyn.'

'I do meet people, Jennifer. There's really no need to worry about me, or,' she said firmly, 'come to stay. I'm absolutely fine, really. I was late getting to the phone when you rang just now because I'd been out.' She prevaricated wildly. 'I went out especially to get some Schwarzkopf extra care vital replenishing shampoo for delicate hair, enriched with vitalising care complex.'

'Oh really, Evelyn? Isn't that just beautiful. I'm so pleased. I'm so thrilled you're starting to look after yourself better.'

'And I was out for much longer than I thought I'd be because I met a man I know, a musician.' She waited for that to sink in.

'A musician?' Jennifer sounded ecstatic. 'What kind of a musician, Evelyn? I'm so pleased for you.'

'He's a noted violinist,' said Evelyn. Well, she thought, a lot of people outside the supermarket did note the playing of the violinist and placed money in the box provided. His presence was noted.

'Where does he play?'

'All over the place.' Evelyn had begun to think quickly.

'Anywhere we know? Does he play at the Top of the Town?' The Top of the Town was an exclusive high-rise restaurant in the inner city.

'Sometimes.' She had actually seen the busker right up at the top of the main street, so this was not actually an untruthful admission. 'Mainly he plays at what you might call big venues.' Supermarkets were large, she thought. This remark was also not untrue.

'How fabulous. Is he in an orchestra?'

'No, I think he's a soloist.' She waited for a moment or two. 'We've never really discussed it.'

'Too busy talking about other things, I suppose.' Jennifer could be very arch. 'Do you like him?'

'Well,' said Evelyn mendaciously, 'it seems like early days yet. It would be hard to say. He does,' she added warily, 'have health problems.' There was the absence of any teeth to consider, and various other unprepossessing details, though the strawberries and cream had been a pretty, if horrifying, thought.

'Has he given you anything yet? Any presents?'

'No,' said Evelyn, 'just strawberries. He left strawberries on my doorstep.'

'Oh, Evelyn,' said Jennifer, 'how romantic! I'm so pleased for you.'

Chapter Ten

The mess was very quiet the night before the sergeant killed himself. Several of the men were on leave of various kinds. Sick leave. Compassionate leave. Home leave. Funeral leave. The father of one of them had died, and the six-year-old daughter of another. Evelyn, in the deep reaches of the night when she awakened, would go over the story slowly in her mind.

The colonel himself had said to the sergeant the previous day, 'We'd better go easy on Smith for the next few weeks. Tragic that little girl of his being run over at the Norwood Crossing, don't you think? You don't easily get over a thing like that.'

'Yes, sir,' said the sergeant. Then, 'No, sir.' Later the colonel said he showed little emotion.

One of the men had had pneumonia and was still in the sickbay. The others had gone to see him during the day and he was sitting up in bed playing Patience on a tray with a pack of cards the staff nurse had given him.

'Red three on black four,' he was saying when they went in. 'Black jack on red queen.' He laid the tray aside — thankfully, they thought — and asked for news.

'News?' said one man. 'You don't want news in a place like this. News don't exist here.' He paused reflectively for a moment or two. 'No word yet on the Front.' They had all thought they might be sent to the Front soon. He sat deep in thought for a moment or two. 'The colonel's still not pleased with the lats,' he said at last.

'Not the bloody latrines again?' The man in bed started up.

'The lats again, my son.' One or two of them groaned in a theatrical way. The latrines had been an intermittent source of irritation in the camp ever since they arrived there and pitched their tents. On the first day the colonel gave orders for the lats to be dug but the wind was coming from an unusual quarter then and his choice of ground, slightly soggy and inclined to be puggy in wet weather, did not help. There had been continuing rumours throughout the unit that one of these days the colonel would give the order to entirely re-dig the latrine block in a different area, downwind.

'Gawd,' said one of the younger ones and, pausing from reading some kind of tattered letter on mauve paper, said, 'Just listen here, this is what my wife says.'

'We don't want to hear what your wife says.' That was a Welshman who could always be relied on to be a funny turn, no matter what. 'We all know what the old trouble and strife says, don't we, lads?' He winked and put on a high voice. '"Just let me know when you're coming home on leave, my dearest, and I'll make sure I've got your favourite oatcake in the tins and also I'd like to be able to go and get a bit of a hairdo." You have to give her warning due to the shortages.' He fumbled in his pocket, took out a small bag of sweets and handed it around. 'If you ask me,' he said, 'my wife wants me to let her know when I'm coming home on leave so she can get all the Yanks out of the house.' He was devoted to his wife. It was well known in the unit that they were a devoted couple and often, in the mail, a large irregularly wrapped brown paper parcel would arrive for him, the wrapping somewhat grease-stained. More oatcake from the kitchen back home. He would sit in his billet, wrapped in a khaki blanket on freezing nights, munching contentedly on these offerings.

'She's a good girl, look you,' he would say, 'My Myfanwy's a good girl. Got to watch her, though.' He would wink at them then. He always passed her the compliment of making her out to be a whore when such a thing would not ever have been possible. They had been devoted since they were children. Her red hair was fine and pale like thistledown and her long white legs fitted beautifully around his waist in the dark when he made love to her with a passion that came from the marrow of his sturdy bones.

The countryside around the encampment was of a rolling nature. The hills stretched away for miles with wooded valleys, some of them deeply grown with ancient trees whose branches were grimly entwined. In these, as winter came deeply down upon them and there was the first snowfall, the crows and rooks cawed and screamed as if they created accompaniments for a death.

It was after a route march at night through this country, one icy week in early winter, that the man in the sickbay had come down with pneumonia. They all said later that the sergeant had marched all night impassively, with no sign of fatigue or emotion. When they finally reached a mini-encampment that had been set up in a forested area so they could have a bit of a rest and a mug of tea the sergeant had said, 'Tea?' in a bewildered kind of way. He might never have heard the word.

'Don't you want a mug of tea, sir?' one of the younger men, hardly more than a boy, had asked.

'Tea?' said the sergeant again.

'Yes, a mug of tea, sir.'

'I'll see about it later.' The sergeant, the boy said, just kept staring into space.

'As if someone had pole-axed him, sir,' he said to the colonel at the enquiry. 'He looked as if someone had hit him on the head with a bottle, sir, that's all I could say,' he said. 'I asked him again later if he wanted a mug of tea and he said, "Tea?" as if I was talking gibberish, sir. I told him I'd asked him earlier and he said, "What?" We noticed after he got the other letter, sir, the night before the march, that he come on a bit funny, sir, and just went off by himself. He usually used to whistle, sir, but he was very quiet.'

'So there was another letter, was there?'

'Yes, sir.'

After the arrival of the hand cream last Christmas Evelyn had remained quietly in the cottage. There were a couple of telephone calls from Jennifer and that was all.

'Evelyn? Is that you? You sound rather muffled somehow. I'm just giving you a tinkle to put off Thursday. Marky says Friday might be better. He's going to be at golf, but you won't mind, will you? He said it might be nice for us two girls to have the house to ourselves for a little chat after Christmas. You can tell me what presents you got. There's still something under the tree here for you, by the way. It's just a pair of tea towels, Evelyn. We thought something practical might be best — you live in such a state these days. Someone stood on the parcel but as Marky said, there was nothing in it that could squash or break and a footprint doesn't matter, does it, not at our age? We're not children, after all. There's still some turkey left, I think. I'll make a little fricassee or something. It's marvellous when it gets that tiny bit gamey, isn't it. Bye bye. See you Friday.' She rang back a moment later.

'Evelyn, I've suddenly thought — you sounded very quiet. You're all right, aren't you?'

'Of course I'm all right. Whatever would be the matter with me?'

'I don't really know, Evelyn. You just sounded very subdued somehow. I wondered if you were well. A while ago — I can't think when — you used to sound quite bubbly.'

'Bubbly? I don't know about that.' That would have been at the time of Charles and his visits, she thought. 'Of course I'm well. I'm usually quiet, Jennifer.'

'You seem even quieter.'

'I'm fine, thank you, Jennifer.' Her formality had not been noted. She noticed that.

'Well, goodbye then.'

'Goodbye, Jennifer.'

She had not got a letter, not like the sergeant did. The knowledge about Charles and the size eighteen fashion-shop owner had come to her conversationally, by circuitous means.

'Can you recommend a restaurant?' She had met some people she once knew, in the city one day before last Christmas. They were on a shopping trip, clutching parcels from designer shops, and were in a flurry about where to have lunch. 'Can you recommend anywhere? You live right in the city, Evelyn — you must know somewhere?' The husband, a small volatile man with a moustache, regarded her fiercely as if the knowledge might have been a secret.

'Well, I don't really know.' She had had to stand in the middle of the main drag thinking for a moment or two, and also trying to remember their names. It was a long time since she had seen them. Fashionable milieus for dining or lunching had slowly passed from her perceptions, as had knowledge of the people she used to know when Frederick was alive. The McLeods, she thought. Their surname was McLeod. But whatever were their Christian names?

Sometimes, when the interest from Frederick's estate dropped alarmingly after bank rates fell, she did not even go into tacky department stores to have a cup of tea in cafeterias filled with old ladies having a day out but, instead, ate an apple while she wandered along the street. When Charles took her into restaurants she had had the peculiar sensation that she might be asked to leave, her presence now being considered unsuitable.

'There's this banker I kind of know,' she had said at last, 'who took me to lunch a while ago to a place in the next block called Ciarino. It was very nice. You might like to try it.' Relieved, she rocked back on her heels slightly. At least she had come up with a name and a place.

'Oh, Charles!' The wife tittered faintly. 'Just the word banker would make anyone think of old Charles. I bet Charles took you there. Don't say you're another one Charles has taken to lunch? Dear God, that man does get about. I suppose you haven't had lunch with him for a while, have you?'

'Well, no,' Evelyn had said, 'actually not.'

'You wouldn't have. Don't you know he's taken up with Matty Rogers? Charles goes through the ladies like a dose of salts. Matty Rogers is that woman who's got a chain of fashion shops, you know — all those shops that have red windows and the outside's all painted purple? Well, she owns all those. They cater for the bigger sizes. Matty's actually enormous, but terribly handsome in a huge kind of way. Her eyes are as big as saucers and she's got these huge feet — at least a size eleven — but everything's in scale. She can't actually lose weight or she might look peculiar.' There was a pause. 'Those enormous people are often very passionate. People say she's had no end of affairs and now she's gobbling up old Charles flat-stick and he's just loving it, by all accounts. They hardly saw the light of day all last weekend, my dear, so my cousin who lives next door says.'

'I don't really know anything about all that.' Some sort of inner strength came to her quickly, standing on the pavement outside yet another bank while the crowds milled past. The main street suddenly seemed to be full of banks. 'He just organised some term deposits for Frederick's estate' — she was absenting herself from the whole thing now, putting it in Frederick's hands — 'and there was some kind of bank lunchy thing that day.'

'Really?' The McLeods regarded her carefully. They had never heard, they said, of a bank lunchy thing.

'Haven't you?' She had been very brisk, laughing curiously shrilly in her raincoat that had a rip in the front — neatly mended in her own careful herringbone stitch with black thread obtained from the super-market — and holding a half-eaten apple. 'It was a promotion of some kind. Every hundredth customer between ten and midday got taken to lunch if they had more than twenty thousand on ninety-day rollover. It was just a smorgasbord. A man called Charles Something organised it.' She paused for a moment. 'I know him only vaguely, of course.'

'Extraordinary.' Their eyes were round and unblinking.

She suddenly remembered the husband's name — Felix. Felix, a short pugnacious man with a bristling moustache and an air of investigation, regarded her fiercely again. 'Funny it wasn't advertised,' he said.

'Wasn't it?' She gazed blandly back at him. His air of enquiry became more pronounced, she thought. 'It actually was advertised, I did hear later,' she said, 'but hardly anyone saw it. It was in very small print on the back page of one of those little throw-out newspapers, those suburban ones.'

'Extraordinary.' They said it again.

Later, walking up the street to catch the bus back to the cottage, she dropped the remnant of the apple in a rubbish bin, its weight suddenly too great to hold. The day was an oddly chilly one due to the usual annual Christmas storm battling up from southerly highlands. She wrapped her coat more firmly around her waist and pulled the belt tight, turning the collar up. At the bus stop she stood with her back to the street and looked at her shadowy reflection in the windows of a commercial building that had ranks of letterboxes beside the front steps and a tatty foyer with a linoleum floor. A worn basket of faded silk flowers stood beside the lift. Outside, traffic at the bus stop rumbled.

Liar, she had thought as she looked at her dark hooded shape. Liar. And fool as well. It had, of course, been absurd to think she might cook a chicken on Christmas Day and imagine that Charles might suddenly arrive like someone in a story that would end happily.

Back home in the cottage the pot of hand cream was still sitting on the bathroom windowsill. *Le Jardinier Crème Adoucissante pour les Mains, Protège et Adoucit les Mains Desséchées. Idéale après le Jardinage.*

But now it was this Christmas, the hand cream still unused.

In the very late afternoon, when the sun was casting long shadows and traffic was beginning to bank up at all the traffic lights, she went skimming northward in her car through two suburbs to collect the hedgeclippers. It was more than a week now since she had dropped them off for sharpening and they might be ready. Around the cottage a shaggy crop of grass was beginning to hang down over the stone walls and a sudden growth of the most common sort of ivy was threatening to strangle her green lilies. An antique rose growing over the pergola near the back door had thrown out long shoots that seemed about to stab her in the eye and the whole garden looked in need of trimming. Up on the higher reaches of the property the olive trees were showing new leaves, silver on their undersides, and these fluttered like some kind of secret currency in the wind that came from the sea.

The first streets she drove along were wide and clean with villas and cottages sprawling in large gardens. Summer was here at last, despite the cold snap, and the beneficence of this showed in some of the properties where sometimes there was a rose or two blooming.

But beyond the second set of traffic lights the road narrowed and was stained here and there with oil and spillages, even with squashed rubbish from collection trucks; broken bottles lay in the gutters and at small commercial premises vans were parked askew in weedy parking lots. Sometimes there might be a boy in overalls, perhaps an apprentice, eating a pie from a paper bag while he stared out at the road. Here and there a determined plant — several times an agapanthus and once a marigold, very upright and brightly yellow, surprised almost — had thrust itself up out of the rough seal in front of a bakery or an engineering works and stood there blooming with a defiant bravado. A supermarket had opened up among this gaggle of light engineering and car-repair businesses and its sign, a hugely painted bunch of luminous grapes, hung from large ropes dyed forest green. Beyond this lay a commercial hinterland of second-rate auction houses, car salesyards, a place where deckchairs could be re-canvassed and the business where Evelyn took the hedgeclippers to be sharpened. There had once been a second-hand shop next door but it was now closed and almost derelict, the windows broken by vandals.

Traffic had been banked up at most of the intersections and she had had to wait for two light changes before she got across. Red to amber, amber to green again. Charles owned a large black car of some kind, an expensive car that smelt of new upholstery, perhaps leather, and had a bewildering array of digital things on the fascia. By the time he collected her in the evenings, in the brief heyday of his attention to her, the rush hour had long passed and they had glided into the city in traffic that had seemed gentle and more serene, perhaps all created by people going on similar outings.

'I do like live theatre, don't you?' Charles would say when they walked into the foyer of some theatre or another. The plays were all over the place: once in a basement that was painted black, another time at the university and outdoors in a serene and grassy quadrangle bounded by old stone buildings.

The traffic today was more ordinary, much more like the plain ordinary world that she inhabited, thought Evelyn. There were mothers driving small cars grimly homeward, the back seats loaded up with shopping bags and tennis racquets, two or three small faces pressed to the windows. One child, a little girl with stiffly plaited hair, poked out her tongue at Evelyn as they passed in an outer lane. Shabby tired men shunted their cars through the traffic, perhaps on their way home to complaining wives after spending a day at jobs they did not like. Sometimes there might be a struggling tree growing on the side of the road, perhaps a slightly vandalised cherry or a silver birch stunted by lack of water and care. They might once have been planted by someone who bought a business and thought it may prosper enough to have a landscaped approach, thought Evelyn.

She inched through the traffic. Her car made a noise like an old sewing machine churning, with difficulty, through fur fabric. Charles's car had made hardly any sound at all. Their progress in it had seemed magical, she thought, and changed carefully and slowly down to second gear as she drove up an incline. The gearbox of the car was showing wear.

'Why don't you change gear?' she had said to him once as they had floated along in the big black car towards a theatre and a restaurant, champagne in the offing.

'It's automatic, darling. Don't you have a car that's automatic? Dear God — what sort of space do you inhabit?'

'Just the usual sort,' she had said, gathering her collar around her throat like a flower closing its petals.

The parking lot of the engineering works when she reached it was unusually empty again. Mostly there were three or four trucks and people, usually men, waiting at the counter for large pieces of equipment, often several of them, that they needed help with to carry out to their vehicles.

'Good heavens,' she said as she stepped in the door, 'where is everyone?' It was a mistake to speak, she suddenly thought. No one really wanted to know what she thought or what she saw. Jennifer said so, and it was probably true.

'The trouble with you, Evelyn,' Jennifer sometimes said, 'is that you've never got over having a fuss made of you and thinking people want to hear what you say. Frederick,' she would say austerely, 'ruined you.'

'He used to think that what I said was very amusing.'

'Evelyn, what you say is not amusing. Someone has to tell you and it might as well be me. Marky says that he just cannot follow your conversation at all most of the time. When I tell him you're coming here for something or other do you know what Marky usually says?'

'No.'

'He says, "That's the woman who says *Oh* a lot? Well, I'm off out, thank you very much." To be quite honest, Marky just can't stand the way you talk.'

The man who usually served behind the counter was leaning against the doorway of an inner office, holding a cup of coffee.

'Mrs Jarrold,' he said. 'Mrs Evelyn Jarrold. How very nice to see you.'

'Really?' she said.

'Really,' he said. 'Extremely nice.'

'I'm sure it isn't,' said Evelyn, 'and I've got this kind of non-friend who keeps telling me that I'm far too inclined to wander about saying hello to people as if they'd want to say hello to me, and making remarks as if what I say is interesting. This non-friend I've got — well, she says I should just shut up. I mean, I shouldn't have even said anything when I came in just now because who wants to know?'

'It's actually quite fascinating that we're not busy,' said the man, putting his cup down. 'I thought it was very interesting myself. Usually we're jam-packed at this hour of the day, with people screaming for things they have to have tomorrow. Or,' he said, 'even yesterday. They all want everything yesterday. But look at it.' He gestured around the shop and the workshop beyond it. There was nobody anywhere. 'Of course,' he said, 'it's the Christmas rush getting to people. They'll be all out shopping this afternoon for presents or groceries and wine, I suppose, or whatever. Now this morning was a different matter entirely,' he said. 'Anyway, it's very nice to see you and I have both good and bad news.'

Good news? Bad news?

'The very good news is that you're my one-hundredth customer since Tuesday and, as we're approaching Christmas, I've been having a little promotion, so you've qualified for a special prize.' He reached under the counter and handed her a gift-wrapped medium-sized box of something that felt reasonably heavy. Chocolates, she thought. 'And the bad news is that I have not yet got your clippers re-set and sharpened. I shall possibly have to deliver them myself.' He smiled at her. A tall man, long-limbed, she noticed, and his eyes were a curious colour, somewhere between blue and green. He seemed to possess, perhaps, an air of delicate pleasure and gentle enquiry.

'I didn't see the promotion advertised,' she said, helplessly holding the parcel. 'And I really think that perhaps you should give this prize to someone who gets more things done. I mean, when I'm here some-times there are big trucks outside with two or three men in them collecting great loads of stuff for businesses that are obviously large. I'm just a very small customer. My hedgeclippers are hardly very important and they wouldn't bring in much money either. You usually only charge five dollars to fix them up for me and that's not going to do a lot for anyone, is it, not five dollars? Maybe I should give this back to you' — she held out the gift — 'and you could give it to the one-hundred-and-first customer, who might be some big business or other that's brought a lot of money into your firm.'

'Definitely not. Definitely, definitely not. You were the hundredth customer and you must have the gift.' He gazed at her blandly, perhaps faintly amused, she thought. Outside the traffic rumbled by endlessly and the sun, sulky at its best that day, was now completely behind clouds.

The silence lengthened as Evelyn held the parcel and contemplated the peculiar echoes and reflections of her life. Having, much earlier, invented the gift of a smorgasbord lunch for every hundredth customer at the bank she was now confronted by an actual gift for a one-hundredth customer at a light engineering and tool-setting works.

'Was your promotion advertised?' she said, turning her face away a little. Was there, she wondered, some kindly airstream that day, a sweet influence in the universe that had come to eventually rescue her from being an out-and-out fibber over Charles? But the business of Charles and what had occurred had to be kept a secret from everyone except the unshockable Andrea. What else, she thought, could I do but try to cloud the issue and cover it up?

'The clippers'll be ready later,' he said, 'but probably not till right on Christmas, and as for the promotion . . .' — he paused slightly as if thinking. Later she wondered if he, too, was inventing something that might be plausible and not easy to check on — 'I advertised it just the once in the local suburban throw-out newspaper. It's got very small print. The chap who owns it is a friend of mine,' he said. 'I thought I'd help him out. He's always trying to sell advertising.' He gazed blandly at her again. 'I think it was on the back page. And some of them,' he said, blandly again, 'got a bit crushed in the press and weren't readable.'

'I thought so,' said Evelyn. It was as if the forces of fate, delicately balanced on the horizon somewhere, had decided quaintly to come down in her favour, that she should not be allowed to be completely mendacious. There had really been, perhaps, an advertisement about a promotion of some kind in a throw-out newspaper somewhere and sometime, on a back page, and in small print. Whether or not it had been on the subject she had so clearly stated to Felix and his wife was of no consequence when viewed within the framework of the universe. Which was, she thought, huge. On that scale the exactness of an advertisement on a back page somewhere, whether it was about a box of chocolates at a small engineering works or a non-existent smorgasbord lunch not given by a bank, was immaterial.

The telephone was ringing again when she arrived home and stepped in the front door of the cottage. Two or three Christmas cards were spilling out of her letterbox. One of them had been tramped on by a large foot wearing a shoe with a thickly patterned tread anointed with mud of an unusual colour. Not from this suburb, she thought. Clutching these missives in her hand she answered the telephone.

'Hello? Is that Evelyn?' The voice was not one she knew.

'It could be,' she said at last. Jennifer's machinations about Christmas and how she was to spend it were making her wary. It did not sound, she thought, like Alan the little ex-headmaster with the very good superannuation scheme and the taste for racial asides in cafés. Nor was it the ebullient Marky with more news of the mysterious Paul. 'Who is speaking, please?'

'It's Mike.'

'Mike?' Evelyn could not recall knowing anyone called Mike,

except for a land agent about four Christmases ago whom Jennifer had failed to jack Evelyn up with. He had subsequently married a woman with flat feet for which she had had three small expensive operations at a private clinic. Her emotions, according to Jennifer, were apt to be volatile. A lot of Jennifer's conversation was about the second and third marriages of insurance agents, car salesmen and real estate personnel. There was something very worn about it, Evelyn always thought, and tacky. Many of the people concerned had had their teeth capped if they had made money or desperately needed root canal work if they had not. Jennifer kept up with all the processes or operations. Some had even had tummy tucks, the stories connected with those the most unpresentable of any and Jennifer usually only touched on them after barbecues and three glasses of an indifferent merlot, or a cheaper bubbly. Tales of liposuction had become quite common, particularly on beer guts and sturdy thighs.

'Mike?' she repeated. Who could Mike be?

'Mike, who left the strawberries on your doorstep.' He chuckled richly.

Evelyn paused. The busker, she thought. The busker.

'I wonder how you got my telephone number?' she said at last.

'The Robinsons gave it to me.' His voice was full-bodied and avuncular.

'The Robinsons?'

'Those friends of mine who live near your house.' He paused again. 'You house looked very pretty,' he said. 'I noticed it again when I dropped in this afternoon.' There was another silence. 'You were out. I thought if I dropped in I could surprise you. I might find you there and we could have a cup of coffee. You could've made me a cup of coffee. I like coffee,' he said. 'I prefer instant.' He paused for a moment. 'Dash of milk,' he said, 'and two sugars.'

'I never drink coffee.' More lies, she thought. 'I seldom buy sugar. I never eat cream. I'm often out. You'd be very lucky, really, to ever find me at home.'

'But I will, my dear, I will.' Arch now, he chuckled again. 'You and

I,' he said, 'are definitely going to have strawberries and cream together. I'll call another day.' He rang off.

She stood by the telephone looking at the mail. *Mein Gott*, she thought. The continental apprentice of the old plumber she and Frederick always used in their house renovations often said *Mein Gott* on his first day when he saw what had to be done: the horror of defunct plumbing to be sorted out, the rusty pipes and broken taps. Frederick had loved buying unsuitably large old houses, often two-storeyed and almost falling down. It had been the challenge he liked, she always thought. He liked making an ugly thing beautiful. After they were married people often said things like, 'Evelyn, I've never noticed your beautiful eyes. And your hair. We've always thought you were so plain.'

The Christmas cards she found in the mail, one of them with the telling footprint, were the usual dutiful kind of thing. Merry Christmas and a Happy New Year from Mary and Tom. We never seem to see you these days, my dear. Life is such a rush for us all, isn't it. We do hope you are well. Happy Christmas from Estelle and Michael. We're off to the States in the New Year. What excitement. Haven't seen you for ages. We do hope you are well.

Perhaps, thought Evelyn, everyone imagined she was ill. The one with the mark of the muddy foot was from the business section of her bank, where Charles headed the investment department. The Christmas greeting was of a general kind, the entire message printed in black ink. There was no personal signature of any kind. The muddy footprint had been, she thought, innocently prophetic, and must have been placed there accidentally by the busker when he had called. She threw the card in the rubbish bin with one hand while she flicked through the telephone book for R for Robinson with an address near her own.

Ting-a-ling. Here was Evelyn ringing the number of a Robinson up on the main road, only a short block away.

A crisp voice answered, one that encouraged no contradiction.

'Hello, this is the Robinson residence.' A woman had answered and she sounded like Jennifer's twin. There was no hesitancy of the very shy or the over-invaded, no hint of uncertainty on any issue at all. The tone was questioning as if saying, in an unstated way, 'What the hell do you want?'

'This is Evelyn Jarrold speaking. I'm telephoning about that man who plays the violin by the shops. I just wondered if it was from you — he said the name was Robinson — that he had got my address.' Evelyn let a significant pause lengthen. 'He seems to have my address and my telephone number.' She waited again. 'He's called in here and left things and I'm faintly alarmed because I don't really know what it's all about.'

'Has he really popped in already? And has he rung?' The voice of the woman at the other end of the line sounded delighted. 'Really? How marvellous. The strawberries, of course. He's left the strawberries, hasn't he. Of course, of course. What a dear man. So quick off the mark.' The voice became confidential. 'I said to him, "Michael," I said, "you must make yourself known to her." But I had no idea he'd take up my idea of a little something on the doorstep. I had thought' — her voice lowered — 'flowers, but then we decided strawberries might be better because you could eat them. We did laugh when he said he'd left them on the doorstep hardly a moment after we gave him the idea and I did really wonder if it was quite true. Michael can get a little carried away.'

'We?' Evelyn, stunned, stood by the telephone. Were there plurals involved in all this? Evening was falling on her garden and the weeds melded into the general greenery. If the hedgeclippers were not sharpened and ready soon the whole place may be covered with a canopy of herbage, herself imprisoned within. And that, she thought, might not be a bad idea at all. At least no one could get at her.

'My husband and I. We do work, you know, at the City Mission and Michael's really a most marvellous fellow. His relationship' — again the tone became confidential — 'with Alison has broken up. The poor dear old girl just got exhausted with the travel. He is away quite a lot. A great one to go walkabout is our dear old Mike.' She gave a hearty laugh. 'Alison just got completely exhausted with travelling around and leading a kind of itinerant life, poor darling, and sleeping in the car and so on. We all said, "What fun," — you know how one does? But she just wouldn't listen. She was once, so they say, the wife of a noted sharebroker but it all turned to custard at the time of the sharemarket crash back God-knows-when and the husband shot himself and then poor dear old Alison evidently took to drink, poor sweetie. She had a bit of a problem with the drink but then she and Michael got together and that seemed to sort it out for them both.' The voice stopped for a moment. 'For a while.'

'But how did you know about me?' It seemed best not to touch upon the subject of the mysterious Alison and her problems.

'You're a friend of Jennifer Clark's, aren't you?' No space was left in the discourse for an answer. 'Jennifer told us all about you — well, she didn't actually tell us about you, she told the Smiths there was a problem with Christmas for you — that you'd be all on your own and they didn't know what to do for the best. We heard it in a roundabout kind of way from the Marchmonts — do you know the Marchmonts?'

'No,' said Evelyn, standing on one leg and gazing into a small cupboard she had opened beneath where the telephone stood. It used to be the drinks cupboard years ago and now contained an almost empty gin bottle. Perhaps enough, she was thinking, for one strong gin and water. There was no tonic.

'Well, the Marchmonts somehow know you vaguely through the opportunity shop. I do hope you don't mind my mentioning it, my dear. They serve in there once a week as their kind of little charity thing and Sophie Marchmont remembered you from when you bought a really nice pink woollen coat. It was hardly worn, she said. Looked lovely on you and had quite a lot of warmth left in it, really.'

'But what has this,' said Evelyn, 'got to do with that man who plays the violin?'

'Well, the Marchmonts thought that it might be a really wonderful thing if we got it all jacked up that Michael spent Christmas Day with you as you're on your own and that would mean we didn't have to have him here because he doesn't really quite fit in, and you'd have someone to spend Christmas with, thus saving your poor friend Jennifer all that worry.'

'I see,' said Evelyn.

'Mike, of course, could go to the Mission Christmas Dinner with all the others — hundreds of them. Indeed, my dear, you could go yourself if you wanted to. But it's just that he was once slightly higher up the musical scale — if you'll excuse my silly little pun — and we thought he deserved something better. Jennifer told the Smiths that you were quite fond of music. Mike used to perform on the hotel circuit once, and I do believe he played in the odd nightclub way back heaven-knows-when. He does tend to like a drink too, just like dear old Alison, and that has posed problems in the past, but I'm sure you'll be able to deal with that. A good woman can find her way through that little minefield. A couple of cans of beer should suffice. Just limit the alcohol and he'll be fine.' Silence fell at last. 'We all thought it was a marvellous idea. And he could play to you — Christmas carols or anything you wanted. You'd just have to say and he'd play anything for you. He plays by ear, you know. He's self-taught.'

'There is one problem with all this,' said Evelyn. 'I do not wish to have your friend Mike here and I do not want people to be making all these arrangements on my behalf without my permission.'

'But he's in a bad state, my dear. You may be able to save him.'

'I don't wish to save anyone,' said Evelyn getting the bottle of gin out of the cupboard now. 'I've suddenly thought that I have to save myself and that is more than enough for me to do. I am,' she said, 'only small. My strength is limited.'

'Jennifer said you were an unselfish lovely person with a heart of gold.' The speaker paused for a moment, to take a breath. 'And the Marchmonts said you had quite good taste and had a nice speaking voice. They thought you'd be a good influence.'

'They were all wrong. I am a wicked, evil, selfish person with no heart at all and no taste and I actually speak very badly most of the time. My language is often appalling and I use four-letter words without even thinking about it.'

'Does the fact that this poor, sweet, lost man left strawberries on your doorstep mean nothing to you at all?'

'Nothing whatever.'

'How dare you pose as a sweet woman in the ordinary world and refuse to help a fellow creature at Christmas of all times? Your friend Jennifer is going to hear about this. I'm going to ring the Marchmonts immediately to tell them what you've said. And after that I'm going to ring the Smiths and the Hendersons. People are going to know about this. We've already told him he can spend Christmas with you so whatever are we going to do now?' The telephone was hung up in her ear with a short, sharp click.

Evelyn went and fetched a glass from the kitchen cupboard and poured the remnants of the gin into it. There was an old ruler in the drawer of the sideboard so when she found it she placed it carefully against the side of the glass. Nearly twenty millimetres, she thought. Nearly an inch. Enough to anaesthetise her for a moment or two. She added some water and swallowed it quickly. The garden was now completely in darkness. Christmas this year, she thought, definitely showed signs of possessing record-breaking awfulness.

Chapter Eleven

Deep in the winter the unit was sent on manoeuvres. This training session was lengthy and involved spending several days in the open and various nights in farm buildings, including barns. They also had to cross a river on a rope-bridge they had made themselves. The second lieutenant fell in the river and swam to the other side and when the company commander found this out he just said, 'Good, good,' as if swimming a river rather than attempting a rope-bridge made by soldiers in training was much the more sensible thing to do.

The weather had been treacherous for some time and the ground everywhere was extremely puggy, especially in the dips and deep valleys they had struggled through. A wrong order was given, or someone misinterpreted a map at a crucial point, and the unit was left behind during the main push by the entire regiment. The unit was not in the correct place at the correct time.

The company commander came on an inspection the next

morning, after the men from the unit had spent a freezing night in yet another barn, and he looked at everything, even the soles of their boots to see if any footwear needed repairing.

He was displeased that they had not been given porridge for breakfast but, when questioned, most of the men said they did not like porridge, which pleased him even less. The company commander believed that porridge did a man good, and he said so. It was implied in his discourse that if they had had porridge more regularly they would be better men who read maps more skilfully and would thus have been in the right place at the right time. As it was they had had to stand aside at some point the previous day while another unit marched through their ranks, like people on a golf course playing through.

'What did these men have for breakfast?' the company commander asked the second lieutenant, who said, 'Liver, sir.' And then, almost as an afterthought, 'And bread, sir. With jam.' There was a silence. 'Definitely jam, sir.'

'Liver? You mean liver?' The commander seemed astounded.

'Yes, sir. Liver, sir.' The second lieutenant waited. 'With bread, sir. And jam.'

The company commander remained deep in thought.

'I see,' he said at last.

The sergeant had been very quiet during the entire exercise. He had been markedly withdrawn for a long time now. It had been several weeks since his initial outburst over the behaviour of his wife and even that was not much of an event. After the letter telling him of her infidelity had arrived he suddenly became quiet when previously he had been a cheery, quite noisy man, fond of jokes and always to be relied upon for some funny story or an amusing aside. He was well liked in the unit because he was good company, but after the arrival of the letter he instantly became quiet, even morose. His whole demeanour and appearance changed. By the time the manoeuvres were held and the men had had to spend the nights in the barns — 'My, but it do stink in here,' said one of the men, a Welshman — he had lost a great deal of weight. He had become thin and pale where once he had been quite a burly man with a ruddy complexion, a jovial man. His face was pallid, his eyes sunken. He looked ill.

The second lieutenant had been extremely busy in the weeks since the first intimations of trouble at the sergeant's home. The sergeant had been given leave then. He had been away for two or three days and had then returned. The men, talking idly among themselves, decided he had probably given his wife a right seeing-to, whatever that might have meant, and everything would be all right now. Maybe they thought he had gone home with gifts — perhaps he had obtained nylon stockings and chocolates on the black market better than the Americans could give — and had carted her off to bed and made love to her violently. Whatever they thought he had done they imagined, in a kind of collective intelligence throughout the whole unit, that he had somehow conquered the problem. There would be no more trouble at home for the sergeant now and everything would be happy. That is what they had imagined. Having been given a seeing-to of some kind the sergeant's wife would now behave.

During a lull in the route march, when the men were settling into a barn and various orders were being given, the second lieutenant suddenly remembered the sergeant and his problems. It was not so much a remembrance of the difficulties, it was just that he suddenly noted the appearance of the sergeant and had a good look at him. The sergeant was very thin, almost cadaverous, his face waxy, the eyes without lustre.

'Things all right, are they?' the second lieutenant asked sometime when he had a moment. 'I'll see about some leave for you when we get back.'

'Thank you, sir,' said the sergeant without interest.

'We might get a good sleep here,' said the second lieutenant. The soldiers always valued rest, loved to sleep. After food and a cup of tea, it was sleep the men valued most, particularly on training manoeuvres.

'Don't sleep well,' said the sergeant. 'Find I don't need the sleep any more like I used to.' He looked haggard, the second lieutenant thought. Perhaps some more home leave could be arranged.

In Evelyn's cottage the telephone rang again.

'Evelyn? Is that you?' It was Jennifer. 'You don't somehow sound like yourself.'

'I was probably distracted. I was reading.' Evelyn put the book down. The pages dealing with the sergeant and how he had eventually shot himself in mysterious circumstances were quite worn now, grubby along the edges. She had read them so many times. 'Do you remember Frederick's gun?' she said. 'Frederick's rifle that he used to shoot rabbits with when we had that ten-acre block up Morrison Road?'

'No?' Jennifer sounded puzzled. 'We didn't really see a lot of Frederick, Evelyn. When you lived up there we kind of lost touch for a while as you may recall. Marky,' she said, 'has never been one for country life.'

'Of course. I was just thinking, though,' said Evelyn, 'that I wish I hadn't handed it in when there was that gun amnesty. The gun licence had lapsed. I forgot about it when Frederico died and when the policeman called to ask me about it I just handed the gun in because I never thought I'd need it again.'

'Gun? Handed in? I never knew anything about this, Evelyn. And what would you need a gun for, for heaven's sake?'

'I wish I hadn't handed the gun in,' said Evelyn, evading the question. 'I could have paid for a new licence, I suppose, couldn't I?'

'How would I know?' Jennifer could be very snappy. 'And I haven't rung you to be talking about guns, Evelyn. I've rung about the Robinsons. Look, I'm awfully sorry about that business of that man called Mike.' Her tone was suddenly conciliatory now, very unlike Jennifer. 'I didn't quite realise what was involved with it all and when those people rang to ask for your number so they could give it to the Robinsons I imagined he was quite a different sort of person. I didn't quite realise exactly what was involved.' She swept on as if she had rehearsed what she was going to say and, being Jennifer, she might well have, thought Evelyn. 'They were all very persuasive and I got the impression he was rather an artistic type, rather Bohemian and quite fascinating. I didn't realise about all the emotional problems and the drinking. And Evelyn, you wouldn't want to be away from home most of the time travelling around in a station wagon like someone in a circus. I didn't realise about all that. I'm terribly sorry.'

'That's all right.' Evelyn was still thinking about the rifle. 'There was also a box of ammunition,' she said. 'I handed that in as well.'

'What? Evelyn, I don't quite underst—'

'The policeman was very nice about it,' said Evelyn. 'He told me they sometimes go through all the records of the gun licences and have a kind of check-up and a lot of the lapsed licences are for guns owned by widows who've just forgotten that they need a licence at all. He said most of them hand the guns in because what does a widow need with a gun, really?'

'Evelyn, I do wonder what you're talking about.' Jennifer's voice was faintly blurred now, as if she had placed the receiver under her chin and was holding it with her shoulder while she did something with both hands. There was a faint sound of scraping. Jennifer, thought Evelyn, was filing her nails.

'Frederick used to keep the rifle in a special locked cabinet when we lived up Morrison Road. He had a Yale lock put on a metal cupboard kind of thing and kept it in there. I had a bit of trouble finding the key when the policeman called, but I did find it and the rifle was in there just fine. I handed it in.' Evelyn stood there, quietly waiting. 'And I wish I hadn't,' she said.

'Nonsense, Evelyn, nonsense.' The scraping had intensified. 'There's nothing for you to shoot in your garden, only snails.' Jennifer tittered slightly. 'Anyway, I'm glad you aren't annoyed about the telephone number. That Robinson woman rang, going mad about it all — she's such a bitch — but I just fobbed her off and I told her it was all just a silly mistake and everyone had got the wrong end of the stick. You're not going to be upset, now, Evelyn, are you?'

'No,' said Evelyn. 'Do you think if I went to the police station and asked about Frederick's gun I could possibly get it back? I'd pay for a licence, of course, and have all the documentation properly done this time. It was just that after Frederico died there was such a lot of work to do and so many things to attend to I never thought about the gun. I had to sell the house and pack everything up. I was exhausted.'

The night was a stormy one, peppered with flurries of hail while lightning flickered over the sea. A vicious wind howled around the cottage and sometime or another, perhaps after the big municipal clock down on the seafront had chimed three in the morning, the storm dropped away into a silence that was almost sepulchral. Evelyn slept uneasily, stirring occasionally. There was an intermittent scraping, a small clatter of dead leaves and twigs, beside her front door and after she heard the big clock strike five she fell into a deeper sleep, dreaming of the busker. He was curled up beside her front door, waiting. Hunched up and with his head forward and resting on his knees, he was sleeping like a peon amid the fallen leaves of her garden, waiting for her to open the door when she awakened. His figure established itself in her mind in mythical proportions as she stirred uneasily in the depths of the dream. Now he was in her kitchen, laughing as he ladled honey from a huge jar onto a thick piece of white bread. He had teeth now and was drumming on the table with a spoon in time to some music on the radio, lounging back so far in one of her old Windsor chairs that one of the back legs must surely break. His drumming with the spoon increased in intensity until it became almost deafening. Evelyn opened her eyes and stared at the bedroom ceiling that held an imaginary map of her life. Stains, errors, miscalculations, just an undistinguished mess. Someone was knocking at her front door. The fantasy about the busker being in her kitchen and drumming on her table was just a dream. There was someone knocking at the front door.

'Good morning,' said an Indian lady in a cerise sari when Evelyn stumbled downstairs to open it. 'My name is Madame Magnolia Sharma.' She handed over a card. 'I am coming to give you your Christmas beauty treatment.' She smiled beatifically. 'By appointment. It is all explained on the card.' She waited. 'I left a message on the answerphone.'

'Ah,' murmured Evelyn. 'I don't check it very often.'

The sea had turned an oily greenish grey and flung itself at the seawall at the end of her street. The dull booming of the waves sounded like a knell. It was after nine o'clock by her own small clock beside her in the hall so she had overslept, she thought. The nightmare about the busker being in the house eating honey and breaking chairs must have been interminable. She began to read the card.

> *Greetings, beautiful and valued customer. The universe can be a place full of cares and worries but, with correct treatment for the stressed human form, many of these can be dissipated. Calmness of mind and tranquillity for the soul are what is aimed for by your own personal therapist, Madame Magnolia Sharma, who has been trained in deep-breathing techniques and also personal massage by none other than the celebrated guru Dhuleep . . .*

There were two or three small red wax seals on the bottom of this missive to give an authenticity to the qualifications. Evelyn stood on her own doorstep, puzzled.

'I hardly ever check my answerphone so I didn't know you were coming,' she said at last. 'Are you just calling along the street, perhaps? Or have you come to see me especially, in which case I don't —'

'But I have not explained properly.' Madame Magnolia Sharma handed over another card.

> *Good and valued customer, you have been fortunate enough to have influential friends who, valuing your beauty and charm, have arranged for you to be given this personal gift voucher. You are*

entitled to: One 45-minute massage using essential oils to promote calmness and well-being, one hair treatment and one 15-minute facial. With every good wish for Christmas from Jennifer and Mark Clark.

'But —' Evelyn began to speak. Jennifer and Marky were not usually so generous.

'Please.' Madame Magnolia Sharma held up her hand, which was covered with gold rings and was as velvety as a flower. 'It is not good talking too much before the treatment. The soul must go into itself in a state of exquisite silence while the body is treated, and then the inner self will be fresh and beautiful. There is too much noise in the world, dear customer, too much talking. The guru,' she said, 'is very against too much talking, particularly on the telephone.'

'I see,' said Evelyn, taking a step backwards. 'But it's much too early,' she said. 'I'm not ready. I didn't know you were coming. I'm not even dressed.'

Madame Magnolia stepped forward. Now she was in the narrow hall and closed the front door behind her.

'That is excellent,' she said. 'We do not have to clear away the worthless beginnings of the day. We can start afresh. Where,' she said briskly, 'do you sleep?'

The telephone began to ring stridently at this moment. Madame Magnolia stepped forward, lifted the receiver swiftly and replaced it on its cradle. 'The guru does not like the telephone,' she said again. 'It tangles the clear silken lines of a mind the guru wishes to be untroubled. I seldom use it myself except to advise about appointments.' The telephone began to ring again. Madame Magnolia sighed deeply and this time, when she lifted the receiver, she spoke. 'Please,' she intoned in a hypnotic voice, 'not to be talking or ringing for at least two hours.'

'Oh, I see, I see.' Evelyn clearly heard Jennifer's voice at the other end of the line. Madame Magnolia terminated the call with another brisk click. This time the telephone remained silent.

'Where do you sleep?' she repeated. Evelyn, defeated now, took her up the narrow wooden stairway to the upstairs room.

'Oh dear, dear, dear.' Madame Magnolia stopped halfway up the stairs. 'May I ask — are you happy here? No? That is because your stairway is running the wrong way. It is facing south-north, which is the wrong sector for you. I have already divined that you have an east-west personality. This is why you are unhappy.'

'Really?' This was a cheering thought. Heartened, Evelyn ran up the last flight of steps from the tiny halfway landing, with the hem of her long white night-dress held in one hand. If the stairs going the wrong way were the only thing that made her unhappy she could hardly be unhappy at all, she thought.

An hour later, soothed by scented oils and with her hair tied up in a turban under which more oil was supposed to be revitalising her hair, Evelyn yet again fell into a light sleep, delicate and sweet this time, and full of the heavy scent of flowers.

Earlier, Madame Magnolia had flitted around the bedroom and got it ready for the treatment.

'A beautiful bed containing many positive vibrations.' She had lightly dusted its brass curlicues and knobs. She flipped the top sheet over the bed end, where it suddenly looked like an arcane drapery in a temple, the effect enhanced by Madame Magnolia Sharma's gold bangles, which she had placed over the knobs for safe-keeping. The blanket she draped over her arm.

'Very beautiful bed,' Madame Magnola had said. 'Very beautiful bed linen. In many places I go there is not good bed linen. Very rich people but not good bed linen. This is very excellent bed linen.'

'I think it was my aunt's.'

'And your aunt was a very beautiful lady who loved you? Yes?' Madame Magnolia Sharma was still gazing at the sheets with admira-

129

tion. 'I thought so. Any bad vibrations here will always be overcome by the good vibrations of your aunt.'

'Really?' Again Evelyn was cheered by this. Charles had been quite disparaging about her bed. Perhaps what Madame Magnolia had said would rid the place of any lingering atmosphere of contempt.

'Good God,' Charles had said. 'You haven't got one of those old brass beds, have you? You don't mean I have to sleep in that? They went out with the Ark, you know, Evelyn, the absolute Ark, those old double beds. I mean, most people these days have at least a queen size, if not a king. However do you expect me to fit in that?' He had screwed his face up into a petulant expression. It would have been better if, at that exact stage, she had shouted, 'Well, why don't you bugger off then?' and had thrown him out.

'And not blankets!' Charles had said. 'Surely not blankets, Evelyn? No one has blankets these days. Haven't you got a duvet? No? All I can say, Evelyn, is Good God, Evelyn, good God. I had no idea, absolutely no idea you lived like this.'

'Beautiful blanket,' said Madame Magnolia. 'Very best wool.' She folded it tenderly and placed it over the bed end as well.

Sometime while Evelyn was in a dreaming state, as the oil enfolded her scalp under one of Madame Magnolia's large white towels, and after the blue extract from a Himalayan plant had been carefully spread over her face to rejuvenate her skin, there was the sound of more vigorous knocking at the door. She was aware of Madame Magnolia's sigh and the sound of little silken-shod feet on the stairs. Madame Magnolia's shoes were made of soft black satin.

'What was that?' she murmured when she smelt the scent of flowers again. Madame Magnolia was wearing an essential oil that contained the essence of many blossoms.

'Very large man knocking at door.' Madame Magnolia sighed. 'In red coat. I sent him away.' There was a long silence. Perhaps it was Mark, thought Evelyn. He was quite large, but seldom called, and Jennifer had already rung anyway.

'Bad vibrations,' said Madame Magnolia. 'A man with a very

unhealthy lifestyle. His vibrations were very bad. His personality was south-west, which would also be wrong for you. You must have someone under the Northern Star. This person had no teeth and very dirty hair and he is wanting to give you strawberries, which I told him are too heating and will lead to a red complexion. Also he is wanting to give you cream. Full of fat.' Her voice became very austere, chillingly contemptuous. 'I told him it was not convenient.'

Evelyn let a silence lengthen. So Madame Magnolia had sent the busker away. 'Please,' said Madame Magnolia Sharma, 'no smiling. Face-pack will crack. None of my ladies eats strawberries. Or cream. It is against the guru's teachings.' Beneath the white towels and surrounded by the scent of oil, Evelyn felt very calm. 'It is also not convenient to have people calling while having a beauty treatment.' Madame Magnolia began to pat Evelyn's cheeks lightly with a sandalwood spatula. 'This will enhance your own natural colour,' she said, and stood back for a moment to view the results. 'Interruptions are not good. I have told the man with no teeth to go away and not come back.'

'Thank you,' said Evelyn. With Madame Magnolia in the house for a couple of hours everything was becoming very well arranged and splendidly explained in the most simplistic way.

'No talking, please.'

Evelyn closed her eyes.

Later, when she awakened, the day appeared to be more luminous. The garden looked less overgrown, the sea more kindly and a warmer blue. A light dappled sunlight patterned the pavement outside her house. The summer leaves were fluttering on the trees and the angle of the sun seemed delightful. A few cornflowers were coming into flower beside her front door so she stood for a while regarding them. Madame Magnolia had remarked upon the presence of blue flowers.

'Excellent,' she had said. 'Blue is your colour.'

'My friend Jennifer says red is better. She says I need brightening up.'

'Red is too violent for your personality. Blue is your colour. Please ignore Mrs Clark's advice.'

Just inside the front door, delicately placed upon the carpet, she had found a card from Madame Magnolia, who must have crept away quietly when Evelyn, soothed by oils and the gentle massage of her shoulders, fell asleep. The clock in the hall struck midday. The morning had gone. As she passed the foot of the stairs the telephone began to ring.

'Evelyn? Have you had your massage? We thought it might be a nice Christmas present for you to have a beauty treatment ready for' — and here Jennifer paused — 'you-know-who.'

'No, I don't. Who?'

'Alan.'

'Oh,' said Evelyn, 'the ex-headmaster. You know, I didn't really like him that much. I didn't actually like him at all.'

Jennifer took this news quite well, thought Evelyn.

'Well, Evelyn' — she gave a sigh here — 'you've got your musician, I suppose, but we do think you could reconsider Alan.'

'Musician?'

'Yes, Evelyn, that one you said plays at the Top of the Town.'

'Oh, him.' The busker again, thought Evelyn. At least he had been useful in deflecting Jennifer from the idea of the ex-headmaster.

'Evelyn, you're in a peculiar mood today. You've gone very grand about men, haven't you? Anyway, I've been thinking about what you said earlier and I thought I'd better ring back. Darling old Marky-Boots was listening to what you said and he said, "Good God, she's not going to be a nun, is she? You'd better get on to her straight away, darling," he said.'

'A nun?'

'Yes. Earlier when I was talking to you, you mentioned something about wanting to be a nun. I thought you mentioned a gun, but Marky says he thought you said nun. Marky says that if you're going to be a nun you won't be wanting your house any more so he could take it off your hands out of the goodness of his heart and use it as a bit of a spec.'

'A spec?' The tranquillity engendered by Madame Magnolia was abating quickly. Evelyn cupped her left cheek, now wonderfully scented and smoothed by the Himalayan treatment, and felt her head begin to ache slightly.

'You know, Evelyn — a spec. A speculation. He'd rent it out over the summer and even though the land's pretty dreadful he thinks he can clap two townhouses on it later and make a bit of money. Later next year your old cottage can either be demolished or it might be able to be sold for removal before they start knocking up some kind of Tuscan-style townhouse development.' She paused for a moment to take a deep breath. 'With balconies, of course.'

'But I'm not going to be a nun.'

Silence fell at the other end of the line.

'Evelyn, will you just excuse me for a moment?' Jennifer's voice was very cold now. 'Marky darling? Marky? She's changed her mind. She's not going to be a nun now.'

'But I've already rung Cadwalladers!' This remark from Marky came from some inner chamber of their house, thought Evelyn, perhaps from his study. Cadwalladers might be a demolition firm, or financiers, she thought.

'I didn't say anything about being a nun,' she said firmly, raising her voice. 'At no time did I mention a nun or say that I was going to be a nun.'

'Evelyn, there's no need to shout.'

'You don't listen to what I say. No one listens to what I say. I might as well never speak, for all the good it does me. I never mentioned the word nun. What I said was that I wanted a gun. I wanted a gun, Jennifer, so I could go out and shoot myself because I'm so sick of Christmas. And I'm sick of everybody and how they go on about Christmas. I said I wanted Frederick's gun back, Jennifer, so I could shoot myself. I very much regret handing the gun in during that arms amnesty. I did not say nun, Jennifer. I said gun.' She hung up and stood staring at the telephone which, now, remained silent. After five minutes she imagined Jennifer would not ring again, at least that day, and went out to look at the flowers again.

The garden had suddenly launched itself forth into summer. The old roses had had new shoots for weeks now, the latest leaves and branches red, but they would fade later to a worn green like the rest of the bushes. The plot of land was steep and rocky and life there was hard. The flowers often lay almost exultantly on clumps of old lilies or on the roses themselves with an air of triumph, as if actually appearing had been a wonder. Up the slope the leaves of the olive trees were fluttering in the wind from the sea.

'Not a good look, Evelyn,' Marky often said when he came to collect Jennifer. 'And your road's totally hopeless to turn around in. It's far too narrow and the parking's abysmal.' Jennifer's Mercedes, a birthday present from Marky, sometimes needed a grease or an oil change and might be in the garage having these jobs done. He would collect her in his own car. 'As I've said to you before, Evelyn, if only you'd asked me about this I'd have advised you against it. There were some very nice little townhouses a developer I know was having a bit of a struggle quitting — nothing the matter with them, of course, but the market was too finely tuned, shall we say, at that moment in time. And a Smeg kitchen, Evelyn. Think of that. And all new whiteware.'

'A Smeg kitchen,' she would repeat, not knowing exactly what that was. The stove in the kitchen of the cottage was of indeterminate make. Its label had long ago been cleaned away. It rocked slightly on the uneven stone floor and cakes she baked in it were inclined to come out higher on one side than the other.

'Dearie me.' That was what Jennifer usually said when she stood doubtfully in the kitchen, fortunately very infrequently. 'If only you'd said.' But said what? What could she have said? The cottage was the only property in the area in her price range. There had been no choice. They clearly assumed Frederick's investments were sizeable, and she did not disabuse them.

Spreading clumps of ox-eye daisies had suddenly rioted at the hint of warmer weather before the latest southerly storm when she had had to go and meet the ex-headmaster. Their tendrils fell over the rocky banks in the garden and over a small stone retaining wall outside the kitchen windows. Some of them were flowering and Evelyn went out to pick a posy of them, and also a bunch of roses. A few of the daisies were a larger species than she had seen before. Perhaps the advent of Madame Magnolia in the house that day had caused blossoms to appear magically, she thought.

With her kitchen scissors she trimmed weeds and grass away from the little stone wall and went indoors with the flowers. The faint scent of roses and daisies filtered through the bathroom, where she placed them in a vase on the washstand. The bathroom had been much improved, she thought, by the leaves and designs she had stencilled after Charles had come to stay so briefly — or perhaps the room had been made more noticeably quaint in the most arcane way by her painting. In this room she had bathed her narrow, pale body and got ready for Charles's various arrivals before he took up with the proprietor of the dress shop.

It was also in this room that she often stood now with a sense of secret horror, almost terror, at her own absurd ideas. How could she have ever contemplated that Charles might love her? she often wondered. Or that she would even want him to? Or that she could love him? What flight of imagination, what remnant of her own sense of herself, could have ever prompted her to think such a ridiculous and unsuitable thing? And Madame Magnolia Sharma would probably say now — if she were consulted on the matter — that Charles had the wrong kind of personality, perhaps going in the same direction as the wooden staircase. It had all been entirely wrong. Absurd. The shame of it made her cringe.

Chapter Twelve

Late at night when she finally went to bed she often stood for much longer than necessary to regard her own reflection in the old gilded mirror that hung above the bathroom washstand. The mirror was too small to show her full-length but she could see her pale face, her hair drawn back and tied with a black ribbon, her arms scratched from gardening encased in the long full sleeves of the Victorian nightdresses she usually wore. They had pintucking on the bodice and the high lace collars around her throat fastened with a small pearl button.

'Ridiculous,' she would say to no one because no one was there, and, picking up the hem of the night-dress in one hand so she would not trip on the stairs, she would go quietly up to her bedroom. The full moon over the sea would shine down like a mocking cheese, or, when it narrowed to a sickle, it would grin at her thinly, mocking again. The sardonic moon knew of her absurdities because she had not drawn the curtains when Charles came to stay — the moon knew everything.

Beyond the back veranda of the cottage a narrow pathway led to a garden shed that was tucked into a fold of the rocky garden. A previous owner had built a trellis framework around it, and upon this old roses grew. The shed itself, thus semi-disguised amid rampant plants, held the garden tools, paint, a sack of potatoes, Evelyn's gardening clothes (which were often too dirty to bring into the house) and gardening gloves encrusted with mud if it were winter, or stiff with dry dirt in the summer. They lay on the floor in a row, neatly placed in pairs, like severed hands.

This afternoon, in the cool, dim depths of this shed, Evelyn stood looking for her paints. When she had painted the mural after Charles came to stay she had put everything away carefully in here somewhere; also the little brushes she had used. She found them on a high shelf. A large spider scuttled away. Another eyed her from a warped beam of the ceiling. It was time, she thought, to make the mural of the tree in the cottage's entrance hall bloom, to fruit, to become an abundant and beautiful thing and not just the skeletal web of branches she had originally painted, the branches as thin as her own thoughts.

Charles would never come back now and if he did he would not be welcome. After he had gone and did not ever return she had slowly and naturally come to know him better than she ever had while he had been there, and his absence was a telling thing in its own worthless way. It had been much more eloquent and much more revealing than his light laughter from her parlour, the touch of his well-manicured hand on her slim arm, the sound of his pleasant voice in the conversations whose content and subjects she had now forgotten, the tickets to plays and the delicate suppers afterwards that had seemed so beguiling at the time. Light, she thought, had played its part at that fleeting time in her life when she had laughed, cleaned her old bracelets and actually worn them, and had gone out in the evening in sequinned sandals. There was the candlelight of the restaurants, the concealed lighting of the bars where Charles sometimes bought her a glass of champagne before a play, the actual and often lurid lighting of the plays themselves. Often they had been about meanness of spirit, deception and unhappiness, she realised now.

The light came into the hall of the cottage in a diffused way, through various narrow doorways. From the parlour door it was clearer and sharper because it was reflected from the sea. The door at the foot of the stairs, at the very end of the hall, led into the spare bedroom, which was always a shadowy room even in high summer. Banked outside its windows were tall old lilies and through their large fleshy dark green leaves came a serene and aqueous light. From the back door the brightness was almost used up, second-hand from passing through the kitchen. By the time it reached the hall there was hardly any left.

In the front of the hall where the light was sharper and clearer Evelyn began to paint apples on the branches of the tree. She made each fruit large and luscious, the skin as rosy as it would be the instant before picking. She gilded the top of each fruit and drew a fine curved little stem with a few extra leaves, also gilded. But towards the door of the spare bedroom she made the apples greener, promising a lusciousness later, but now at the stage of ripeness that would make an orchardist imagine he had to wait a fortnight before picking. Those stems she gilded with a darker paint, almost bronze, and made the leaves smaller. In one or two places she painted clusters of flowers and touched them with bronze again, fading the pink of the blossoms to a faint shade of sepia on the shadowy edges. The myth of her tree could cover all stages of a season, she thought, from blossom to decay, and then painted a few withered apples, rotting, in various shades of brown at its foot.

After this she went into the bathroom and painted an extravagant tendril of ivy around the bathroom mirror, and more ivy up the window frame to surround the casement with a luxuriance of greenery. She looked at herself in the mirror again and her own steady eyes stared back at her, without expression or lustre.

'What are you doing, Evelyn?' Jennifer rang as twilight began to fall. Her activities had kept her occupied all afternoon, thought Evelyn. The whole day had nearly gone.

'Painting.'

'Painting? Whatever are you painting? No, don't tell me — I haven't really got time to listen. I've just rung for a moment. Evelyn, I've been thinking — maybe I've been a bit short with you lately. I do get a little impatient but it's because I'm so busy.'

'Have you? Are you?' Having Madame Magnolia there in the morning had done her a lot of good, thought Evelyn. Aspects of her life which she had imagined were chillingly close and unable to be viewed philosophically had now retreated to some middle distance of thought.

'Yes, I honestly do think I've been a bit short with you lately, Evelyn. It's just that I haven't been well. And I've been rather worried about various things. Frantic, actually.'

'You never seem worried,' said Evelyn, 'or unwell. I always think you and Mark go through life completely untouched by everything and you've got no idea of worry or pain or anguish or anything.'

'Oh, Evelyn, that's nonsense.' Marky must be out, thought Evelyn, or Jennifer would not say 'oh'. 'At the moment we're just about worried sick. I really can't tell you what's the matter but it's something to do with Marky's work and various aspects of things. Evelyn, it's just too complicated to explain even if I were able to which I'm not because there's an embargo on everything. Well, all the financial stuff anyway. If the press got hold of it we'd be absolutely dead lumber, as Marky would say.'

'Really? An embargo?' This sounded much more complicated than her own humble counting of potatoes to see how long the bag would last, or her painting of a couple of dozen mythical apples on empty branches and rotting fruit beneath them.

'Even Jared's in trouble, I think. He hasn't said much but it's something about winding odometers back on cars, Evelyn, and all the dealers do it. I can't imagine why they've picked on him. He's always been so sensitive. His relationship with that lovely girl I told you about

— well, all that may be in jeopardy now. As I understand it she's going out with another of his dealer friends now, one who's not being investigated.' She sighed deeply. 'Anyway, Evelyn, you've been slightly on my mind. You didn't really mean it, did you, when you said earlier you wanted to shoot yourself?'

'Yes.'

'Oh, Evelyn, you mustn't think like that. Don't be ridiculous.' Mark must definitely be out, thought Evelyn. There had been two 'ohs' now.

'I can think like that if I like.' She stood looking out at the garden for a moment or two. 'And I'm not ridiculous. But I can't get Frederick's gun back, Jennifer, and I've looked in the telephone book for gunsmiths and they aren't advertised there any more. I suppose it's the gangs and the bank robbers and so on. I suppose shops that sell guns don't advertise they've got them any more, do they? I simply don't know. It seems impossible, anyway, for me to get a gun so it'd be unlikely I'd shoot myself, for that reason.'

'But Evelyn, you always seem all right, don't you? You always seem cheerful.' Jennifer waited for reassurance. 'Anyway, be that as it may — let's just leave the business of shooting yourself for the moment. How did your massage with Madame Magnolia go? We thought it might be' — she paused here for a moment — 'a timely Christmas gift for you.'

'Lovely,' said Evelyn. 'It was lovely, thank you. I felt quite different afterwards. It was quite surprising, really, because it gave me rather a shock when she arrived and I couldn't be bothered at all, but afterwards I felt quite different. I've been painting all afternoon.'

'You're painting that dreadful kitchen at last?' Jennifer's voice contained a faint degree of excitement. 'Marky'll be so pleased. He thinks you should just do a quickie on the place, Evelyn, and flick it over as soon as possible.'

'I've been painting apples,' said Evelyn, 'or some kind of mythical fruit a bit like apples on my mural of the tree, that's all. But I feel quite different since this morning. After Madame Magnolia gave me the massage and put the blue Himalayan stuff on my face I felt marvellous.'

'Not the blue Himalayan stuff, Evelyn?' Jennifer's voice was rising now. 'Not the Himalayan stuff, Evelyn, did you say that?'

'Yes.'

'Oh, Evelyn, it's slightly hallucinogenic. You might feel rather let down tomorrow. Do be prepared, my dear, do be prepared. This explains everything.' She rang off with a slight exclamation. 'I must go, I must go.' Her voice came urgently into the receiver as if she might be talking about something else entirely now. Late in the evening Evelyn got out the paints again and put more apples on the spreading branches of the tree. They glimmered there, gilded and glowing, like a fruit from an ancient land, enticing and delicious. The leaf tendrils she had painted in the bathroom seemed a little ungenerous so she added another branch above the window frame and painted more large green leaves to hang down the architrave to mirror and exceed the sudden growth outside the windows. If the hedgeclippers were not sharpened soon the cottage might be engulfed in greenery by Christmas, she thought. At the little bay window of the spare bedroom the lilies had suddenly spread to almost touch the glass and self-sown begonias clutched at that stony ground in generous swathes. The weeds and grasses, though, were taking hold and sprouting in every direction. There must be, thought Evelyn, definite warmth in the soil to signal the beginning of summer growth even though the weather had been dark and stormy on many days, never more so than when she had had to go and meet the ex-headmaster.

As if prompted by this recollection, not at all savoury, the telephone rang again.

'Hello? Is that Mrs Evelyn Jarrold? I don't know if you'll remember me but this is —'

'Yes, I know. It's Alan, isn't it?' It was the ex-headmaster again.

'I'm sorry this is a little late to ring' — he sounded slightly apologetic — 'but I haven't been well lately and I'm a bit behind with all the little jobs I wrote on my list today.'

A list? So she had been on a list, like a task, thought Evelyn. *Ring*

Evelyn Jarrold. Or perhaps *Ring that mad friend of the Clarks.*

'I write out a list every day so I don't forget anything. It's only nine o'clock. I didn't think you'd have gone to bed yet. The Clarks said you were a night owl.' His voice sounded hesitant.

So, thought Evelyn, the Clarks had been talking about her again. Jennifer had probably given an admonitory screech and said, 'Poor old Evelyn usually has her head in some book or other in the evenings. Reads till all hours. Lives in another world. The one she's reading now's all about someone who shot himself, so she says.'

A night owl? She let the pause lengthen. 'I was actually painting and I forgot the time myself. I don't know if you could say I'm a night owl. I am,' she said, 'myself.'

'Quite so,' said the little man and gave a dry cough. And then, 'Painting?'

'Yes, painting,' said Evelyn. 'I've been painting a mural — a huge spreading tree with apples on it. I've been gilding them so they catch the light of the moon really well. The moonlight comes in through the old glass panels in my front door.'

The ex-headmaster sighed.

'The Clarks said you were artistic,' he said. It sounded like a crime. 'But I mean there are quite a lot of good people in the world who're artistic. Don't imagine I think it's a fault. Everything in its place, is what I say, and I do have my own very deep interest in the bowling club. I've been on the committee for the past five years and I have hopes of being honorary vice-president one day. We've had a mural painted on one of the walls of our clubrooms.' He waited for a moment of two. 'My neighbour's taken up sculpture since he retired,' he said, 'and he always seemed such a down to earth man. No one had the faintest suspicion that he was at all artistic.' He waited again. 'He makes,' he said, 'model aeroplanes out of beer cans — all undone and flattened, of course.'

'Really?' said Evelyn.

'Anyway,' he said, 'I've rung because I've reached a bit of a dead end with these interviews I've been doing. I did have hopes, very great hopes I might add' — he sighed — 'of one very, very lovely lady I met further north. But' — his voice became fainter — 'there were various difficulties that presented themselves and —'

'Of course, of course.' Evelyn was once more doubling up on her remarks to provide a generosity of conversation that did not actually exist. That would be the cross-dresser who danced all night. And wasn't there also someone who owed a lot of money somewhere? Jennifer had gone on about that at least twice.

'None of us is getting any younger,' said the ex-headmaster gloomily. 'One must think of the future and what it might hold.'

'I never do.' Evelyn dabbed another apple with a little more gold paint that had not yet dried on the brush. The mural was looking remarkably life-giving.

'Do you not?' The ex-headmaster sighed heavily. 'The Clarks said you had odd ideas, but never mind. I shall just have to bear with that.' He sighed again. 'What I was thinking was — would you be prepared to meet me again one day? I was rather preoccupied when I last spoke to you and perhaps I didn't give the matter my best attention.'

Evelyn remained silent, breathing carefully so he would hear no noise from her end of the line.

'The Clarks said you suddenly had this other man in your life.' The ex-headmaster continued his discourse. 'A musician, they said.' There was a silence for a moment. 'And of quite some note, it seems. Plays at the Top of the Town, they said, but what I thought was that maybe I might have a chance to meet you again and perhaps we might get on better this time.' He waited. 'Musicians can be unreliable,' he said at last, 'and as far as I know it's an uncertain lifestyle. What's in fashion one year is out of fashion the next so, using your friend as an example, he might be playing at the Top of the Town now but he might not be playing there always. It won't always be like it is now.'

'No, I don't think it would be — I think he's planning to travel.' Fragments of her conversation with the Robinsons were beginning to come back to her now. What was it they had said? The busker went walkabout quite often and took his girlfriend with him, if he had one, in the car? They had had to sleep on the side of the road. Was that it? 'He tours,' she said at last into the telephone receiver, and listened to the ex-headmaster's small intake of breath.

'Probably Las Vegas,' he said at last, 'and the nightclub circuit. I couldn't compete with that.' He sighed again. 'And you seemed quite a nice woman, too, if only I'd thought about it properly. I was exhausted,' he said. 'I've had a sort of little breakdown. Interviewing everyone exhausted me, and there was all the driving too.'

'Miles and miles of it,' chimed in Evelyn, 'over hill and dale.'

'Indeed. So you remember,' he said, 'I did think you were a bit too tall — and possibly too young. I did have in mind an older lady with, perhaps, more ordinary interests. I thought,' he said, 'croquet.'

'Croquet?'

'But, of course, nothing's set in stone.' He spoke hastily now, as if eager to make amends. 'China-painting would be fine. Even tennis.' Set in stone was one of Jennifer's favourite phrases, thought Evelyn. He must have had quite a long conversation with her before ringing. The ex-headmaster was speaking quickly now, perhaps anxious to make up for any imagined offence. 'If I met the right person I could always rene-gotiate my stance on height and interests and so on. After all' — he swallowed a couple of times — 'the human heart knows no bounds.' He sounded semi-strangled now, as if his words had almost choked him. Jennifer must really have given him an ear-bashing, thought Evelyn. 'At the end of the day,' he said, 'it is only true love that counts.' He went into a paroxysm of coughing. 'Even at our age.'

'I'm not that old,' said Evelyn at last.

'Of course not, of course not.' Eager to make amends again, he tripped over the words. 'I was just speaking figuratively.'

'Ah,' said Evelyn. By making such a non-comment she was committed to nothing, she thought.

'A chap I know' — the ex-headmaster was becoming desperate now — 'recently married a woman second time around and she's turned out to be quite nice, really. They've had a few problems and we all turn a blind eye to a lot, she says, but they aren't really unhappy and things haven't turned out too badly I suppose,' he said. 'Now, she's quite an artistic person that you might like. She does' — he paused again — 'freehand ornamental cake icing in primary colours — and not by the book either. We've got quite a nice little circle already, haven't we, what with my neighbour who makes the aeroplane models.'

'Dear God,' said Evelyn.

'Good. I thought you'd be pleased.'

Later, as the moonlight was shining on the gilded apples, Evelyn went upstairs in her white nightie, taking with her a jar of perfumed lotion left behind by Madame Magnolia. It had been gift-wrapped and had a label saying it was a Christmas present from Jennifer and Mark but the day had been so enervating, the shock of the ex-headmaster's second approach so tiny but telling, the visit of Madame Magnolia so bizarre that she felt in need of a gift right now.

'Perhaps we could meet again,' the ex-headmaster had said. 'I was thinking — perhaps I could take you out to lunch this time, perhaps to that place I go to that you spoke so warmly of, that place where I get the roast meals.'

Oh no, thought Evelyn, not the blasted roast dinners again. Not them. Enticed by her silence he continued.

'They do roast pork on a Wednesday, and Thursday's usually beef day, but if you'd prefer lamb, Monday might be the best day. Parking's good on a Monday.' He seemed hopeful, she thought, of lamb.

'I see,' said Evelyn. She was standing on one leg now, one small foot in a black velvet scuff her only hold upon the face of the world. Perhaps, she thought, she might float away in a blessed way, or just miraculously disappear.

'You could choose.' Magnanimous and suddenly generous, he was spreading himself before her. The other women must have turned out to be absolute disasters, she thought, if his inspections of them had prompted this.

'I'll have to think about it, and I'll let you know.' He gave her his telephone number, each digit carefully enunciated, and he made her read it back to him.

'I'll say au revoir then,' he said and gave a thin little laugh. 'Your wish is my command, but I'd recommend the lamb. And, by the way, the surname's Fosdyke. I don't know if I've told you.'

Fosdyke, thought Evelyn.

The dizzy moon rose late that night and Evelyn, watching from the upstairs windows, saw its sharp outline come from behind scudding clouds almost shockingly as the wind rose. The sky was full of foreboding, and the moon shone fitfully and almost fretfully — a glimpse here, a glimpse there and then darkness for many moments as more clouds passed. It would be a stormy night again, thought Evelyn, possibly with thunder and lightning by morning. The sharp moon had seemed to grin at her again, perhaps horribly, she thought, but she was aware this fantasy, this imagined derision, was probably caused by her own guilty conscience. In happy households where everything was secure, sanguine couples would merely imagine it was a night of intermittent bad weather illuminated by a fragment of the moon and would think no more of it, she imagined. They might not even note the shape of the moon. It would be left to fanciful and self-lacerating souls such as herself to stare sadly out into the gloom and imagine a kind of punishment was being thrust upon them. The thin, mean smile of the moon, the darkness and uncertainty of the sky — all of these were just chastisements she had invented for herself.

Thunder had begun to growl from the east by now, and further over the harbour, quite a distance away beyond other far-off bays, lightning began to flicker. The storm, she thought, might drift away and would possibly not touch her cottage or the little bay in which it stood. Everyone might sleep peacefully with just the sound of soothing rain upon tiles.

As for any peacefulness of thought — that was another matter. As always when she looked out into the night, her thoughts were dark. She had imagined, somehow, that Charles would be like Frederick and because she wanted this to be so then it would be. But it had not. Charles was so unlike Frederick that it was like comparing a dog and a cat, or a calf and a lamb. How could she have been so inept, so gauche? Evelyn stirred uneasily, and clasped both arms across her chest like someone carrying out an act of supplication. The dishonour to herself, the ravishment of her small house's privacy, the disrespect to her possessions had all been caused by her own hopeful stupidity.

'You must make an effort, Evelyn,' Jennifer often said, and she had done so and this is where it had led.

Silenced and stilled by her own secrets, Evelyn stood and wept as the thunder growled further east now, hardly discernible, and the lightning flickered on the horizon. The night might be peaceful after all, Evelyn thought. The storm may not be coming this way even vaguely. The moon continued to appear and disappear behind clouds like a smile playing a game and she thought of Charles and how he had sometimes smiled, but not often and mostly without genuine humour, particularly at the end.

He had read the labels on the bottles of wine she bought at the supermarket when he ceased to bring her wine himself, and as she poured him a glass he would say, 'Not a year I know,' turning away, preoccupied. When he came to visit she would always give him a glass of wine and some little sandwiches.

'Not a vineyard I know. Not a variety of bread I've ever bought,' he sometimes said. 'Not a company I've heard of. Not a label I've seen. French?' He would look doubtfully at the bottle and might turn it in his hands as if seeking a secret from its actual glass, the label having proved deeply unsatisfactory. 'Often,' he would say in that dismissive manner he had, 'they don't travel well.' She would just say, 'Oh,' in that way Marky particularly disliked.

'The thing about you, Evelyn,' Marky had said last week, or was it the week before, 'is that the way you talk is just so bloody silly. I know you think I don't like you, but I don't really care about you one way or the other. I couldn't really say I disliked you, so don't think that. It's just the way you talk, Evelyn — it's so bloody silly. People say things to you and you just stand there and say, "Oh".'

'It's because I'm polite.' She had raised her voice, she remembered that. Her voice, she thought, had suddenly possessed a hard note. 'I'm polite and when people are rude it puzzles me and I don't know what to do or say. I suppose I say "Oh" because of that.'

'I'm terribly sorry about Marky.' Jennifer had telephoned later. 'He's had a really terrible day and they had a few drinkies afterwards. The poor darling's come home slightly under the weather and I've put him to bed. He's been under a lot of stress. Don't take any notice of what he said, Evelyn. It was just the booze talking.'

'Was it?' she had said.

Chapter Thirteen

The horror of Christmas was a reasonably recent thing. Christmas used to be a calm and measured festivity.

'Any cards?' Frederick used to say when he returned home from the office. By then the grip of summer would be upon everything and on some days the landscape almost used to shimmer with heat. The days and nights now seemed colder, Evelyn thought, and she drew her wrap more closely about her shoulders. She was standing at the upstairs windows again, looking out over the sea, which was a steely grey in the very early morning, gulls crying as they drifted on eddies in the wind.

The Christmas cards then had been more cheerful, certainly more numerous and had contained ordinary news. Now they often had excuses and little else. Evelyn considered the excuses unnecessary. The first Christmas she had spent alone had passed almost unnoticed. There were hardly any cards or gifts. It was as though most of the people she had known stood breathlessly silent as far as she was concerned, in a desperate hush of their own manufacture, perhaps so she would not notice them.

But by the time her second Christmas alone approached everything had become more crowded in a peculiarly silent way, the strident ringing of the telephone often bringing the only real sound of a human voice.

'Evelyn?' The voices were often conspiratorial, as if the speakers possessed an unpalatable secret that only she knew: that she was to be by herself at Christmas. 'Evelyn, just a tiny word, dear, literally as we rush out the door. Yes, darling, I'm coming.' There were often faint cries in the distance. 'Yes, darling, I know we have to be on the motorway early. I'm just having a tiny word with Evelyn. Evelyn Jarrold, darling. You must remember Evelyn? Evelyn, we do hope you're all right. Did you get our card? Lovely. We're not doing presents this year, except for the immediate family, but we sent you that lovely picture of the Holy Family so you could be guarded from above.' A worn and ashen Madonna might hold an emaciated yellow baby that looked on the point of death while in the background a darkly bearded figure lurked. I must be sensible, Evelyn would think. It is not gloomy. It is just that with Old Masters, and not just the ones on Christmas cards, the colour alters over the centuries and everything goes dull and brown. The real sky, when she looked up, seemed empty, though. An aeroplane. An advertising balloon. Some seagulls. Another aeroplane, smaller this time. A helicopter. More seagulls. Clouds. No clouds. Emptiness.

By the third Christmas people seemed to have a renewed capacity for effort. The letterbox began to be almost crowded with messages, cheerily dressed in red or green and liberally gilded or garlanded with holly, an occasional brave Santa Claus beaming from the front covers of cards that had become guiltily elaborate. Cards piled up in her letterbox, stacked on top of one another and vying for position, many of them sent by air and at the last moment, often deeply religious. She had opened them and regarded them carefully in the evenings, sitting in her kitchen as the dinner cooked. There was always an abundance of blue-robed females riding donkeys and clutching infants of various shapes, sometimes alone in a nameless desert, occasionally accompanied by a distant male figure in sandals and a hooded cloak. Deserts figured a lot. Men on camels riding through a desert. Just the desert itself with the odd palm tree. Animals grouped in a stable staring at a bundle. Just the bundle. It was hopeless, Evelyn thought, to imagine that much of this luridly printed correspondence contained sincere thought because the messages were so at variance with the printed pictures. Awfully sorry we haven't been in touch all year. It seems to have gone by so quickly and now we're off for three weeks with the Hendersons, who've got a time-share in Noosa. It should be fabulous fun. If you feel like a walk do pop over and pick some lemons from the garden. The tree has a wonderful crop. Don't worry about Adolf — he'll be in the kennels. You may need to give the gate a good push because it jams. The children have really grown up and you would probably not recognise them now.

By the fourth Christmas everyone had settled down. Most had given up entirely: a relief. The few cards that flicked into her letterbox were of the most determined kind now. Madonnas proliferated, Holy Families in the ascendency, possibly because most groups contained some kind of looming masculine figure. There were a few jolly Santa Clauses, elves who mysteriously seemed to be sitting in shoes, ditto clothed mice wearing red coats, hats and scarves but no pants, more deserts, quite a lot of camels, fewer bundles. By the next Christmas most mail ceased, except that from the truly determined and mostly containing just a scrawled signature and long printed serial letters about what their families had done over the year. Qualifications in dentistry abounded, there was the odd doctor, grandchildren born, grandchildren in football teams, more grandchildren expected, late babies for the middle-aged, an occasional divorce, superannuation funds lost in unexpected swindles, a daughter gone to jail, the confession of this firmly typed as if it must be faced, uttered and thus made semi-presentable.

Her own news she kept a secret. The move from the house on

Fitzroy Point into town and then to the cottage. Her job with a publisher, only intermittent, and accomplished at home when she was required occasionally to give an opinion on a small volume of artistic reminiscences by an antique dealer, or a gardening book on an arcane and specialised subject, perhaps bulbs.

'You've got a desk, Evelyn.' Jennifer had been astonished when she first saw it. 'Whatever have you got a desk for? You're working? Working at what? Editing? I never knew you could do that.'

'Did you not?' she had said, each word clearly spaced and enunciated like three little raps on the knuckle for Jennifer. 'I can do anything. You may not be aware of it, but I can.'

'Don't be so silly, Evelyn. Just leave all that and come with me. You can do it later, or tomorrow, or something. I'm going to collect Cynthia' — the Mercedes was parked askew at the gate — 'and we're going into town for lunch. You can come too. It's only thirty dollars. Surely you've got thirty dollars? Everyone's got thirty dollars, Evelyn.'

'I can't come. I have to work. And I haven't got thirty dollars.'

'But you can work anytime, Evelyn. I can lend you thirty dollars. And Cynthia's trying to give up smoking. We have to help, Evelyn. We need to be supportive.'

'I don't actually like Cynthia. I have to work now. Cynthia can give up ciggies or not, just as she pleases. I don't care.'

'You've become very hard, Evelyn.'

'I know,' she would say, grinning.

The work, the protective idea of the work, had become her buffer. It kept the curious at bay.

'Why haven't we seen you, Evelyn?' The tone was often accusatory, as if she had done something wrong.

'I've been working.'

'Have you, Evelyn?' They often seemed relieved, she thought. Evelyn's got herself a job — the best thing to do, really. It'll keep her amused and out of trouble. She'll meet people. She might meet someone she likes. She imagined they might talk about her like that. No need to worry about Evelyn. She's working now. Someone said she's editing something, I think that's what it was. She's working anyway. Oh super.

So she had deliberately dropped out of sight and her slowly emptying letterbox as one Christmas became another was, she thought, a sign of her success. The Christmas cards from people she had once regularly seen had seemed horrible in their difference from the friendships she had once enjoyed with the senders, and their absence no longer reminded her of this. The empty letterbox was a benediction.

The card from the bank this year was the only really disquieting message and that was innocent enough. The secretary or clerk who had sent it to her would have done so in a disembodied way, simply because her name was on a list of depositors. It was just a business thing and contained news of interest rates and a new banking facility, a public relations exercise masquerading as a festive message. Thousands of people might have received one, she thought as she put it in the rubbish bin. It was nothing to do with Charles who, at that moment, could have been romping in a black and gold bedroom with the enormous shopkeeper, licking her navel and simultaneously spanking her robust thighs with a new hairbrush bought especially for the purpose.

When she returned to the letterbox later in the day another card rested therein, possibly delivered by the postman to the wrong address and correctly re-delivered by a punctilious neighbour. The picture was of a miniature Santa Claus valiantly standing at the front of a huge sleigh that was a massive half-circle of Christmas moss. With a delicate and inadequate piece of string he was trying to control two huge half-circle moss reindeer who were wildly galloping through a completely empty landscape on extremely thin legs. The message inside was from an elderly lady whom she had once known well and who was now in a very distant home for the aged. Love and blessings from Norma. That was all. Evelyn placed this silent message in the middle of her mantelpiece. It seemed to her that she and Norma both understood how things were now.

The telephone rang again, as if trained to do so.

'It's me again.' It was Andrea. 'Look, Evelyn, I know I've told you millions of times, but you could come with me on Christmas Day if you wanted to — only you'd have to wait outside in the garden. Hilda's a total recluse and I'm the only person she lets into the house from one year's end to the next. She's cash-strapped but asset-rich and I've just got to keep in with her.' She paused for a moment to draw breath. 'This business of Christmas always drives me crazy.' She hung up.

Chapter Fourteen

'Have I ever told you exactly' — Andrea paused and took a gulp of an acidic cabernet shiraz sold on special at the supermarket for only six dollars ninety five, perhaps the end of a line — 'how my marriage, or if I'm to be specific, my non-marriage, actually ended? Evelyn, this is terrible wine.'

'I know. But it was cheap.' Evelyn watched the large hand of Andrea's clock falter slightly and the clock, waveringly, struck eleven. 'I hadn't realised it's so late. I must be going.'

'Eleven's early.' Andrea pulled a contemptuous face but whether this was about the wine or the time Evelyn could not be certain. 'I blame my father.' Andrea slumped down in her chair and gazed morosely into her wine glass. 'As there isn't anything better I suppose you'd better fill this up again, Evelyn.' She held it out. The remnants of a pizza lay in its box on a trunk Andrea used as a coffee table, and among an untidy clutter of recent and ancient *Vogues* the crumbs of pizza crust, olives, smoked chicken and much else glimmered. 'One day,' said Andrea, 'I must tidy all that up. Anyway' — she gave a deep sigh — 'I haven't ever really told you the full story, the entire thing.'

'You told me once that you were glad and you were only slightly depressed for two days, then you went to the cinema and never thought another thing about it.'

'I did not. I never said any such thing. I was broken-hearted for four years.'

'You never told me that.' Evelyn poured herself another glass of the shiraz. 'There's not much of this left. Have I ever told you that theory of mine that there should be a supplementary tiny bottle on the side of each main bottle so you could press a little button and get just one more glass out? I always seem to want just one more glass but the bottle's empty.'

'I'm sure I never told you I was only depressed for two days.' Andrea stared across the room, bellicose and at bay in a large green chair. It seemed that she was not to be deflected.

'You did so.'

'I did not.'

'You did so.'

'I would never have said any such thing. I was absolutely destroyed. I couldn't even choose any colours for the house or any redecorations or anything. My confidence was absolutely shattered. I'm sure I told you. It was three years before I finally decided to have the kitchen painted yellow and another year before I called the painter.' She sighed deeply again. 'I blame my father.' Andrea continued to stare into space, occasionally sipping the wine. From far away, down by the sea, came the sound of a foghorn. A mist must be rising, thought Evelyn, and she would have to drive home through wreaths of fog. Blast.

'What for?' After a long silence she spoke. Andrea's eyes were shut and she might possibly have drifted off to sleep.

'The break-up of my marriage, of course.' Andrea's eyes snapped open again immediately. Not asleep at all, thought Evelyn. Just contemplating, or resting like a lizard on a rock. 'For the whole attitude I used to have to men, and myself. I blame him entirely.' She snapped her mouth shut like the end of a lemon. 'The whole thing was my father's fault entirely.'

'Really?'

'Absolutely. If he hadn't had such a demonic power complex and if the sociological demographics of our household when I was a child had been more even, vis-à-vis my mother having some power instead of being crushed by his chauvinistic attitudes re domesticity, I might have had a better self-esteem level and therefore I wouldn't have imagined I needed to see myself reflected in someone else's eyes and therefore I wouldn't have married Patrick so the whole thing, the entire mess of my life, is absolutely my father's fault.' She gazed fiercely into space, then stood up suddenly. 'I'm sick of this awful wine,' she said, and put her glass down with a bang on the trunk. 'I'm going to see if I've got anything better under the stairs. I'm sure there's something there that's been recommended by *Cuisine* magazine. We need something nice, Evelyn. Our fathers have ruined our lives.'

'Have they?'

'Definitely.' Andrea's voice came, muffled but nearly sonorous, from the cupboard under the staircase now. In a moment there was an exclamation of satisfaction. She marched back into the sitting room with another bottle of wine and began to attack it with an implement of bewildering design.

'Whatever's that peculiar thing you've got there?' Evelyn put her reading glasses on the end of her nose. What Andrea had in her hand looked like a cross between a small hammer and the miniature scale model of a chromium staircase.

'My new bottle opener, of course.' Andrea was back in snappy mode. 'It's the latest design from Scandinavia — don't you know anything, Evelyn?'

'Probably not.' Evelyn held out her glass. 'I've just got that old corkscrew thing that's years old.' It was going to be a much longer evening than she had anticipated. More foghorns were hooting now from the sea. The fog must be thickening.

'What I think we'd better do,' said Andrea as she filled their glasses again, 'is just stay here while I tell you the complete story of my marriage — it's a very long story, Evelyn, so it's going to take ages. I'll get an eiderdown each. We can just go to sleep where we are. You can't drive home now and the weather's terrible. Best to stay till morning. Shut up. Shut up!' She was shouting towards the windows now. From down the street a dog was barking. Evelyn closed her eyes. Andrea was always so energetic, so undeterred, so violently active. It was amazing — admirable, really — where she got her zeal from. 'Shut up, shut up!' Andrea continued to shout at the dog.

'The thing was' — she was settling back in her chair again and arranging the eiderdown, the dog now silent — 'that I had no idea at all about what was going on. I mean, Evelyn, how pathetic can you get? I just thought when my best friend was waiting on the beach for us with a freshly made quiche for lunch when we came ashore — did I tell you we had a catamaran then? — well, I just thought she was being a very kind friend. How silly can you get? How silly could I get?'

Evelyn took a sip of the new wine. Miles better than the other one, she thought. A merlot.

'This is nice,' she said after a long pause. It might be best to get Andrea off the topic of her failed marriage at this time of night.

'It ought to be.' Andrea was back in snappish modus. 'I told Patrick that if he was going to give me some wine as part of our separation agreement it had better be good.'

'That was kind.' I sound like someone at a vicarage afternoon tea, thought Evelyn.

'Evelyn' — Andrea was wagging her head from side to side — 'you're just pathetic. It wasn't kind of him at all. He was just trying to get out of paying actual money. Probably someone gave him the wine as part of some deal or other and he never even had to pay for it. You'd never know what Patrick was doing from one day to the next. He could have been fucking some winemaker's wife and robbing the poor bastard's cellar at the same time.'

'It was a nice thought, anyway. It's a very nice wine.' Evelyn sipped reflectively. The room was beginning to look faintly blurred. 'Are you painting that wall?' She gestured towards the fireplace. 'Are you changing the colour scheme?'

'No, I'm not. And it wasn't a nice thought. Patrick's just a bastard.' Andrea perked up in the chair now, glaring across the room at Evelyn, her face set, the juggernaut jaw thrust out. 'Don't expect me to be grateful. Four years I spent here in a state of terrible agony, never knowing what he was doing or when he was coming home or anything. And I'm definitely not redecorating again. Whatever made you think I was?' She put on her round owlish glasses and stared at her friend. 'Are you drunk, Evelyn?'

'Certainly not.'

'You are.'

'I'm not.'

'You must be to think I'm redecorating the lounge. That's a painting up there, Evelyn. It's been hanging there for years.'

'Well,' said Evelyn rearranging herself slightly in the chair and tucking the eiderdown under her chin, 'I don't remember that great big square of just plain green up there before.'

'It's been there for years. It's by Anton Smikhend.'

'I've never heard of Anton Smikhend.'

'Wherever have you been, Evelyn, wherever have you been? Anton Smikhend was very big in the eighties. Whatever were you doing in the eighties? No, no, don't tell me.' Andrea fell about again in mock horror rolling her eyes a bit more. 'You were living in a state of oppressed domesticity on that big property you and Fred had up past the point.'

'I used to make bread then.' Evelyn took another sip of wine. It would be best, she thought, not to take up the challenge of discussing domestic slavery, oppression or, really, even Anton Smikhend.

'You were shackled, Evelyn, in domestic slavery.' Andrea glared belligerently across the room.

'I was not. I liked making bread. It made the house smell nice. I was perfectly happy living in that place.'

'It was chauvinist slavery.' Andrea always claimed to be an anarchist.

'It was not. It was a perfectly nice life. I loved all the ducks and hens.'

'Oh God, how many ducks and hens did you have to look after?'

'How should I know?' Evelyn was staring at the patch of green on the wall. I'm sure I've never seen that before, she thought. I am either mad or possibly drunk. 'It depended on the shooting season and so on. When the shooting season began we used to get a lot of ducks on the dam because Frederick never allowed any shooting there. And as for hens,' she said, sipping the wine again, 'it all depended on what battery hens needed rescuing. If Frederick had rescued a lot of battery hens we'd have a lot of hens for a while. The numbers fluctuated.'

'How chauvinist.' Andrea gave a contemptuous snort. 'So Frederick so-called rescued the hens and then he left you to look after them. How disgusting.'

'No it wasn't.'

'Yes, it was.'

'No, it wasn't.'

'Yes, it was.'

'I liked them. I liked looking after them. How could Frederick possibly look after all the hens and ducks and the whole property all the time when he was away on business such a lot? Be reasonable.'

'I am being reasonable.' Andrea glared at Evelyn. 'You're the one being unreasonable. You can't blame me for being totally opposed to male neo-nazi ideas and stereotyping.' She snapped her mouth shut.

'I liked the hens.' Evelyn was staring at the picture again. Surely those wavy lines across it had not been there before? Or had they? 'I used to give them names. There was Philippa and Jane and Antonia and Emily and Mary and Louise and Adeline —'

'Oh, shut up. Just shut up.'

Evelyn took a deep breath. The room seemed to have shrunk and wherever she looked there appeared to be only a narrow corridor to see through, the rest surrounded by a blackish mist. With a final scrap of energy she roused herself, assembled her wavering thoughts and spoke.

'Weren't you telling me about' — and here she grasped for the name of Patrick's second wife — 'Stinkerbell?' It might be just possible, even at this hour of the night, to prevent a fight and get Andrea wafted into a safer harbour. 'Surely,' she said, 'Stinkerbell can't be her real name?'

'No, it isn't. That's what I call her.' There was a long silence. 'Her real name could possibly be something like Marilyn or Helen or Samantha.'

'You must know, Andrea.'

Andrea gave a horrible cackle and the light from her new avant garde milled-steel standard lamp made her spectacles glitter strangely.

'I do,' she said. 'It's actually Annabelle. Spelt with two 'n's and two 'l's, of course.' She spoke with stinging clarity. 'Her background,' she said briskly, 'is, of course, neo-liberal.'

'How do you know?' The things Andrea knew were quite remarkable, thought Evelyn.

'How do I know? I just know, that's all. You can tell.'

'How can you tell?'

'She makes quiches. That should have told me a lot from the very beginning. Neo-liberals always make quiches. The quiche is a neo-liberal kind of cuisine thing. I should have known something was up from the very first time we beached the catamaran and there she was in her Gucci yachting jersey and her little loafers and her linen jeans, carrying a smoked chicken and olive quiche for our lunch. I should've known. I should've suspected something. I never knew he was fucking her in the boatshed.' Andrea began to cry. 'It took me four years to find out.' The sobs reached a crescendo as the dog down the street began to bark again and the clock struck one. 'Oh shut up, shut up!' shouted Andrea, flailing one arm as if to hit them all.

'Boo hoo hoo.' Andrea was wailing thinly now. 'I thought she was just being very kind and cooking our lunch to save me work but the little fucker was fucking my husband in the shed. Boo hoo hoo.' She rocked back and forth, her mouth wide open. 'Boo hoo hoo. My best friend. Boo hoo hoo. It took me four years to find out and four years to get over it when he went off.' The sobs settled into a nameless murmur followed by an enduring silence. 'How could you possibly say it only took me two days to get over it all and then I went off to the cinema with someone else? How could you say such a terrible thing?'

'I don't think I said that, did I?'

'Yes, you did, Evelyn.'

'I'm sure I didn't. I haven't any recollection of saying any such thing.'

'You certainly did.'

'I did not.'

'You did so.' Andrea's eyes closed, her mouth opened again and silence fell.

After some time Evelyn propped herself up on one elbow.

'The sheep,' she said tentatively, 'were hardly any trouble at all and some of them were quite tame.' She waited for a moment or two. 'And the horse was really sweet. She was very old. You couldn't ride her or anything. Frederick rescued her from a pet-food man.' But Andrea's eyes seemed still to be tightly shut, and from her open mouth came a faint snort on each inward breath. Evelyn closed her own eyes and the roaring in her ears increased in intensity until it sounded like the sea. I'm going to float away, she thought.

In the morning the sound of the dog's inevitable barking awakened them.

'What are you doing here?' Andrea sat up suddenly, the stare characteristically bellicose, the jaw jutting again. The night seemed to have left little impression on her except that her very thin hair, which usually clung, perhaps fondly, to her scalp, was standing on one side of her head. The effect was rakish and slightly vivacious.

'Andrea, you told me to stay.' Evelyn spoke from beneath the eiderdown. During the night a late frost must have settled and the air was piercingly chilly.

'I never did any such thing. The last thing I remember was us having dinner here.'

'But we talked for ages after that.'

'Did we?'

'And then you told me to stay all night.'

'Whatever would I do that for?' Andrea's stare became even more pugnacious.

It may be a really bad day, thought Evelyn as she gazed at what she could see of the world past the black piped border of the eiderdown. On the right-hand side of her small view there appeared to be something peachy pink giving a glow. She reached for it discreetly. Her hair tie.

'And why you wear those silly things in your hair —' Andrea must have awakened fully alert and was missing nothing. She glared at Evelyn again.

Definitely, thought Evelyn, it would be a bad day.

'I just use them to tie up my hair. They're not a political state-ment.'

'What you need is a decent haircut. You should go to Sick, like I do.' Andrea went to an anarchist hairdresser who had changed his name by deedpoll. He had once owned a salon called The Martin Scrimegeor House of Beauty but since his conversion, well documented in Andrea's conversations, to anarchism, he had become known as Sick.

'I don't want to go to Sick.'

'You need shorter hair.' Andrea glared across the room. Her eyes looked very small and glittered palely.

'I must go home,' said Evelyn.

'I'd better make you a cup of coffee before you go. I suppose.' Andrea's mouth was turned down at each corner and her tone was grudging. 'Come out to the kitchen. I'll give you Sick's number so you can give him a call but he won't be able to fit you in till after New Year. His waiting list is endless.' Jennifer, thought Evelyn. The sudden conversational likeness was daunting.

'The thing is' — she was following Andrea out to the kitchen now, trailing the eiderdown. Amazingly she did not seem to have a bad headache, though the makings of one were there, she thought. 'The thing is, I don't want to have my hair very short like just a few strands of old string tossed against a golf ball and glued on with paste. I like my hair the way it is.'

Andrea turned around slowly, her silhouette almost devilish against the light coming in through the sole kitchen window. This casement was considerably obscured by the rampant growth of a giant and very prickly cactus, which tore some kind of living from the bricks of Andrea's back porch. Occasionally it flowered, a grim bilious yellow bloom, and Andrea ripped this off with various epithets bandied about like, 'Flowering little motherfucker, see what I'll do to you,' or 'Filthy fucking flowers — I hate you.'

'Do you mean,' she said now, 'that my hair looks like a few bits of string tossed against a billiard ball and glued on with paste?'

'Yes, I do actually.' Evelyn waited. Somehow, in the past few days, her enveloping reticence, her silence over her sometimes very differing opinions, must have been stripped away. Perhaps it was the wine last night, or the pizza, or spending the night curled up under an eiderdown in one of Andrea's definitively sculptural but very uncomfortable chairs that had done it. Every time she had opened her eyes her first view had been of a pen and wash sketch of the word 'FUCK', with curlicues and various embellishments, by an artist with, as Andrea always said, a large reputation. The night had been bleak. 'I can't imagine why anyone would pay seventy-five dollars to look as if they'd had a basin haircut and were just about bald.'

Andrea drew a deep breath. Her eiderdown, wrapped around her shoulders like a cloak, trembled.

'Get out,' she said.

'I will,' said Evelyn. 'Cheerio.'

'Don't imagine,' said Andrea, 'that I'm bothering to throw a few clothes on and drive up the road to the patisserie to get you fresh crois-sants for breakfast that are so marvellous they're to die for from the very newest place that everyone's going to. There's not a thing worth eating for miles around since the new patisserie opened. Don't imagine after telling me that I look bald —'

'I never said you looked bald.'

'You distinctly said I did.' Andrea's voice was rising now. 'Don't argue with me. Don't imagine I'm making you coffee and buying you croissants after that, thank you, you neo-liberal little middle-class shit.' Andrea was famous for foul language.

Outside, the air was fresh and clean. Evelyn took the eiderdown from her shoulders, folded it and left it on Andrea's front veranda. It had been much easier than she imagined to escape, so there were marked benefits in incurring such rage. If she had been as accommodatingly pleasant and malleable as she usually was she would have had to stay for at least another hour, by which time the faint sign of a headache now beginning at her right temple might have developed into a full-blown migraine. This way she could get home to the Disprins in plenty of time and not be abused for being a fucking neo-liberal who needed pain relief. Her car started at the first turn of the motor and glided quietly away from the kerb. What a gorgeous morning, she thought.

Chapter Fifteen

The upstairs bedroom still smelt faintly of Madame Magnolia's oils and lotions. Evelyn stood by the little windows and looked out over the city. There must be many people, she thought, embattled by the idea of Christmas and there must be, within the framework of that enormous collective intelligence, some way of managing the festivity. The scent of oils was very calming and centring. Evelyn clasped her hands and stared out over the street to the sea again.

At the end of the road, by the seawall, the water was quite deep even at low tide. Berths for boats were available there and their owners kept little rowing boats in a shed near the wall so they could row out to their craft. The moorings for these were about twenty metres out and in rough weather the boats bobbed dangerously, sometimes even dragging their anchor chains a little. None had ever capsized. There were two or three quite lavish yachts, a small motorboat encrusted with sea moss and barnacles, a modest little fishing boat, two small yachts.

If she had a boat, thought Evelyn, she could row out to it early on Christmas Day and hide in it until Boxing Day. In fact Christmas Eve could be a better time to embark on the subterfuge because that would get rid of the last-minute callers.

'Evelyn, just a tiny Christmas message, dear. We're just off on holiday and having a few people around for a drink and whatever, and just thought of you. Too late to ask you now, of course, but you're such a quiet old bird these days anyway. Do hope you have a happy Christmas and we all feel sure you'll have wonderful plans. Lots of love.' The spoken messages sounded very like the ones on the Christmas cards.

Other Christmases she had experimented with not answering the telephone at all but it rang and rang, endlessly rang. She used to stand in front of it counting the rings. Twenty-four, twenty-five, twenty-six. It was better to answer it as quickly as possible: that way the small ordeals of non-inclusion were shorter.

The thing to do, she thought now, was to have a plan. There must be a plan. If it was impossible to isolate herself on a boat because she did not have one, surely she could isolate herself in her own house? Or on her own property? That seemed a better idea.

The shed out in the back garden had possibilities when she inspected it. Used for the garden tools, it was lined with shelves on one wall and had a stout wooden floor. This door was slightly loose on its hinges but the roof had been mended shortly after she bought the property. One of the roof beams had been rotten but all that was fixed now. The shed was dry, but not warm. The sea breeze filtered in through joins in the tin walls but, overall, it was not too bad. If she went camping she would have to stay in a tent, which would not be as weatherproof as the shed. It was definitely a possibility. If she spent Christmas quietly in the shed the ringing of the telephone would not reach her. If the busker decided to call again with strawberries and cream she would not even hear him knocking at the front door. She could be peaceful. It seemed, when she did another circuit of the shed inside and out, an agreeable solution to it all.

'I'm going away at Christmas,' she said experimentally to Jennifer later in the day. It would be sensible to get some kind of reaction to her plan, she thought.

'Away?' Jennifer sounded only slightly surprised. 'Where?'

'Camping.'

'Camping?' Jennifer's surprise increased markedly. 'You?' she said. 'Camping?'

'Yes,' said Evelyn, and waited.

'Where? You've never been camping before. Who are you going with? You can't go camping by yourself, Evelyn. It mightn't be safe.'

'I'll be with friends. We're going camping.' Again she waited, eyeing the shed out of the kitchen window. If the sea was south in relation to her cottage, the shed must be north, she thought, because it was on the opposite side to the sea view. 'Up north,' she said.

'It's lovely up there. The beaches are gorgeous. How long will you be away?' There seemed, as usual, the sound of faint grinding or rasping from Jennifer's end of the telephone line. Jennifer would be filing her toenails, Evelyn thought, possibly absent-mindedly and looking idly at her appointment diary, which always lay on the low Chinese table where the telephone sat. Marky had once had business links with various Asian capitals and there was quite a conglomeration of carved serpents and dragons that grimaced from various screens and tables in their house, the telephone table one of them. 'If you're away any more than a week you'll miss out on my festive turkey fricassee,' said Jennifer. 'You know I always do that about the twenty-ninth.'

'I may be home by then.' Evelyn stood with the telephone in her hand, thinking deeply. The draughts in the shed might make it uncomfortable for too long a stay. Maybe two nights would be enough — Christmas Eve and the evening of Christmas Day — and she could creep back into the cottage from time to time to collect a ham sandwich or boil an egg, have a bath and a comfort stop or even sleep in her own bed just as long as she didn't put a light on. Maybe she could even have a secret barbecue, she thought now, set up behind the shed. Perhaps a grilled sausage or two? And she might be able to do toast.

By midday she had decided it was a crackpot notion. It would be best to be sensible and endure it all, she thought, including Jennifer's fricassee on the twenty-ninth or thereabouts. Answer the telephone, take the messages, read the mail, answer the door. Be a good girl.

By mid-afternoon she had had another idea — all Christmas Day at the cinema — then discarded it almost immediately. She could go from one film to another and return to the cottage late in the evening saturated with a mixture of violence and cultivation in bright colours. But, like the idea about going to stay in her own shed, this also had to be rejected. The cinemas were all to be closed on Christmas Day. Even the homeless and dispossessed were supposed to be busy then, having Christmas dinner at the City Mission or anywhere. The City Mission! she thought joyfully. She could hide at the City Mission. She carefully dialled its telephone number.

'I wondered,' she said, 'if I could volunteer to help you on Christmas D—'

'Good gracious me, no,' said a jolly voice. 'It's very good of you, of course, but our volunteers for Christmas Day are all listed and notified by the beginning of August each year. We just don't have any vacancies.'

'By August?' Evelyn was stunned.

'Yes,' said the jolly voice. 'There's great competition to help here on Christmas Day. You've really got no idea what it's like. We do have a waiting list of helpers — could I place your name on that perhaps?'

'How long,' said Evelyn, 'is the waiting list?'

'We do have four hundred on it at the moment. I really don't think there'd be much hope of your actually being called upon this Christmas or even next, but the Christmas after that might be more likely. A lot of people have to wait five years.'

'Thank you,' said Evelyn faintly. 'I think I'll leave it for the moment.' She hung up. The city must be full of people wanting to avoid Christmas, she thought: hundreds and hundreds of them out there — she looked out over the sea — wanting to hide the fact that they are frightened of jolly but dismissive cards and telephone calls, seeking a refuge by doing good works. Those who actually went and ate the dinner were braver, she thought. At least they admitted they needed the anonymity of comfort and company on Christmas Day. She went and looked at the shed again. Impossible, she thought.

'Dear girl.' The telephone had rung once more, the moment she put her foot on the cottage's back doorstep. 'Look, Evelyn' — it was Jennifer again — 'I've been thinking about this business of your going camping and I don't think it's a good idea at all. There's the traffic to consider, for starters. You know as well as I do that the whole place is jammed up with traffic at Christmas. I don't want to seem morbid, but you could easily have an accident, even just a tiny nose-to-tail can do a lot of damage, and, as Marky always says, your car, Evelyn, is far from young. What was that?' Jennifer seemed to be shouting to someone further away, perhaps Marky in his study, thought Evelyn. 'Sorry, Evelyn, that was just Marky. He says he's going to write you a note about your car.'

'A note about my car? What about my car?'

There was some murmuring at the other end of the line. 'Marky says the note'll explain it all,' said Jennifer firmly. 'And please do think again about going camping. I know it probably sounds very romantic setting yourselves up on some isolated promontory surrounded by beautiful trees and rocks, Evelyn, but life isn't like that. When he sits by the campfire playing to you in the evenings you'll be bitten alive by mosquitoes and heaven knows what. The sandflies are virulent further north. Marky says they're the size of horses. And everywhere's so crowded at this time of year. You'll have to queue for hours just to buy an ice-cream.'

'Yes,' said Evelyn, again faintly. So Jennifer and Mark thought she intended going camping with the mysterious and non-existent musician from the Top of the Town and he would serenade her with music at sundown each day. 'I'll think about what you've said,' she said at last, 'and I'll get back to you.' Already, she thought as she hung up the telephone, she was becoming more duplicitous and deceitful than she ever would have thought possible.

My Dearest Evelyn —

It is the next day and the threatened letter from Marky has arrived in the post; the news in it must be bad, thinks Evelyn, for him to address her so fondly.

> *As you know, Jen and I are very proud of our garden. I think you sometimes come to our annual Open Day when everything is at its best and this, as you also probably know, is part of the city-wide Open Gardens scheme. Competition to be included is very fierce and for the last two seasons Jen and I have had to beat back rivals from other gardens in the area whose hybrid clivias have almost matched our own.*

Whatever is all this about? thinks Evelyn, eyes on the horizon. The sea today is a deep and glittering blue, the boats moored at the end of the street look so picturesque they seem to have been placed there deliberately. Further down the road someone is mowing a lawn. She continues to read, leaning on the letterbox with one elbow and with one hand cupping her head.

> *Not only is each garden assessed by officials from the council before the Open Gardens season but surroundings such as drives, paths, and garden accoutrements like furniture, statues and gazebos are inspected as well.*

> *It is upon the subject of paths that I wish to confide a small difficulty. I wonder if you would mind parking your car around the corner if you visit in future. We have had the Italian paving at the front of the house water-blasted in preparation for the viewing season and occasionally I have, in the past, found the odd tiny drip of oil out there, particularly when you have visited. For this reason I have blamed your car for the discoloration. I have enclosed a little map I have drawn with good parking places marked out in the street. I particularly recommend Anderson Crescent, where you would have a walk of only two and a half blocks after parking if you wanted to pop in and see Jennifer during the day. At night it would be very dark around there, though, because of the overhanging trees, so if you came here in the evening it would be best to remember to bring a*

torch. Anstis Close, which branches off Anderson Crescent, is a bit difficult because some of those old bridge-playing harridans there regard the parking in the street as their own and kind of reserve it for their friends. If you parked there I feel you may be moved on by some old bitch or other, so I therefore recommend Anderson Crescent as being the best bet.

Yours is a dear little car, of course, but I do also recommend that you consider trading it in on something newer and smarter, even though you have that sentimental attachment for it because old Fred bought it for you. I could always put in a word for you with a friend of mine who has a motor business and I could get you a good deal on, say, an el-cheapo ten-year-old BMW that might have had only two or three owners. It would have to be a Japanese import though, for that kind of price. But once you get those oil drips I think the news is all bad, Evelyn. The old banger could need a valve grind and you've also got a bit of rust by the back window, I don't know if you've noticed. This is just a word of warning, my dear.

Every good wish, Mark.

There were some other things in the letterbox so Evelyn continued to stand out on her own front path, much marked by age and the passage of her own muddy feet when gardening, and read the offerings. There was a prettily printed card of a laden Christmas tree festooned with glitter from the Smiths. We do hope your weather might be better than ours, they have written, but we live in hope. A raucous Santa Claus was shouting Merry Christmas in big red letters on a card from Mavis King, who was a widow. The message inside was telling and revealing and was written in tiny letters as if the words were a deeply held secret. I am abolishing Christmas this year, it said, and going on holiday to Vanuatu. How wise, thought Evelyn. On another card two campers in bright clothes were sitting on deckchairs on a cheerful and over-populated beach. Mysteriously, in front of them stood three lugubrious sheep being stared at malevolently by a huge butterfly. We never see you, Evelyn. The tone was perhaps accusatory. Every good wish at

172

Christmas from an indecipherable signature. A very circumspect Christmas garland with a discreet trim of tartan ribbon, hardly any red, mostly green, contained the following austere message: Your continued success at managing is most pleasing. The handwriting was elderly, the name almost forgotten but the sentiments were not unkind, thought Evelyn. Three wise men in gaudy robes, partially gilded, plodded stalwartly across a desert at night with an angel flying overhead blowing a trumpet. The camels must have run away, frightened by the noise. More indecipherable writing on that one. A blue and silver card with Christmas trees in the best of taste from the doctor she used to go to before she moved to the cottage. I wish you the best of health in the future. They would sit there in the surgery talking about books after she asked for more sleeping tablets, and possibly cough medicine in winter. It used to be quite pleasant, thought Evelyn. A scrawled message inside a card showing an empty house — Jingle bells, Santa smells, Love from Gordon. Gordon had an alcohol problem and must have had a few drinks while doing his cards.

And the cards that had already arrived, the ones standing in a little uneven row in her sitting room, were not so bad. The whole emergency about Christmas was something created by other people, thought Evelyn. One Christmas two or three years ago, when her lies and evasions were more successful than usual, she spent a tranquil and not unbeautiful day. It possessed the miniature stillness of a painting on ivory. In the morning she had got up and looked out over a city that seemed silenced. From far away there had been a faint hum of traffic — people going out to Christmas lunch, perhaps. In the cottage she had bathed and dressed carefully in clothes laid out the night before. She wore a sapphire bracelet Frederick had once given her. Like a second donation of the same gift, it glittered on her wrist. For lunch she had ham and some French bread and she opened a bottle of a French wine, a sauvignon blanc, and drank a large glass of it, then ate a chocolate from a box of sweets someone had given her. In the afternoon she had walked around the nearby streets looking at flowers in gardens, roses over trellises, huge clumps of daisies. Everywhere there was silence. Houses had a peculiarly untenanted look, even though they might have had several cars parked outside. There was the occasional small child playing with a new toy, often red, on a veranda, but of adults there was little sign. No music, no sound of a television, no laughter broke the abiding silence of that afternoon. She walked gently and peacefully as if through an empty land.

In the evening she had cooked a small chicken and gone to a lot of trouble over the stuffing. Red peppers, olive oil of the best sort, garlic, herbs from her garden, lemon zest. Tiny new potatoes lay on her plate like kindly eyes. The beans she grew in her garden had thrown out a sudden crop so she had gathered those. It had been, she thought now, a beautiful little meal. Peaceful, stressless, solitary, exquisite. Like a meal a hermit might have in an eyrie on a high mountain pass, or a repast served mysteriously to a travelling stranger in a castle that was almost wrecked, the dinner she cooked that evening had a quality of care and charm that was beautiful. Afterwards she told some lies to cover up the silence and peace of the day. In the invaded season of Christmas it did not do to be serenely alone. It was a dangerous thing to say or do. She had learnt that.

'Don't be ridiculous,' Jennifer had said afterwards. 'I've never heard you mention friends called the Cunninghams before.'

'Haven't you?' She had been evasive. 'The Cunninghams always have a lovely Christmas. They asked me to their place.'

'Nonsense.' Jennifer's face had turned a faint pink as it always did when she was angry. 'Don't give me that.' She had looked assessingly around, as if Evelyn's house might tell her something. 'I wouldn't put it past you, Evelyn, to have just stayed here moping by yourself.'

'Not at all.' She had been very cheerful, even courageous and combative. The silence of the untenanted, uninvaded Christmas had been delightful. She had marched into the serenity of her unpopulated Christmas with all the faith and heart of a pilgrim. 'I had a really beautiful Christmas. It was lovely.' She waited for a moment. 'With the Cunninghams.'

'I don't believe you, Evelyn. And I've never ever heard you

mention any people called the Cunninghams before. Next Christmas I'm going to see to it that you have Christmas with someone if it kills me, Evelyn. You can go and have Christmas with Mother. Mother loves to spend Christmas with someone and at the home they're very good about people having an extra on Christmas Day.' So that is what had happened. Christmas with Jennifer's mother.

Jennifer's mother had died three or four months after that and was mentioned now far more fondly and more frequently than before.

'Jennifer, I haven't seen that bracelet before. Isn't it beautiful?' people might say, and Jennifer, with a pleased little pout and a shrug of her shoulders, would say lightly, 'It was Mother's. I'm sorting out Mother's things, you know. She did have quite a lot of nice stuff.' And Jennifer's plump hands, fattened by her well-fed years with Marky on a rich diet of cocktail crackers, pâté and champagne among other things, would be scrabbling in Mother's drawers and boxes discovering all the loot, Evelyn used to think.

On that Christmas Day Jennifer's mother had looked at her with pale blue eyes that had faded to almost white and had stretched out a skeletal hand. 'Jenny,' she had said.

'No, it isn't Jenny. I'm Evelyn. Jennifer sent me.'

'Jenny.'

'Jenny's busy. I've come instead.'

'Jenny.'

'Just let me tie this around her' — a nurse was holding a sort of bib — 'and you can give her her dinner.' Very carefully Evelyn had fed the old lady. A little bit of chicken soup, perhaps two spoonfuls. A fragment of the white meat of chicken, a few peas, a crumb of potato. In the end the old lady held up her hand.

'Jenny,' she said again. 'Jenny.'

'I'm not Jennifer, darling. I'm Evelyn.'

'Jenny.'

'She doesn't have many visitors,' the nurse said when Evelyn was ushered out. 'She likes to sit at the window and watch the birds. We're not sure what she notices and what she doesn't.'

Evelyn turned and waved to the still figure at the window. It raised one hand and the lips moved slightly. 'Jenny.'

'I'm not her daughter.' Evelyn looked at the nurse uneasily. It was impossible to imagine what she might be thinking. 'I'm not Jennifer. Jennifer sent me,' she said as if that might make the day seem better.

'Oh, that's all right,' said the nurse, turning now from the door. 'We don't see the daughter very often. Her mother does wait for her but as long as somebody comes she thinks it's her so that's all right. She does wait, though. She does wait.'

'Jenny.' The old mouth opened again, bird-like. 'Jenny.'

About April, Jennifer's mother died.

'I've had to cancel my manicure and my massage.' Jennifer had been quite brisk on the telephone. 'I've had word from the home that Mother's gone so we're going to have to make arrangements about things.'

'Gone? Has she run away?' Jennifer's mother had looked very infirm, anchored to a small armchair.

'No, gone, Evelyn, gone. You know — gone.'

Within a short while Jennifer had begun to sprout the new crop of gold bangles and the odd large diamond ring in rose gold settings of an antique sort.

'They were Mother's,' she would say.

'People have been really marvellous,' Jennifer had said at the time of the funeral. 'They've rallied around. I've had quite a few little cards and notes — oddly, nothing from the home and I haven't had anything from you, Evelyn, but as I said to Marky, "She does live in her own little world." Do you like this ring, Evelyn? It was Mother's.' She flapped one manicured hand under Evelyn's nose. 'I've had my nails done just a pale plum this week — red isn't very fitting at this time, do you think? — and I'm going to wear black to the service, of course. Poor Marky can't come. He's got a meeting. If it's a nice day I'll wear one of my big hats, otherwise something small — velvet, I think. Do you know the Harbertsons are putting on a little luncheon party for me, just very quiet and only a few people there, perhaps only thirty or forty? I could drop in to your place, Evelyn, and have a cup of coffee with you sometime later in the week. I know you don't entertain, dear, not any more, but you could give me any flowers or anything then. Maybe a casserole because I'll be too upset to cook.'

'Could I?' But Jennifer had gone. The longer she had been married to Marky the swifter she had become at hanging up the telephone.

But that all happened on another Christmas and now it was this Christmas and time for a little bit of what Jennifer would call retail therapy. Cards, thought Evelyn. She would send a few cards, and set off for the shops along the seafront. There were two stationery shops where cards were sold so she would buy six and send them to people.

On the way — it was now only a few days until Christmas — the landscape most peculiarly presented little idea of the festive season. Where Jennifer saw parties, presents and pleasures Evelyn saw nothing at all except a reflection of her own worries. Mail had been placed in various letterboxes along the road to the shops, but there it remained, envelopes poking out of the letter slits askew and sometimes dampened by overnight rain so they must have been there, neglected and forgotten, since yesterday. Doors were firmly closed and only one had been decorated with a Christmas wreath whose holly and baubles were shabbily faded. It was a tired relic of many festive seasons and the door upon which it was fastened was also firmly closed. It did not look a friendly scenario. The blinds in that house were down and gardens all along the way possessed dedicated drifts of unwanted junk mail. Notices from supermarkets about turkeys at reduced prices and highly coloured brochures from department stores mingled with used wrappings from sweets and the occasional ice-cream stick.

'They're very picked over,' said the shop assistant glumly when Evelyn asked about Christmas cards at the first stationery shop up the little main street. The wind from the sea eddied in the door with chilling force as she spoke. There would be another flurry of thunder and lightning overnight, thought Evelyn, and more rain. Nothing seemed very summery at all this year. With a small packet of cards depicting cheerful mice wearing red beanie hats, and no pants, she set off for the post office.

Just a quick message before Christmas, my dears, before I rush off. Thank you for your kind card. May see you in the New Year. Love, Evelyn. With these small and saving messages of concealment arriving (she hoped) at their destinations before Christmas Day she could avoid the exposure of her planned festivity. She had decided she would take the old deckchair out into the garden behind the shed and would remain there for most of Christmas Day, reading under the shade of the old banana palms. If it rained or was too cold she could get set up in the shed with the same chair. By evening, when she re-entered her own cottage with all the furtive side glances of a burglar, everyone would be anchored by a large Christmas lunch or they would be preparing to be anchored by a large Christmas dinner. The day might pass, if she were very lucky, uninvaded and uninspected, and her own privately planned Christmas dinner of a piece of fresh salmon, new potatoes and a salad could be a delicious secret eaten alone in a state of great peace, the inadequacies of her house and her life and her thoughts unjudged.

As she made her way back to the seafront she noticed festive writing and holly berries scrawled on the window of the fish shop. *Open as usual Christmas Day from 5 p.m.* In an instant she changed the menu. In the evening, as the sun was setting on Christmas Day, she would filter quietly through the little streets that led to the shops and she would buy fish and chips, which she would eat in her own peaceful kitchen with a salad of cos lettuce, olives and cucumber. She would have a glass of white wine. Even two glasses, she thought. Or three. And then, faintly squiffy and dazed from reading out-of-date *Vogues* all day, she would watch an edited broadcast of the Queen's Christmas message on television. And perhaps the Queen might say, as she did last year, that the year had not been altogether personally successful — or, in ordinary parlance, bloody awful — and Evelyn could then, with kindred feeling, raise her glass to the screen and have another mouthful of an unimportant little riesling or perhaps a sauvignon blanc from a smaller vineyard. It might not be, she thought, too bad at all, and would contain no sense of nostalgia from previous Christmases.

The toothless busker had not returned with more of the threatened strawberries and cream. Alan, the little ex-headmaster, had not telephoned about the roast dinner in the place where wine sauce was two dollars extra. Jennifer seemed peculiarly preoccupied with herself, her voice coming over her cellphone in a muffled kind of way from her own en suite bathroom, the calls often abruptly ended with a faint exclamation. The people to whom Evelyn had sent the cheerful and obfuscatory pantsless mouse cards might put them on their mantelpieces without another thought. Perhaps, after all, it would be peaceful.

Outside the windows of her cottage, as if sensing this reassuring thought, a small bird began to sing with piercing sweetness.

Chapter Sixteen

Here was Evelyn the next morning going through her old magazines to find suitable articles to read on Christmas Day. The novel about the sergeant who shot himself would not be suitable then, she thought. Recipes could be appropriate, however, because she could psychologically eat dishes she could not possibly cook, and could also remain thinner.

In the novel the sergeant, at the end, had appeared to get himself into a neutral mood and other soldiers in the unit thought he had improved in temperament. They imagined he had assimilated the shock of his wife's infidelity and possible continuing semi-defection. He no longer looked quite so gaunt or in a state of noticeable disarray. He had lost a lot of weight since the news about his wife had reached him, but he seemed calmer. He was seen to be quietly eating his meals in the mess.

'We must do something about your home leave,' said the second lieutenant when the unit was out in the field on manoeuvres.

'Yes, sir,' said the sergeant, seemingly without much feeling or interest, and the second lieutenant, reassured, turned away. There would be plenty of time to arrange leave for the sergeant when they returned to camp, he thought. The man looked a little better. There was less need for concern.

'You do want some more home leave, don't you?' he asked.

'Yes, sir,' said the sergeant, again without much interest. There was a silence. 'Just a bit of trouble at home, sir,' he said, 'that's all. Just a bit of trouble at home.'

'Indeed.' The second lieutenant was already consulting the map again. They were miles off course, he decided, and would certainly not reach the designated point of contact with the other unit at the specified time. There would probably be one hell of a row later with the colonel.

Looking Good: Change Your Life, Here's How. That would be a good article to read, thought Evelyn as she flicked through the index of one of Jennifer's discarded magazines. It might give her a few pointers about how to be more successful at pretending to be a retail therapist and successful luncher like Jennifer, if she really wanted to be like Jennifer, which she did not. But Christmas Day had to be passed somehow. *Eight Women's Summer Survival Kits.* Maybe this would say to wear your old clothes back to front to give a new look? Or to tie hair that needed a cut on top of your head in a vertical ponytail to save on hairdresser's fees? *The Forty People You Need To Make You Beautiful.* Definitely not that story, she thought. Too depressing. Even Jennifer did not have forty people working on her to give her that glossy look. Two people did her artificial nails every second Wednesday, and there was Madame Magnolia Sharma for the weekly massage with essential oils, Chanteuse the hairdresser, the podiatrist and so on, but the total would hardly be forty, even for Jennifer.

Survival Tactics. This, thought Evelyn, could be interesting and she turned to the page for a quick pre-Christmas look.

> *'City noise is so disturbing,' says former model Louise Bleckley-Smith (photographed far left wearing a cerulean blue silk jacket found in a Berlin junk market and jeans given to her by a jet-setting friend). 'I do not feel I can get through the summer without my portable radio which I listen to all the time,' laughs extravagantly beautiful Louise, now the live-in partner of celebrated musicologist Pierre Blanc and exponent of the currently ultra-fashionable grunge-shabby-chic school of good looks . . .*

Somewhere in the cottage she had a blue jacket that could possibly be called cerulean, thought Evelyn as she stretched out her hand to turn on her own radio. And she did have a pair of Calvin Klein jeans that she bought at an opportunity shop for only six dollars fifty and the person who had previously owned them could have been friendly, if only she had known Evelyn. Perhaps Christmas Day spent frivolously reading magazines could have a definite charm.

Pip, pip, pip. That was the signal for the news on the radio.

'Here is the ten o'clock news,' said the announcer, 'read by Brian Michaelson.' The voice was deep and reassuring. 'Mystery surrounds the arrival of five crack members of the banking fraud squad at the Main Street branch of —' The bank was her own, thought Evelyn. The fraud squad? She turned the radio's volume right up. 'According to a statement issued a few minutes ago by the bank's legal advisers, a high-level investigation is continuing within the bank's investment structure. Investors who are concerned have been ringing an 0800 number listed in morning newspapers throughout the country. An additional one hundred staff have been taken on to cope with the overload of calls.'

'Jennifer?' There was no one to telephone about this but Jennifer, and since she had become so grand with the marriage to Marky she would not be at all supportive or sympathetic, thought Evelyn after she dialed Jennifer's number.

'Well, stupid,' said Jennifer predictably, 'ring the 0800 number then. You haven't got a morning paper? Well, hang on a minute and I'll find the number for you in ours. You really are hopeless, Evelyn. I'm in the bathroom. I really don't want to talk to anyone right now.' In the bathroom again?

'Hello? You have reached Myra. How can I help you?' The tone of the person Evelyn eventually reached on the telephone at the bank was reassuring, elderly and very calm. Evelyn had had to wait for eighteen minutes listening to music and being told by a computerised voice that her call was extremely valuable to the bank and would she please just wait for her turn in the telephone queue. Myra, whoever Myra may really have been, seemed to do something on a computer because Evelyn heard the odd squeaking and tapping noises of a keyboard.

'Yes, Mrs Jarrold, I have you here now.' There was the faint sound of breathing as if Myra might be leaning closer to the screen. Evelyn's banking had been found in the system. 'There's no need for you to worry, Mrs Jarrold. Everything in your accounts is entirely in order, except your cheque account is overdrawn by sixty-four dollars and nine cents, but you would, of course, know that.' Evelyn gritted her teeth. 'Can you just give me your investment numbers, please, Mrs Jarrold? You have them right by the telephone? Excellent.' There was a slight delay and more tapping noises. 'Everything's fine, Mrs Jarrold. No, I can't tell you anything more at the moment.' The voice was very circumspect.

'Everything's fine,' Evelyn told Jennifer later. 'The money I've got in the bank's fine. I thought for a moment someone might have stolen it in a robbery or maybe there'd been an embezzlement of funds or something. It all seems most mysterious.'

'Evelyn' — Jennifer's voice was very preoccupied — 'of course no one would embezzle your funds because you've hardly got any. As I've often told you, Frederick left you in a bad state. If anyone was going to embezzle funds they'd choose a bank account worth embezzling funds from and, Evelyn, it wouldn't be yours, I can tell you that in a moment.'

'But —'

'Evelyn, I'm in the bathroom. I really can't talk to you right now.' Yet again Jennifer hung up.

Far away to the north the city evened out into sparsely spread suburbs. Then the ten-acre blocks began and it was almost the countryside, with just a house here and there, sometimes a gateway leading to an avenue of trees and a farm cottage in the distance. Barns and farm sheds dotted the landscape and children kept ponies in small paddocks close to the house. The roads were good because everyone was always driving into the city for dancing lessons, piano lessons, music lessons, choir practice, appointments with podiatrists, beauty therapists, hairdressers, marriage counsellors and so on. The trees were often large and fine and spread a dappled shade on the roadside verges where the grass grew deep and lush, and sometimes drifts of wild flowers like buttercups grew rampantly if the site was damp, or cornflowers if it was dry.

Could her plans for Christmas be altered, Evelyn wondered, and might she go out into the countryside on Christmas Day, driving along in her car that dripped oil about which the celebrated Marky had complained? Parked in the lingering shade of some tree or other she could spread out the old tartan rug and open up a picnic basket all alone amidst the singing of birds and the faint ruffle of a friendly breeze in the treetops. There were various alternatives to spending Christmas Day hiding under the banana palms behind her garden shed. In the meantime, though, the grass and weeds were continuing to grow wildly and there was no news of the hedgeclippers, which she needed to cut everything back.

'Hello?' This is Evelyn on the telephone again, enquiring about her clippers. 'This is Evelyn —' She was going to say her full name and explain her business but the replying voice cut in swiftly.

'Yes, it's Evelyn Jarrold, isn't it? You're ringing about your clippers.' It was the man with the very measured voice who always served behind the counter at the small engineering works, the man with the greenish eyes and the steady gaze.

'Yes,' said Evelyn, 'it is, and I do want to know about the clippers, please, because my garden really needs cutting back.' She waits for a moment or two. 'Before Christmas if possible,' she said. 'I want to cut my garden back before Christmas or, failing that, straight after Christmas, otherwise I might be strangled by the weeds.' Everyone was having things done before Christmas. Jennifer was having her hair touched up and her nails done, also a pedicure; Marky was having his Range Rover and the Mercedes cleaned and serviced, and the firm that looked after Marky and Jennifer's prize-winning garden had to come and give the whole place a complete clean-up or Jennifer said she was going to die and Marky, in addition, would kill the entire staff — even the Alsatian dog that sat on the truck to guard the tools. 'And how good of you,' said Evelyn to the man at the engineering works, 'to know who I was and what I wanted.'

'I'd know your voice anywhere,' said the man. 'Now, let me see.' He seemed to be rifling through pieces of paper. Evelyn listened to the rustling noises. 'Ah, yes.' From his voice she could tell he was smiling. 'We'll have to deliver your clippers to you — it's a special service we do at Christmas for a few customers. Would Christmas Eve be all right? It would? Oh, good. I'll just double-check your address. Now,' he said, 'would five-thirty be a suitable time?'

'I suppose so. I'm not really usually doing a lot at that time. By that hour of the day I've kind of finished my work.'

'And you'll definitely be home?' He seemed quite anxious about this.

'I think so.'

'You'd definitely need to be there,' said this man at the engineering shop, 'because there's another delivery in conjunction with the delivery of the clippers.'

'But —'

'No "buts", Mrs Jarrold.' He paused for a moment again. 'Um, Evelyn,' he said. 'Evelyn. You have qualified for our special customer-of-the-year award in the Christmas draw. Something else will also be delivered to you with the hedgeclippers but I can't say anything more about it at the moment. It is,' he said enticingly, 'a surprise.'

'A surprise? What sort of a surprise?' Alarmed, Evelyn looked around. The cottage was tiny and the entire property was on the small side. Even the three banana palms growing behind the garden shed all came off the same trunk if you took a good look at them. Surely she could not possibly have won a ride-on lawnmower or a small tractor? 'I've only got a tiny garden,' said Evelyn, 'and a tiny house. There isn't much room for anything.'

'Worry not,' said the man. 'It's nothing at all, really. You wouldn't have a problem with it.'

'Oh.' And it was only much later that she realised she had not thanked the man, that she said only 'Oh' and rang off.

'I'm terribly sorry' — she had telephoned the engineering shop again — 'I know I'm probably a nuisance phoning again when you're busy, but —' She was going to say her name, but he seemed to know this already.

'Hello, Evelyn. Hello, Mrs Jarrold.' Perhaps he did not know what to call her, thought Evelyn, and was hedging his bets by calling her everything.

'How did you know it was me again?'

'I recognised your voice, of course. Like I said before.'

'Oh,' said Evelyn and took a deep breath. 'I just rang to thank you. I forgot to say thank you before. I wasn't ungrateful or anything like that. It just gave me such a shock to think I'd won a prize because I never win prizes and I've already won one at your shop because I won a box of chocolates for being the hundredth customer, don't you remember? Do you think someone else should get this new prize because I've already had a prize?'

'Not at all,' said the man. 'The prize is for you. I'll be bringing it, and your clippers, on Christmas Eve at five-thirty. I did the draw for the prize myself and I can assure you that your name leapt out of the hat when I put my hand in. It's all completely fair and you have to have it. The other prize — the box of chocolates — is irrelevant. How were they, by the way?'

'Lovely,' said Evelyn. 'I don't eat chocolates very often, but I must say they were delicious. They were those lovely Belgian ones shaped like shells and in two colours, but I suppose you know that.'

'I do. I chose them myself.' He rang off.

Much of life seemed suddenly to be conducted on the telephone this week. Jennifer was busy having all the last-minute touch-ups before Christmas.

'Evelyn, I'm terribly sorry I won't be able to ring tomorrow —'

'But —' Evelyn got no further. She was going to say, 'But I didn't think you were going to.'

'I'm really busy with last-minute Christmas things. I've simply got to get my roots re-coloured and I must get all these last-minute cards to the courier, and the plumber's coming. Something needs doing in the bathroom. The cistern's gone peculiar. Something seems to have broken or worn out or something. I've got to get it all done by Christmas or I don't know how I'm going to manage. The painter's let me down. He promised to repaint my kitchen by the middle of December and there's been no sign of him. I've rung and rung and he just never returns my calls. The woman he lives with has been really rude on the phone. She sounds drunk even in the mornings. I really wanted to get it all done by Christmas and I'm terribly disappointed.' Jennifer rang off with what sounded like yet another muffled exclamation.

'Evelyn?' This was another telephone call half an hour later. 'It's Imelda Robinson speaking.'

'Yes?' Evelyn was deeply suspicious.

'Evelyn, we just wondered if you'd given any more thought to Christmas. Our poor dear old musician friend has somehow got new teeth — he's gone especially, Evelyn, and got a new set of dentures in your honour — and we just wondered, Evelyn, if somehow your arrangements about Christmas had fallen through and he could come to your place on Christmas Day after all?'

'No,' said Evelyn. 'Definitely not.'

'Oh.' The sound was a short, sharp exclamation like a bang on the knee with a stick. 'Really.' The voice was very irritated. 'Well, it's quite embarrassing, but we've already told him he can go to your place, Evelyn. I feel I may call you Evelyn, may I?'

'I don't really mind,' said Evelyn, 'but he can't come here. I'm going to be elsewhere.' Outside her kitchen windows the garden shed glimmered faintly among the rampant weeds. The tiny building was repainted last year and the paint still had some gloss, even after the storms of winter and liberal doses of windblown dust and sea spray. 'I'm going northward.'

'Northward? What do you mean — northward? Do you mean you're going up north?'

'Yes.' Definitely, thought Evelyn, she was going up north for Christmas — to her own banana plantation, even though it was only three thin trunks coming off the same bole and positioned behind her garden shed. Even if she took a picnic out in the country that would be north as well, because she would have to drive through what the land agents called the northern suburbs so, therefore, that must be north too.

'I see.' Imelda Robinson's tone was very cold. 'The teeth don't fit very well,' she said, 'but he's made every effort, Evelyn, that he possibly can. He's almost moved heaven and earth to get the teeth in time and we both think you, similarly, could —'

'He can't come here for Christmas. I'm going up north.' Repetition did not make it sound any better.

'Really.' Imelda Robinson spoke very sharply. 'But we've told him he can come.' It sounded like an edict from somewhere very important, each word given a telling emphasis. 'We felt sure you'd change your mind. Now, can you really not manage to fit him in? Could you not take him up north with you? I'm sure he'd be willing to travel. He loves travelling.'

'No.' Evelyn's voice was stony. 'You'll just have to un-tell him, I'm sorry.'

'Well, really. I think your attitude is disgraceful.' Imelda Robinson terminated the call without saying anything more.

The postman, burdened with mail, trundled up the street on his bicycle and placed a few bits and pieces in most letterboxes, Evelyn's included. There was a mysterious postcard in lurid purple and gold addressed to an equally mysterious Mrs Smith, which read, 'May next year be *your* happy year, my dear. Love from Jane.' No return address was included so this message could not be sent to its correct destination. The power bill had arrived, and also a notice from the garage saying the car was due for a grease and oil. The letterbox had almost taken a voluntary holiday from the Christmas rush of mail today and sat on its painted stand surrounded by lilies and roses, a few self-sown forget-me-nots at its foot. It was like a peaceful miniature house in a peaceful miniature wilderness.

There were deadlines to meet with Evelyn's work so she spent the rest of the day at her desk. The book she was editing was a volume about gardening, about old bulbs in particular, and she sat immured in ancient terminologies, much of it in Latin, checking spelling in her various dictionaries and watching the slow passage of the sun across the small bay window of her study. With half a dozen sharp pencils at hand and wearing a little quilted jacket she sat at her desk peacefully as if Christmas was not happening and Jennifer, far away in another suburb, was not fretting about the colour of her hair or the condition of her kitchen walls. *Chionodoxa lucillae, Narcissus leedsii (flora), Moraea bicolor*

— with her immaculate lettering Evelyn corrected the proofs and double-checked everything, and by evening the work was finished.

The following morning the seafront was very calm. The sea, glassy with lack of wind, lay enticingly at the end of the street. There was hardly any sound of lapping at the seawall when Evelyn walked along the seaward path to post the manuscript away, her feet crunching on the crushed shell surface. The post office was four short blocks away and most of the houses looked closed and shuttered.

The little boats moored out from the seawall were bobbing gently in the faint wash from a passing vessel but that craft, well out in the harbour, seemed to be proceeding by sorcery. There was no sound of an engine. The large ship sailed along silently, its deck mounded with large metal containers. If three or four had been stacked up they would have taken up an area about the size of Evelyn's entire house.

But among the gaggle of small, familiar, shabby little craft was a new yacht, larger than the rest and much smarter. The moorings at the end of the street seldom changed. The little boats were mostly of the more utilitarian variety, owned by local people who liked to go fishing. Some of the boats were never used. They were just moored there week after week, their hulls encrusted with sea moss and barnacles and their portholes covered with canvas that rotted slowly in the summer sun and winter rain.

But on this particular day a new yacht was there. Fastened to a buoy on the northern side of the moorings, it rested easily in the current, its turquoise sails furled and the brass trim to its decking brilliantly polished. Trim, discreet and much larger than any other boat there, it was also noticeable because it was immaculate. Evelyn stood for a long time regarding the harbour, and the new boat.

In her time living in the little street the people around the area had slowly become known to her. At first they seemed to be just faceless, nameless passers-by, but now she knew most of them. The Sullivans were wealthy and lived in the street behind hers but were not yachting people and would not have a boat like that. It rose faintly in the current, its immaculate black hull and white trim glistening with newness and also with care. Its portholes glittered brilliantly as if they might have been crystal and at their edges she could see turquoise and white striped fabric. Perhaps little curtains, she thought. The new yacht had little curtains to match its sails. Very smart.

The Sullivans held parties in their landscaped and refurbished back-yard and often kept people awake at night for a block or two, and when she looked out her little windows to see where the noise was coming from it was always from the Sullivans' place. But they were backyard barbecue-type people, parties on the terrace their speciality. Although they were rumoured to be wealthy, the husband well placed in business somewhere, the new yacht was probably not theirs because, even though quite big, it would not be large enough to accommodate their entertainments. The deck would hold only — she screwed up her eyes to stare at it — a few people.

A large and spreading tree in the Sullivans' back yard had been fitted with spotlights and from there would come the sound of laughter, ice chinking in glasses and sometimes wild splashing. They had a swimming pool and gave pool parties in the summer for twenty people whose cars were parked right up the road as if the Sullivans owned all the parking as well. Such numbers could not fit on the new yacht.

Further up that street most of the residents were quite elderly and lived quiet shuttered lives behind net curtains in small villas and bunga-lows that were often painted uniformly cream. Mrs Smithson hardly ever went out because of her arthritis. A saintly man who lived in a large bungalow at the top of the hill often had extra people to stay who pottered around in the witless way of the homeless and dispossessed and sometimes, if they felt energetic, painted parts of his house in a sporadic and slapdash manner. The chimney had been done sometime during the previous winter by a youngish man who spent a lot of time sitting on the front porch talking to a brindled cat and whittling away at pieces of wood. A girl with long fair hair had washed the curtains in the front room as spring settled on the area but she was gone by the following week. The owner of that house was known to be kind to birds because there was a feeding tray on the ragged front lawn and occasionally on this reposed the large and irregularly shaped bone from a forequarter of hogget. The birds feasted deliriously. He was not the sort of man, though, who would have a yacht with turquoise sails.

Further up the street a large and decaying mansion perched on a slight promontory, its windows covered by old-fashioned brown Holland blinds. From that house on some fine evenings came the sound of classical music. The people who lived there were called the Burnses and were seldom seen. Elderly and rumoured to be infirm, they kept an old Rover car, immaculately polished, in a garage in the basement and the pavement outside the house was cluttered in summer with a rampant growth of gladiolus gone wild, and also purple spraxias that flowered luridly in spring. They would not have such a yacht either, thought Evelyn.

At first when she had moved to the cottage nothing about the area meant anything to her and that was partly why she chose to live there. When the big house she had lived in when Frederick was alive was for sale she would wander around her local area disconsolately, seeing everywhere reminders of how things used to be. When that property was for sale she would flee the house while the agents held Open Homes, and sometimes almost running down her own drive would encounter groups of people preparing to enter. The agents always called them parties. *Five parties came through*. They would leave notes on her kitchen table saying things like this. *Seven parties today*. It was as if they turned it into a festivity, which she supposed it was in a way. Like gulls feeding on the drifting and bloated carcass of a dead fish, the parties usually seemed cheerful, the sound of their feet on the gravel drive often containing the excitement of invaders. Sometimes, when she passed them on her way out, she would say things.

'A really beautiful house,' she would say as if she had come early

— earliest — to the Open Home and, gazing back at it, would smile ruefully at them as she posed as a disappointed would-be buyer, perhaps lacking the funds or the energy to attempt such a place. 'I'd really love to buy it.' With the sudden duplicity of the truly desperate she always hid photographs of herself before these Saturday afternoons of invasion so they would not know she was the actual owner of the place. Once she came upon a man and his wife staring into a little basement room built into the old stone foundations of the residence.

'A playhouse,' the man had said with authority.

'I think it might be nice to use it as a storeroom.' She heard the assumed cheerfulness in her voice become almost genuine. 'I think I'd use it as a storeroom. See how dry it is? See how clean it is?' Indefatigably she pointed out the good things about the place. Then, vaguely, she looked about as though suddenly distracted. 'I'd use it as a sort of garden shed,' she would say. 'Oh, see — look. The people who own it do the same. Look at all the lovely garden tools.' And there would be Frederick's long-handled clippers and the hedgeclippers she used now to keep the growth down on the cottage's rocky section, the lawnmower, the sprayer. 'Marvellous,' she would say, as if she had become a salesman working on her own behalf. 'They seem very tidy people, don't they?' Then, having made herself plural in the minds of the viewers, she would go running down through the trees to the gate and around the corner where her car was parked and would speed away.

A couple of hours later when she returned there would be the notes on the kitchen table, the house silent and empty but with the aghast atmosphere of a property invaded. Sometimes a cushion might be askew as if someone had sat on a chair. Other times the curtains would be differently arranged. *Six parties today, one of them seemed very interested. Four parties today, one young couple rapt.* They had bought it, that young couple. And when she moved out she left a note for them on the kitchen bench. *I do hope you will be happy here. I always was. It is a really beautiful house in its own way and you must not let it frighten you because of its size. A lot of people say it looks creepy with the chimneys rearing up above the trees but they do not know the charm of the rooms or the way the light comes in the leadlights in the moonlight. I have lived here for a long time, the last two years by myself, and I have never been frightened. Good luck.* She left a bottle of wine for them, and some crackers and a nice piece of cheese, and imagined that they might picnic happily among the packing cases, the sound of their laughter splintering the silence of the house.

The neighbours back then had already begun to complain about weeds on the boundaries, the height of the trees, the size of the hedges, though before she lived in the house by herself, when Frederick was alive, they had always seemed friendly. The area was mapped in her mind with a series of easy familiaries. The shop right up on the corner where Mrs Barclay had worked for thirty years and knew everyone's order off by heart. Old Miss Simmonds who knew everyone's business before they knew it themselves and was the neighbourhood Miss Know-it-All. Ronald and Evadne Gage, who owned five acres on the southern end of the road and ran stock on it. Evadne also bred Siamese cats. And so on.

When Evelyn went and lived in the cottage the streets around were a mystery to her, and had in many ways remained so. The area was not one she had ever known and that was one reason she went there. There were no old familiarities to seem different now. She knew the houses by the characteristics of their architecture, not by their owners, though some, like the one occupied by the saintly man who took in the homeless, became a continuingly populated story in her mind. Like episodes in a melodrama she watched the slow procession of people who came and went from that house. Other houses in the streets near her own she knew only by the colours of their gates or their windows. On her daily walk late each afternoon she passed them and slowly learnt off by heart the nature of the area. The house that always looked closed up. The house with the trellised veranda. The house with the garbage on the front lawn. In her mind they were all clearly listed, as were the boats moored at the bottom of the road beyond the seawall.

One of the little launches was owned by an old fisherman who lived three blocks away and sometimes, in the late afternoon, Evelyn would see him plodding along towards a house owned by the widow of one of his old friends. He kept her supplied with fresh fish. Slowly the mythology of the area had been revealed to her, and she supposed that her own mythologies had equally slowly become apparent to anyone interested enough to study them. How she worked in her garden which had never been a garden until she went there. Nothing had ever grown on that barren little tract of land until she put in her roses and her lilies. How she occasionally had a visitor in a large and expensive car (Jennifer). How she lived very quietly and could be seen daily bent over a desk in the front room doing some kind of work. How she kept the blinds right up as high as they would go to get maximum light because the cottage was deeply shaded.

But the yacht with the turquoise sails moored at the end of the road was a sudden and delicious discordant note. In the evening she walked down to the seawall again as the sun set. The yacht still lay gently at anchor, rising and falling with the faint swell of the sea. Glimmering with immaculate paint, it was set upon the surface of the sea like a smile. Its curtained portholes had all the promise of closed eyes before a wonderful day begins. The old fisherman was rowing ashore from his little launch so she went to the slips while he pulled the dinghy up. Across the harbour the city floated like a myth in the last rays of a rosy beneficent sun.

'What sort of yacht is that?' she asked, pointing to the one with the coloured sails.

'Cavalier.' He was a taciturn man and he was busy with the oars and a rope that he was coiling around one arm.

'I've never seen it before.'

'No?'

'Do you know who owns it?'

'No.'

'Catch anything?'

'No,' he said, though she could see the glitter of a fish in a sack. She went quietly away up her own street, then to her dictionary.

Cavalier, it said. Noun: courtly gentleman, or horseman.

In the moonlight, much later, she made out the shape of the yacht again, still rising and falling faintly with the wash of the tide. Faintly visible from her front windows, it lay at anchor at the bottom of the street like a promise and she wondered who owned it. To whom did this luxurious and charming craft belong?

Chapter Seventeen

The following day, just after ten in the morning, Andrea approached Evelyn's cottage on foot with a wide skirting movement along the opposite pavement. From time to time she stopped behind a lamp-post to observe Evelyn's cottage. Evelyn, accidentally hidden behind a vine on her balcony, observed all this closely. Andrea held a brown-paper parcel in one hand and her smallest electric coffee machine in the other. One of her jacket pockets bulged markedly. She must have left her car parked down on the seafront. Evelyn screwed up her eyes and stared intently. Yes, definitely. Parked at the end of the street was a vehicle of a luminous yellow. Andrea's Volkswagen.

'What a dreadful colour,' Evelyn had said when Andrea bought it the year before last.

'What do you mean — what a dreadful colour? It's a statement.' Andrea's jaw jutted dangerously.

'A statement of what? It looks as if it was the last one left because it was so ghastly. Did you get it cheaper?'

'Don't be silly, Evelyn. Just come to terms with the fact that you've got no taste. This car is a statement of my contempt for neo-liberalism and middle-class fascism.'

'Oh,' Evelyn had said. And then, 'Would you like a cup of tea?'

'Tea is such a middle-class drink, Evelyn. When will you ever learn?' There had been more grimacing and eye-rolling after that. 'I despair of you. I really do.'

This morning Andrea seemed to be approaching her cottage with care, thought Evelyn. Presently there was a knock at the front door.

'Evelyn, I'm terribly sorry I was so rude. I've come to say I'm sorry.' Andrea, uncharacteristically, stood hesitantly on the wooden duckboards that led to the cottage's front door. On either side the mud was being encroached upon by lilies, a pink rose and some robust begonias that had seeded themselves. There were also salvias in a drift by the front wall. 'I've brought some croissants from that new place where everything's to die for' — this was one of Andrea's favourite complimentary phrases — 'and I've brought my own coffee machine because your coffee's so disgusting. No one uses a plunger any more, Evelyn. Except you.' Her glare, though, was fairly friendly this morning and there seemed to be a faint smile lurking there some-where. 'And I've also brought some of my own specially ground exclusively blended coffee because that stuff you buy at the super-market's dreadful.'

'That's all right.' Evelyn opened the door wider and Andrea tramped in. 'You could have a cup of tea if you like. I was just having one.' Andrea was wearing a pair of semi-boots in black leather of a construction so solid and so heavy-soled they looked as if her feet had been dipped in dark concrete. 'I suppose,' said Evelyn as they walked down the thin hall in single file, 'that your new shoes are by that chap Bing Olsen, are they?'

'They certainly are.' Andrea's jaw showed signs of jutting again. 'I never wear any shoes but his. These ones cost six hundred dollars.' She waved one foot in the air.

'Good God,' said Evelyn.

'You really ought to get some decent shoes, Evelyn.' Andrea's tone was quite mild, though, thought Evelyn. She was obviously proceeding as pleasantly as she could. 'Those sort of ballet shoe things you wear are insane.'

'I know,' said Evelyn, 'but I like them. I particularly like,' she said dangerously, 'pink.'

'How disgusting.' Andrea put the coffee machine down on Evelyn's wooden kitchen bench more gently than usual and opened a paper bag she took from a very large pocket in her jacket. This garment looked as if it might be made of sacking for workmen to wear when they were plastering but, Evelyn supposed, it was probably designed by anarchist artists. The buttons, she thought, had been formed from bent fish-hooks.

'Do you like my jacket?' said Andrea as if divining these thoughts.

'No,' said Evelyn.

'I didn't think you would.' Andrea cackled less noisily than usual. She was certainly wanting to make amends, thought Evelyn. 'It's by Sick's cousin Bill.'

'Bill who?'

'Bill nothing, Evelyn. He just calls himself Bill. Surely you've heard of him? Everyone's heard of Bill. He just calls himself Bill as a statement of opposition. He was on television last week.' Andrea was a television addict.

'Was he?'

'Evelyn, you're so innocent. Don't you think the buttons are marvellous?' Andrea spun slowly around on one leaden leather-covered toe. 'He imports them especially from the United States. They're made by prisoners on Death Row out of their own bed springs. Imagine that, Evelyn. Their own actual bed springs.'

'I'll put the kettle on,' said Evelyn. Best to change the subject or they might get into another fight. 'I think my pot of tea's gone cold anyway. I'll have to make a fresh one.'

Andrea swallowed convulsively at this mention of tea.

'I've just got to have coffee,' she said. 'I can't drink tea. And I've brought some croissants from that new patisserie —'

'— where everything's to die for. Yes, I know.' Evelyn paused. 'I've got some very nice olive bread. I got it from the Salvation Army.' It was a day, she thought, for living dangerously.

'Does the Salvation Army make bread? I didn't know the Salvation Army made bread.' Andrea looked bewildered.

'No.' Evelyn was very firm. Unrepentant. 'They give it away. A bakery gives them the bread that's not sold and you can go there, if you want to, and get free bread. I quite often go. It's yesterday's but it's still quite fresh.' Stunned, Andrea remained silent. 'Would you like a piece? When interest rates drop to four per cent I go there to get my bread.' Andrea took it wordlessly and began to eat.

She munched for several moments. 'I think this might come from that new place. It tastes just like theirs. So you get it free, Evelyn, do you?' She paused and looked pensively out at the garden. 'I often,' she said, 'buy a loaf one day and don't have it till the next so I suppose that's about the same. I pay five dollars for one of these Italian loaves.' A concession indeed, thought Evelyn. 'God, your garden's disgusting. You've got flowers, Evelyn. Flowers? What are flowers? I only grow plants with thorns and spines.'

'I know,' said Evelyn. 'My garden's really horrible. Come upstairs. You can have your coffee up there. The view's nice today, and there's no wind. You can have the big velvet chair to sit in. It's really comfortable. I'll perch somewhere. I'll perch on the edge of the bed.' It would be wise, she thought, to let Andrea score a point or two because she had scored the odd point herself and had, uncharacteristically, got away with them. Andrea must be in mellow modus today.

'Anyway,' said Andrea, 'what I wanted to say was that I'm sorry I was so awful. I didn't really mean it. I actually felt quite sick. I think I had a hangover. I had to go and take some Disprin and I hate the idea of that sort of middle-class pretension.' She sighed and looked out to sea as she sank down in the old green chair and continued to eat the olive bread, the croissants forgotten. The sound of her big shoes banging on the stairs still seemed to echo through the place. 'This bread,' she said slowly, 'is quite good. What I really wanted to tell you the other night, and I never did, was the full story of how my marriage broke up. You're my best friend, Evelyn, and I've never told you.'

'Yes, you did. You told me about Stinkerbell and the quiches and the boatshed and all that. You told me all that, Andrea.'

'Did I? I must have been more out of it than I thought. I haven't told you about my boyfriend, though, have I?' There was another of her cackles. 'I'll just go downstairs and make the coffee and I'll tell you all about Fergus. And I'll bring up the croissants. This might take some time.'

Evelyn sighed and sat down on the edge of the bed. It was going to be a long morning.

'Wasn't he the one,' she shouted down the narrow stairway, 'who wouldn't sit with his back to the door?'

'There was a lot more to it than that.' Andrea's reply came darkly from some inner downstairs corner of the cottage now. 'That was only the beginning. Did I ever tell you, for instance, that he also always slept with the light on and the radio playing? Where are your coffee cups, Evelyn? I must say you've got a very strange way of arranging the storage in this apology for a kitchen. You need to get kitchen designers in — when you've got enough money, of course.' It certainly would be a long morning, thought Evelyn. Clattering came from below.

'I'm just loading up one of your trays with some apples and some of your cheese and my croissants.' Andrea was attending to the catering. 'I might as well stay and have a peculiar kind of lunch with you, Evelyn, and tell you the entire unexpurgated version of my flingette with Fergus. The sex was good but he had so many hang-ups I gave him the heave-ho in the end. My word, you do seem to have a peculiar assortment of food here.' The refrigerator was being opened vigorously. Its door slammed again. 'Don't you have any olives? I despair of you, Evelyn, I really do.' There was silence for a few seconds. 'And what you really need is a Miele stove, Evelyn. A Miele stove is to die for. And a stainless steel refrigerator. You need a stainless steel refrigerator, Evelyn. Evelyn? Are you listening?'

This discourse was interrupted by what sounded like an explosion down the street.

'What was that?' Andrea's voice had risen to almost a shriek. Activity in the kitchen ceased suddenly. Evelyn went to the upstairs windows and stared out. A bus had hit a power pole down at the corner. Passengers were slowly clambering down the bus's steps, looking shaken.

'A bus has hit a power pole, Andrea. I don't think anyone's hurt. They seem to be climbing out.' From far away came the wail of an ambulance. As she gazed out a police car slid in to the kerb near the bus. 'It all seems to be in hand, Andrea. The police have already arrived.'

'Oh, good.' Andrea was climbing the stairs again now, her large bespoke footwear once more clumping loudly on the wooden treads. 'I'll probably have to stay for a while until they clear the street. The bus hasn't hit my car, has it? Oh, good. Anyway, I've got plenty of time now to tell you the entire story of my flingette. I shall leave no stone unturned.' She paused to take a deep breath. 'At the end,' she said, 'I just ran into his office and threw all the Tupperware that he'd left at my place at him. But at the beginning, just after his wife had tossed him out, things didn't seem so bad.' She approached the bed briskly. 'Here's a fresh cup of coffee, Evelyn. And here's a croissant. I'll just put them beside the bed for you and you can eat while I'm talking. Please don't interrupt because it's a long, long story.'

Evelyn lay down and put her head exactly at the centre of a large feather pillow. It was going to be an interminable morning.

Chapter Eighteen

In the evening Evelyn sat on the balcony and looked reflectively out to sea. Beyond the immediacy of the small moorings at the end of her street the harbour stretched out into a great gulf across which large shipping moved. In the final minutes of twilight, before darkness finally came down upon the city, a large shabby container ship passed silently by, hugely burdened and mysteriously soundless, the noise of its motor drowned out by the sea and the city and the screaming of the gulls. In its wash the beautiful new yacht with the furled turquoise sails bobbed gently.

Inside the cottage there were signs of Evelyn's own ideas of how Christmas was spent now. The cards that meant something to her stood in a row on the mantelpiece. The rest, like the one from Charles's bank, had been thrown away. There was a Christmas cake cooling in the kitchen on the table and in the morning she would ice it with brandy frosting, the ingredients for which lay, neatly stacked, upon that kitchen table. There was sliced ham in a parcel in the refrigerator, a chicken in the freezer, a bunch of asparagus hidden away somewhere in an old French basket. The materials with which to manufacture Christmas dinner were all at hand, if she decided against the anarchic but delicious fish and chips; and the garden shed, neatly scrubbed and swept in the last day or two, its shelves meticulously tidied, awaited tenancy for the day. Behind the shed she had weeded and prepared the garden in case the weather was extremely hot, and in that case the deckchair could be placed there, under the banana palms. The little padlock was ready to lock the side gate that led to the back garden so her hiding place could not be discovered, and if people knocked at the front door in a sudden agony of conscience about her she would be found to be not at home.

Everyone would be happy. Callers would think they had done their duty. She would imagine her inadequacies were unexposed, her secrets still her own. *Oh Evelyn, you're not here all by yourself, are you? Why didn't you say? And whatever are you doing in the shed?* Somehow, the clear enunciation of her festive situation always made it seem absurd, any quaint happiness she had manufactured suddenly dispersed, all sense of solitary tranquillity besmirched. *You should have said, Evelyn, you should have said.* But what, she would always think, was there to say?

You could say that to spend the day alone with no reminder of solitariness in the observation of others who were not solitary was a happier state to be in than enduring a day of watching the connubiality and caresses of others who were often ostentatious in their displays of mutual affection. Jennifer, draped gallantly against Marky's expanding stomach, would chew one of his sunburnt ears as she licked his mottled cheek and say, 'It must be awful for you, Evelyn. We must try to think of someone.' And, immediately, even though the Christmas barbecue or the picnic lunch had seemed bearable until then it suddenly would not be. The perception of her isolation, firmly stated in bright sunlight, made it as obvious as the stink of fish and people would turn away. Jennifer's Uncle Barry, recently a widower, had plodded through the crowd at last Christmas's post-festivity barbecue to say, without preamble, 'I could never replace Monica. Jennifer said I had to meet you, but I could never replace Monica,' and Evelyn had snapped, 'Who asked you to, buddy-boy?'

'Uncle Barry said you were rude, Evelyn.' That was Jennifer while they were loading the dishwasher later.

'Rude?'

'Yes. Uncle Barry said you were very rude. It's the festive season, Evelyn. People aren't rude at this time of year. He's gone home early now and it's all your fault. You were rude. He said you were rude.'

'Was I?'

'He's just recently been through all that trauma, Evelyn, of poor Auntie Monica's illness and then the funeral, which was absolutely awful. The weather was terrible. I ruined a perfectly good pair of Italian shoes and I chipped my nails on the car door and as for my hat — I don't think I can ever wear it again and it was a Pooh Corner too.'

'A what?'

'A Pooh Corner, Evelyn. Haven't you ever heard of Pooh Corner hats? They're handmade by that woman who's supposed to have been a Hungarian countess and then she married a Turk and then she came here and now she makes hats.'

'I see,' said Evelyn, who did not.

'I do think you, of all people, could've been a little bit kinder. You, of all people,' Jennifer had repeated, 'could've understood.' Jennifer had returned relentlessly to the subject of Uncle Barry.

The trouble was that she did understand. Absolutely. Understood the whole thing.

Jennifer would have said, 'My friend Evelyn's going to be here. Maybe you two could get together. She's really quite a good little cook when she tries and even though she's got a lot of funny ideas, particularly in recent times, you could easily get her out of all that, Uncle Barry. Do try to make yourself known to her and perhaps you two could get along? It's ghastly being all by yourself at Christmas — these are things you'll have to think about now, Uncle. I'll introduce you to her — she'll probably be wearing one of her funny crushed sunhats made of dried hyacinth root or something like that but she's not a bad old soul, really, our funny old Evelyn — and the rest's up to you. You've just got to think, Uncle — do you want to eat carbon for the rest of your life? You can't cook and you burn everything. Monica's saucepans are all ruined already.' It would have been something like that, anyway. 'You could just be married quietly and have the reception here in the garden, Uncle Barry. Everyone would know it was just a convenience kind of thing but it'd get the two of you settled. You wouldn't need to get a cleaning lady, Uncle. It could be a great saving. Think about it.'

Uncle Barry would have been put in the position of being perceived as a man who could not cook and who would be forced to eat only grimly burnt food forever. The doom and horror of it would have made him aggressive. As it made Evelyn.

'So why don't you push off,' she had said. 'I never asked to meet you. Why don't you stuff your barbecued sausages up your arse and leave me alone. I do not,' she had said, 'want you. I never asked to meet you. I don't want to meet anyone. So bugger off.' That part of the conversation had perhaps not been repeated, she thought as she put dishes away in Jennifer's especially designed kitchen with granite benches and doorknobs made to a unique design by a well-known potter. Uncle Barry had perhaps stopped short of repeating all that.

'You were rude,' Jennifer had said.

'I was.'

'I think you should apologise.'

'I won't.'

'In that case I think it might be nice if you went home now.'

'Good. I intended to anyway.'

In the novel the new waiter in the mess was considered insolent from the moment he began work there. He was punctiliously polite but there was something in his manner that was instantly perceived as insolent by some of the men who dined there. In that curious way people have of classing a person, they imagined immediately that he had once been somehow superior to them and this antagonised them. He was better educated than they were; they could tell this immediately. He had a better background. This also they knew at once by social osmosis. He had come down in the world obviously and yet dared to retain a musicality of modulation, the well-rounded vowels of the aristocratic, and the graceful movements of one who must have gone to the best schools and had been trained to dance, to play cricket, everything. He had not been working as a waiter in the mess for more than one evening when the complaints began to roll in.

The second lieutenant was in an impossible position. He had once known the new waiter in circumstances far different from those pertaining now. The idea of the man who was now a waiter ever being a waiter would never have been imagined. But there he was — a waiter, and in the mess.

If he had arrived as a colonel or a major, even a captain, it would have been all right. They would have accepted him instantly, grappled successfully with his slightly louche attitudes, his quietly drawling voice, his sidelong humorous glances, his odd brand of faintly disrespectful humour. Even his cynicism could have been considered an advantage in warfare, because who must be more cynical than a soldier who does not know which friend he will still have alive by nightfall or in what billet he will be sleeping next week? What sounds may assault his ears before and after battle? Who will be a hero, and who not? If he had arrived, with advance warning from HQ, in a staff car, fully uniformed and with a neatly trimmed moustache everything would have proceeded according to a universal plan.

No one knew how he had arrived. Perhaps by services bus — some kind of army transport anyway. Perhaps on the back of a truck, in the fallow stretches of the late morning when the officers were drilling or on manoeuvres. His arrival was unremarkable.

'My God, I'm looking forward to some grub,' someone shouted

before dinner began that night. He called the new waiter a slow bugger and told him to hurry up. Most of them sitting at the tables said what a day it had been. An awful day, and one after which you needed a good dinner.

After a slight delay the waiter appeared, a tall slim man who gave an impression of being too shrunken for his uniform. He looked as if he had been ill, possibly for a long time. His eyes were red-rimmed and his complexion slightly waxy. He began to hand around dishes of potatoes.

'You can tell the cook,' said one of the men, 'that he can stuff these potatoes up his arse. They're not cooked properly.' He dropped one or two onto his plate in a theatrical way and they splashed gravy over the cloth.

'Yes, sir,' said the waiter.

'What are you going to tell the cook?'

'To stick the potatoes up his arse, sir.'

'And that they're not cooked properly.'

'And that they're not cooked properly, sir.'

'Righto, then. Dismissed.'

The waiter moved away to another table. There was something about him, some lost familiarity that slowly provoked the second lieutenant's interest and he realised that, long before the war, he had known this man very well.

The new waiter, though, had suddenly attracted a spate of odium from a goodly proportion of those dining in the mess. Some began to say it was so difficult to get a waiter there, why did the previous one have to disappear so suddenly? He, too, had been appalling but they knew him. His appalling habits and attitudes, the dereliction of his duties were all well known to them and his understanding of their contempt was also a familiar thing. They were all at ease with their mutual scorn. But the new waiter was a different matter. Their sudden disdain for him was tinged with slight fear because they had a suspicion he may once have been better than they were. When one of them claimed loudly that the soup was like monkey pee he did so with a guilty air, knowing that a gentleman would never say such a thing.

'When did the new waiter arrive?' the second lieutenant asked carefully. He had been to school with the man who was now the waiter. He was remembering it now with nostalgia and hopelessness.

'About lunchtime,' said someone. Someone else chimed in to say the waiter had a la-di-da voice and needed taking down a peg and someone else said being a waiter was not as bad as being on sanitary duties.

Several days later the second lieutenant was told it was a rule in the army not to interfere with the ranks. He had wanted to get the waiter who had once been his school friend a better job, a better place — anything. Subsequently the waiter was sent to Singapore to work in an army laundry, where he was captured by the Japanese and died, but that was a long time after the sergeant shot himself over the faithless wife. That all happened when the unit was still in training, quite early in the war.

'I do wish you wouldn't always read those silly books.' This was Jennifer on the telephone again. 'Every time I ring you, you say you're reading. I haven't got much time, Evelyn' — but when did her non-friend Jennifer have any time these days? thought Evelyn — 'but I just saw something quite peculiar on television and I thought I'd better let you know. There was some kind of announcement on suddenly about a statement from your bank in greater detail later. Have you got the news on? No, I thought not. Well, for heaven's sake turn it on, Evelyn. It might be something of interest to you. There was something about your bank the day before yesterday, was it? Or was it yesterday? I've forgotten. But there's going to be something else on now so turn your television on and have a look. I thought you'd be interested apropos what we were talking about earlier in the week. But I've got to go now.' Jennifer's voice sounded somewhat faint, even strangulated. 'I'm not very well. I really do think you could at least watch the news without having to be told.'

Oh dear. In trouble again, thought Evelyn. Her television set was a small one, perched among the books on some shelves in the little room where she worked, and the view it gave of the world was compact and almost jewel-like. Terrorists looked a manageable size. Tanks looked quaintly unreal, children throwing stones at the tanks hardly more than naughty animated dolls.

'What you need, Evelyn,' Marky had said on many occasions, 'is what is called a home cinema. Something with a wide screen, so you get a decent look at things. How do you think you can keep up with world events by staring at something about the size of a postage stamp?'

'It's a fourteen-inch.' Her own defence was usually delivered deadpan, the remarks almost monosyllabic.

'A postage stamp, Evelyn, hardly bigger than a postage stamp. Your problem is you read too much. That's what I don't like about you. I mean, I came into the house yet again the other day to find you sitting up beside the kitchen bench rabbiting on about some book you've been reading for generations about some soldier who shot himself. Well, Evelyn, who wants to know? Certainly not me for the fortieth time as I step in my own front door, and certainly not poor Jennifer who's done her best for you, Evelyn, and what gratitude has she got? I'll tell you — none. And she's not a bit well at the moment, for reasons I cannot specify. She just doesn't want to discuss it. She's been very good to you, Evelyn. She even introduced you to her Uncle Barry last Christmas and you told him to shove his lunch up his arse. What sort of talk is that, may I ask? Don't imagine for one moment that we don't know all about that, my dear. And while I'm giving you a talking-to I might as well say my piece yet again about how we think Teddy's the limit. What he needs to do is come back home, get a decent job and do a few things for his mother, including spending Christmas with her so the rest of us don't get clobbered with the job. And get a haircut.'

Outside the windows of the cottage evening was falling and the last rays of the sun shone on the skyscrapers across the harbour so they glimmered like buildings in a heavenly land. The little room in which Evelyn usually worked had a remarkable view of this through its tiny windows, and from the book-filled shelves the television set began to present yet another manageable view of the world.

The weather is going to be good tomorrow, the announcer said, and pointed at various parts of the map. Winds tomorrow in the north, fine weather most places, rain over the country within the next forty-eight hours. Now back to the news.

'And now, just to hand.' The newsreader's expression was serious, the eyes unremittingly unblinking. 'The police were called today to . . .'

Evelyn sank on to the floor, almost into a foetal position. The picture on the screen was of her bank. 'Officials connected with the bank and members of the banking fraud squad are continuing to invest-igate alleged irregularities and are being helped by a bank employee.' The camera flashed wildly in an arc and captured a black official-looking car into which a man was being bundled. His jacket had been pulled up over his head but on the well-turned wrist was a gold watch that looked frighteningly familiar. And there was a distinctive signet ring on the little finger of the left hand, which Evelyn recognised instantly. The intaglio centrepiece of this ring had the coat of arms of some notable family or another, possibly now defunct, uninterested or dying of starvation. Charles had bought it last year for quite a lot of money at an antique shop.

'That's rather a nice old ring you're wearing.' She had said to him once when she handed him the little tray of sandwiches. 'These are mushroom pâté,' she had said. 'I don't really think it's a good thing for you to have a glass of wine and then drive, so I've made some little sandwiches to sop it all up.'

'Darling.' He gave her one of those very fond looks. 'And who says I'll be going?' He had slipped the ring off and placed it on the middle finger of her left hand. 'You're so observant, Evelyn. No one else has noticed it. It's rather a nice one, don't you think? Bought it the other day over at McCutcheon's.' McCutcheon's was an exclusive jewellery store handling a lot of antique items in the eastern suburbs where people bought lavish presents for each other, or themselves. He gave a careless wave of his hand. 'It's very old,' he said. 'An antique. Just the best, Evelyn, just the very best.'

'Of course.' She had slipped it off and given it back to him, the intaglio with its ancient coat of arms glimmering at her. It was a dark reddish colour, like old dried blood from a wound that was healing, perhaps from a bullet.

'It cost mega, mega bucks, Evelyn. You have to pay mega bucks for this sort of thing.'

'I suppose so,' she had said.

'And there's nearly an ounce of gold in it — eighteen-carat gold. And the coat of arms is very rare and very special. It's just not an ordinary armorial ring, Evelyn; it's the best.'

'Would you like another glass of wine?'

'I don't think so. It might be a little corky. I feel it's a little corky. Did you get it at the supermarket? I thought so.'

Chapter Nineteen

Ting-a-ling. Evelyn's telephone was ringing again.

'Evelyn? Is that you? You sound rather odd.'

'I've just ru—' She was going to say she had just rushed in from the garden but there was no time.

'Evelyn, I've told you before, you've got a very bad habit of interrupting. Anyway, it's Mark speaking. It's suddenly occurred to me that I haven't really ever got back to you properly about Paul — you know that friend of mine, Paul? That one I told you about who's got this property you'd be just marvellous on, Evelyn? And, by the way, I dare say there hasn't been any word from that son of yours? No, Evelyn, don't even speak. I felt the answer was no before I even finished asking the question. So it's up to us, I suppose, to get you placed at Christmas.' He sighed.

'But —'

'Don't interrupt, Evelyn.' There was another sigh. 'You'd have been fantastic on Paul's farm, too, with all that digging and chopping and whatever, and it wouldn't matter to you, would it, dear, that the old house has got a dirt floor? I felt that you and Paul would have been ideal, just absolutely a couple in a million, and you could've had a wonderful time out there at Christmas helping him kill a chicken and pluck it and all that stuff, Evelyn. Back to our roots, Evelyn, back to our roots. We're all country souls at heart but' — he sighed heavily yet again — 'it seems it is not to be.' A silence now. 'And that's what I rang you about, Evelyn. To tell you what's happened about Paul. And I do hope you're not too disappointed.'

'Disappointed?' A Paul-less life stretched out before her and Evelyn, illuminated by the notion that she would now not have to use the many excuses she had invented to avoid meeting him at all, and particularly being taken to see the potato paddock and the house with the dirt floor and all the shovels and garden spades, saw her garden through her own kitchen windows equally illuminated in a sudden glow of brilliant sunshine. It all looked very beautiful and desirable. And it was all hers, including the garden spade. Which she could use or not, as she pleased. Evelyn did not have a shovel.

'It seems,' Marky began again, 'that Paul has decided he has got a calling.'

'A calling?'

'Yes, Evelyn, a calling. A calling to the ministry, my dear. He's had a calling for years, as I've already told you, to campaign on behalf of wildfowl I think you'd call it, particularly ducks, Evelyn, particularly ducks. Paul has always been very devoted to the idea of ducks. But his mind has been taken over now with the idea of human beings and he's decided he wants to be a vicar. I gather, from what he's said, that he's going to enter some kind of ecclesiastical college very soon. He may even be there now, studying as I speak. His little sort of farm thing's been let out to a couple of hippies who've left a commune somewhere further up north. They want to grow things — God knows what, but let us not enquire into that too closely.'

'I see,' said Evelyn.

'I did hope you would, my dear. And as far as I can gather, the course he's going to be on is somehow designed for older people who decide they want to enter the ministry and it's kind of encapsulated, so to speak, so they become a vicar quicker.'

'A vicar quicker?'

'I think he'll be out, fully qualified, in a year or two but in the interim everything's socially in limbo with regard to Paul, so Jen and I definitely thought Christmas on the farm would have to be a no-go zone for you.' He paused for a moment of reflection. 'Shame, really, because there'd be haymaking coming up and you could've been wonderfully useful. I'm not really sure he actually did have paddocks shut up for hay, but if he had you could have helped, Evelyn.'

'But —'

'No time for ifs and buts, Evelyn — I've got clients waiting so I must away, my dear. Jennifer told me to tell you she'd have rung you herself with the news about Paul but she's in the bathroom. I've come clean to her about the whole thing.'

'The bathroom? Again?' He had gone, but in a moment the telephone rang again.

'Evelyn? Mark again. I'm terribly sorry I forgot to tell you about the Finnigans.'

'The Finnigans? But I don't know anyone called Fin—'

'Please don't interrupt, Evelyn. Time is of the essence for me right now. The Finnigans are our new neighbours and they're terribly sweet people, really. She has a slight problem with one leg, and he's been behind bars, according to rumour — but only, and I do stress this, for some sort of white-collar crime, Evelyn: nothing really nasty that might frighten anyone. Some kind of minor embezzlement thingie or a small error in a balance sheet, I imagine. Could have all been some kind of ghastly mistake, really, or even a frame-up, but he's paid the price and we find him quite a wonderful chap, really.' He paused to draw breath. 'Grows wonderful baby carrots,' he said. 'And beans. He's marvellous with beans.'

'Beans?' said Evelyn.

'Don't be silly, Evelyn. Beans have nothing to do with it. What I meant to tell you is that the Finnigans would have liked to have you for Christmas, even though they don't know you, but they have to have her mother with them and it's just too difficult. I gather the old girl's out of it. She could possibly think you're Hitler and try to strangle you. That's one of her things. And the other thing is that she's a tiny bit unreliable downstairs in the pantaloon department so there's the odd puddle here and there and sometimes something larger. Otherwise,' he said, 'they'd have loved to have you over to help load and unload the dishwasher and keep an eye on the barbie. They do hate the steak to be overdone. We told them,' he said, 'that you're very handy. We just happened to mention to them that you were on your own and a good little worker and they said they might ask you for the day — to help, you know, Evelyn, to help you all. Sadly, it's all off.'

'But I —' Too late.

Evelyn stood looking out at the wild mess of flowers in her back garden. She had cleaned the kitchen windows yesterday and the view was pristine and almost glittering. Pink roses rioted beside purple dahlias. Peach-coloured canna lilies thrust themselves up between the waving stalks of blue biennial salvias. At the back of the garden the silvery leaves of her olive trees fluttered in the wind from the sea and the blooms on three large hydrangea bushes seemed to gaze at her kindly like big blue faces. Whatever could have given Mark and Jennifer the idea that she could be touted about like an unwanted parcel at Christmas to be foisted onto batty neighbours and their incontinent mother or matched up with a man who preferred ducks and whose house had a dirt floor? And Jennifer immured in the bathroom yet again? What did all this mean?

The newspaper the following morning carried similarly enigmatic pieces of news. Weather over the festive season was expected to be stormy due to the approach of an easterly low-pressure zone. But, equally, a slightly stronger high-pressure area to the west might drive this away and the weather could, thus, be excellent. The Prime Minister's office had announced that a high-level meeting of some leaders might be held in an Asian capital but, due to various bits of trouble in some of the Third World countries, this may have to be postponed until next winter. The French fashion houses had come out with a mixed view of hemlines: Chanel's were right down; Ungaro had gone up to the mid-thigh and had navel cut-outs in daywear.

Tucked away at the bottom of page five was the news that the fraud squad was continuing to go through files at the bank where her investments were held. A man was also continuing to help them with their enquiries. An investigation throughout the entire investment department had ascertained that the difficulty was not widespread and pertained to just one area. A fraud squad spokesman had issued the following statement: 'A high-level investigation is continuing and it is hoped that a firm statement can be issued tomorrow.'

Perhaps, thought Evelyn as she looked out of one of her small windows, they were using the word 'area' to mean 'person'. Perhaps only one person was actually involved. There was a slightly blurred photograph of someone in the back seat of a police car, a man with his well-tailored jacket pulled up over his head — Charles always dressed well, and there was that very recognisable ring again. Charles had been up to tricks of a more diverse sort than she had hitherto imagined. A newspaper photographer must have pressed forward for a fleeting view of the people getting into the car before it sped away and a television crew must have been there as well because last night's view on the Channel One news had been from exactly the same angle. There might have been a rope to hold people back, she thought, and that might be why the view was the same. Could there possibly have been a crowd of concerned people worrying about their money and being held back by a hastily erected barrier of some kind so they could advance no further? If the street outside the bank had had to be prepared so thoroughly for the exit of the man with the signet ring and the well-cut jacket pulled up over his head then the investigation must be a major one.

The harbour today looked more jewel-like and distant, the sea a warmer blue, with the yachts around in their moorings at the end of the street. The large one with turquoise sails was still there, she noted. Two men in overalls were out on the deck doing something to the brass portholes, possibly polishing them or refurbishing them in some way, and a third man was putting up a turquoise and beige striped awning over part of the deck. Through her binoculars the view was much clearer and she noticed that there seemed to be activity inside the yacht as well. Sometimes a hand came up from inside a hatch and more little tailored curtains with very tight tie-backs, also in turquoise and beige stripes, were being put up inside. There was also a stack of teak deckchairs with turquoise covers beside a ladder, up which these workers must have climbed, she thought. Beneath it, bobbing cheerfully about on the warm and lovely sea, was a dinghy on which the work team must have arrived. Someone, she thought, was getting the vessel ready for a Christmas party on board.

The telephone rang suddenly. Probably Jennifer again, she thought.

'Jennifer, I'm absolutely sick of hearing about Christmas.'

'It's not that awful Jennifer. It's me.' It was Andrea.

'Oh.'

'I know you came around here ultra-recently' — Andrea's voice sounded very tense — 'but why don't you come around again this evening? This business of Christmas is really getting to me. Bring a pizza and a bottle of wine. I think it's your turn, isn't it? The thought of Christmas Day yet again with my cousin Hilda in that terrible house full of cats and empty tin cans is just hanging over me, Evelyn. I can't bear the thought of it. I'd much rather come to your place for Christmas.'

Chapter Twenty

Evelyn awakened just after dawn on Christmas Eve. The day before Christmas. Oh, hell, she thought. And she lay in the big comfortable brass bed staring at the ceiling. The map of its cracks and faults, as always, gave no clue to the course of her own ridiculous life — except that it, like the ceiling, was much flawed.

The sun was rising and, reflected in the calm and silvery sea, looked like a blush for the hopeful, or a fire for the damned. In her current mood she leaned more towards the idea of fire.

With a cup of tea in one hand and a small slice of dry toast in the other she watched the early morning news on television, an unaccustomed diversion prompted only by the idea that there may be something more about Charles being charged, arrested, murdered in the police cells overnight by an unknown and mysteriously enraged fellow prisoner, or similarly harmed. Even only stabbed slightly by a drug-enraged inmate using a biro would be okay, she thought. The intaglio ring, together with his Rolex watch, would by now have been taken off him and placed in a coded envelope by some glum policeman, in case he decided to swallow them both or poke them in his ears or up his nose, both these activities highly improbable in one so sartorially correct and fond of his own appearance.

The news announcements were made by someone with blue hair and a slightly nasal voice. Main access to a southern city had been completely blocked by an unseasonable flood. A top Parisian model had announced she was a lesbian after strutting the catwalk for Karl Lagerfeld in a minute bikini made entirely from sterling silver chain and silk gingham gardenias. Sixteen people were unaccounted for after a mudslide buried a Paraguayan village. Evelyn watched intently, toast in hand. After being helped by a man overnight the fraud squad had announced that an arrest had been made in the matter of irregularities at such-and-such a bank. Further investigations were pending and in the meantime the man's name was suppressed. A court appearance was expected after New Year. In the meantime bail had been refused and the man's passport had been confiscated.

Evelyn ate the piece of dry toast and, with a sudden burst of energy, skipped out to the kitchen to put another piece of bread in the toaster — a bigger piece, sliced more generously — and when it presented itself browned perfectly she spread it with butter and marmalade. It was nearly Christmas, after all. And how delicious, she thought, to have a minuscule celebration about Charles being arrested. Other news was not of great interest. A certain model of car had been recalled by the manufacturers due to problems with the brake drums. Weather was expected to improve over the whole country for Christmas Day with the approach of a high-pressure front from the west. The Cancer Society had issued its usual warning about the use of sunscreen lotions both in and out of the water for those who were planning to spend the festive season at the beach if the weather improved. And so on.

In the midst of these announcements the telephone rang again.

'Jennifer?' Evelyn picked up the receiver in one sharp movement, the tone terse. 'Jennifer, I'm watching the news on television — could you ring back later?'

'Mother?' The voice sounded very far away. 'Is that you?'

'Teddy?'

'Mother — I've got hold of a cellphone and I'm ringing to wish you a happy Christmas.'

'Oh, Teddy.' Evelyn sank down and sat on the floor. 'Teddy — how lovely to hear your voice. It's so lovely to hear you.'

'I can't talk for long. One of the tribesmen coming through here has a link-up with a tour company and he's got a cellphone. I kind of lost mine a while ago — some sod stood on it — so I haven't rung, but I've sent you something for Christmas and I'll be home again for a while next Christmas. I've got you a coat, Mother, a Mongolian coat. It's got lapis lazuli tassels and I thought it was very you. We're miles from anywhere right out here but I've given it to the same man I've borrowed the cellphone from and he's promised to post it for me. I don't know when it'll arrive. Probably not till months after Christmas if I know anything.'

'Oh, Teddy — just what I wanted.' She paused for a moment. 'I didn't really know where you were, dear' — it was like kindergarten all over again, she thought, but just with an adult-sized infant — 'so I got the bank to transfer some funds for you. It seemed very dull but it was all I could do.'

'Oh, Mother, how lovely.' He was not her son for nothing, thought Evelyn. 'When I get back to Ulan Bator I'll buy myself a present and another woolly hat. Don't worry. Don't let the buggers get at you. I'll be home for next Christmas but I'll have to go now. We're starting a move east today and everything's loaded. I've got a terrible hangover. We all got pissed last night on mare's milk.'

'How could you do that, darling?'

'They ferment it somehow and turn it into booze. Now, if you have a glass of Moët at Christmas raise your glass and think of me. Even a gin and tonic would do. The throat singers here are fabulous but I'll tell you all about it when I see you.'

Evelyn continued to sit on the floor for a long time. It seemed only a moment since she and Frederick had wheeled Teddy outside for the first time in his pram. Both of them had peered anxiously under the pram's hood at this curious infant who looked like no one in particular and whose great dark eyes glowed back at them from beneath the brim of a hand-knitted blue woollen helmet done entirely in two-ply moss stitch. He had always seemed to gaze far beyond the environs of that pram and when able to stand had perched stalwartly beside his bedroom windowsill to look at the stars at night and the great wide sky during the day. Possibly it was natural now that he would roam obscure parts of the world studying the music and habits of remote tribes and recording them for the BBC. While she watched the telephone it rang again.

'Evelyn? What were you doing? I rang just now and got an engaged signal for ages.' Jennifer this time.

'I was talking to Teddy.'

'Teddy? Don't say he's rung?'

'He couldn't ring before because he lost his phone. He borrowed one from someone passing through.'

'Passing through? Passing through where, Evelyn? Where actually is he?'

'Mongolia.'

'I beg your pardon? Where?'

'Mongolia.'

'You never told me that, Evelyn. I feel sure that if I'd known Teddy was in Mongolia I'd have remembered.' There was a long and significant silence. 'I really don't know why, Evelyn, you and Fred didn't bring Teddy up to be an ordinary person who works in a bank or whatever. Now just look at my gorgeous boy. He's doing very well in the vehicle industry and next year he's going to upgrade his BMW to the latest model bar one. He's got a very beautiful new partner who's about to break into modelling and the sky's the limit for them, Evelyn, the sky's the limit. Her legs are more than eighty centimetres long.'

'Teddy loves music.' Evelyn stood defensively on one leg, like an embattled heron. 'He always did. And art. He loves music and art and he loves the sky and the flight of great flocks of birds in northern migrations.'

'For heaven's sake, Evelyn. Look, I've been really, really tactful up till now and I've only mentioned Teddy a few times but it's been very much on my mind, Evelyn, that you've never said a word about him and both Marky and I think he's been very neglectful — very, very neglectful, Evelyn, to coin a phrase — not to have done something about you at Christmas. We've been waiting and waiting for you to say something about Teddy and now we find he's been in Mongolia all this time.'

'He's working under contract for the BBC. He's recording the music of migratory peoples, particularly the throat singers of Mongolia.'

'Don't be ridiculous, Evelyn. The way you talk sometimes is just too absurd.'

Later in the afternoon Evelyn stood, as Teddy might have done if he were there, looking up into the great wide sky thinking about music and art. It was as if her mind had become faceted so it could hold many images and impressions, even apprehensions, at the same time. In part of it she silently heard the opening bars of her favourite Beethoven Symphony — the fourth. In another part she was once again standing before a tiny oil painting by Boudin which she had once seen in London and had never forgotten. Its miniature splendour had been such that, at the time, she felt she might fall down on the floor in front of it. This impression had never left her.

And there was Teddy far away but gazing up into that same huge cup of the sky, listening for the approach of horsemen and perhaps a great bird, perhaps an eagle or a hawk, floating like an eye above them all. There was Charles in his cell under twenty-four-hour surveillance now, according to the very latest news, having been found trying to hang himself using strips of his torn sheeting. And someone else who, according to the same news broadcast, had been helping the police with their enquiries into the case. A blurred picture of something or somebody quite large and definitely female had appeared momentarily on the screen, all blocked out with flashing little squares. Possibly the fat shopkeeper. The house of that person had been searched, said a poker-faced announcer, and various items had been taken away for forensic examination. Would that perhaps include the shopkeeper's large-sized knickers in black silk imprinted with the impression of Charles's hands? Evelyn wondered. Or would the items taken away be fifty-dollar notes that Charles and the shopkeeper both counted in the evenings by the light of a guttering candle with fingers stained by vintage wine, bodily fluids of varying kinds and Chanel No 5? Time would tell. Charles and his lady friend might even have bought expensive electronic equipment, first-class tickets to faraway places and watches by Cartier. Sad-eyed and cynical policemen might be, at that very moment, sorting through them and making lists of the illicit shopping.

But now there was the visit of the man delivering the hedge clippers to contemplate. If he was arriving at five-thirty there was not much time to prepare for the visit, but what did one do to get ready for the mysterious delivery of hedgeclippers by a quiet man with eyes of uncertain colour? Perhaps some tiny sandwiches, she thought, and could she offer him a glass of wine? She placed a bottle of a more than ordinary chardonnay bought on special at the supermarket in her refrigerator where it jostled an over-ripe tomato and a half-empty jar of Marmite.

Perhaps he may prefer a cup of tea? She buffed the old silver teapot with the duster she used as a bookmark. The portion of old tea towel could have somehow, magically, taken on the aura of some of the more beautiful words in the novel about the sergeant who shot himself and may, thus, make the visit more charming. Then she washed her long hair, rinsing it in water in which she had steeped leaves from the old rosemary bush in the garden, and pinned it up behind her ears. There was no more time to do anything else and all of these activities were mercifully not interrupted by Jennifer who seemed to have been silenced by the news of Teddy being in Mongolia. Or perhaps it was the throat-singing that had shut her up, or the job with the BBC, or just the idea of someone following obscure tribes to listen to them singing. Jennifer, though, was quiet.

Her hair was still slightly damp when there was a vigorous rapping on the doorknocker at the exact moment the clock struck five-thirty. Perfectly on time, she thought. How terrifying. And she ran down the stairs to answer the door.

'Good evening.' There was the man from the repair shop with a newspaper parcel under one arm and a bunch of pink roses in one hand. 'I've got your clippers, and your prize.' The sky had turned a pearly colour and some people ran up the street laughing. It suddenly seemed a happy evening, a joyful kind of twilight. The sea shimmered at the end of the road, the new yacht rising and falling gently in the swell.

'Would you like to come in?' Evelyn opened the door wider. 'It's Christmas,' she said. 'It's nice to ask people in at Christmas. Could I offer you a glass of battery water and maybe a little sandwich? If you've got time? Which you may not have, because often I find people are kind of busy.' She stood there awkwardly, like a visitor in her own house unsure of a welcome.

'No.' He stepped in the door. 'I'm not too busy at all. But what was it you offered me a glass of?'

'I've got a very silly sense of humour.' Evelyn was leading the way down the tiny hall to the sitting room. 'I said battery water but of course I didn't really mean real battery water. I just meant that perhaps the wine I've got isn't the most marvellous sort of wine. I got it on special at the supermarket.' I must not babble, thought Evelyn. Pink roses, she thought. No one had brought her pink roses for years. 'I can recommend the green velvet chair' — they were in the room now — 'because it's by far the most comfortable.' And I mustn't be bossy, she thought, and go on like someone's grandmother. She watched him sit down carefully, still holding the parcel containing the clippers, and the flowers.

'Perhaps I could put this down.' He put the package on the floor. 'There's no charge, by the way. You were the one-hundredth person to return to have their clippers re-sharpened and so qualified for our Christmas freebie.'

'Really?' said Evelyn.

'Really.' He was very firm about it.

'Thank you very much. But I've already won a box of chocolates for being the one-hundredth something else. It seems hardly fair that I'm winning another prize now.'

'Yes, I know.' He grinned faintly at her, just a flicker of a smile. 'And you've also won another prize,' he said, 'if you'd like it, but I'll tell you about that when you've given me a glass of your very excellent battery water.'

'I've made some little sandwiches too,' said Evelyn. 'Would you like a little sandwich? Perhaps?'

'Good. What I like best in the evening is to have a glass of battery water and a little sandwich. Yes, I'd love a little sandwich.'

'Would you really?' She stopped in the doorway and looked around at him. Quite a tall man, she thought. He had tucked himself into the old green velvet chair as if he liked it.

'Really. Yes,' he said, 'I would.' He waited. 'I would indeed.'

'I'll go and get the tray then, and I'll get a vase for the roses. They're very lovely,' she said. 'Thank you. It's a long time since anyone gave me roses.' Kind of hazel eyes, she thought as she went down the hall to the kitchen. Bluish greenish brownish eyes. Hazel.

'You mustn't bore people, Evelyn.' Jennifer often said that. 'People like to be asked to biggish things, Evelyn. Big dinners and big cocktail parties where they can make contact with influential people who might be useful, Evelyn. They don't like just being asked on their own to talk about gardens or flowers or heaven knows what and have a glass of that awful plonk you buy at the supermarket. Even your tea's ghastly.'

'It's Chinese green tea.'

'Precisely.' Jennifer was often snappy about the tea. 'No one wants it, Evelyn. Just get real.'

Perhaps, Evelyn thought now, Jennifer was wrong. Perhaps there were people in the world who liked to sit in small delicately furnished cottages and drink doubtful wine from excellent glasses and eat small sandwiches with the crusts left on or have cups of Chinese green tea on sultry afternoons when the light in a tiny sitting room could be shadowy and delightful.

'I didn't ask whether you'd rather have tea,' she said when she went back to the sitting room with the tray. 'I could have made tea? Chinese green tea?'

'No, no. The battery water's fine. Exactly what I'd like. Perhaps another afternoon I could have the tea, could I?'

'Certainly you could, if you'd like.' She poured the wine and handed him his glass, and put the roses in the vase. 'And a little sandwich? They're lettuce and Marmite.'

'One of my favourites.' He took one and munched reflectively. Definitely hazel eyes, she thought, and one a little darker than the other. Feet of a medium size and well shod in rather old-fashioned polished brown brogues with punch-hole decoration. Never trust a man with small feet, her mother used to say. Never trust a man with a cleft chin. Never trust a man who smiles too much. Never trust a man who doesn't polish his shoes. Never trust a man with his eyes too close together. She looked again. His feet were definitely a good medium size, even verging towards the faintly large. His eyes were wide apart, the chin uncleft. He regarded her gravely. Certainly he did not seem to smile incessantly.

'This is not at all bad,' he said, raising his glass slightly.

'Good.' She took a sandwich herself, watching him carefully.

'You'll be wondering what I want,' he said, 'and when I said you'd won another prize it's not a prize at all, really. It's nothing to do with the business or anything, but what I wondered was, if you aren't doing anything tomorrow — on Christmas Day — would you have lunch with me?' The silence seemed endless. 'And dinner, of course. Lunch and dinner. The whole day, actually. A sort of picnic.' he waited for a moment. 'But I suppose you'd be all booked up? Someone like you would be all booked up?'

Evelyn held her sandwich in one hand and the glass of battery-water wine in the other, silenced and stunned. A parade of loathsome Christmas Days glimmered in her mind. Jennifer trying to palm her off on Uncle Barry who didn't want anyone. Telling Uncle Barry to shove his dinner up his arse. The Christmas Day she had spent with Jennifer's mother. The busker with no teeth. Jennifer and Marky's friend with the ready smile and narrow eyes who had married the woman with troublesome feet. Good old Andrea always telling her she could come to Cousin Hilda's place but she'd have to wait outside because Hilda was a recluse. The parade of horrors seemed endless.

'It's quite all right,' he said, 'if you're doing something else. I've obviously given you a bit of a shock. Perhaps I've intruded. Perhaps I'd better go.' He moved to put his glass back on the tray. 'Oh, hell,' he said. 'I've messed it all up.'

'No, no.' Evelyn stood up. 'It's quite all right. It's just that I was thinking about other Christmases. I sort of lost myself for a moment. It's living by myself, I suppose — I've got unsociable. I've lost my social skills. I go into a daydream because mostly I'm left on the edge of things and no one notices what I do.'

'Look, I'll show you,' he said. 'Just come with me for a moment, and I'll show you.' He took her hand. 'Come with me and I'll show you what I mean. Please don't worry.' He led her out her own front door and they stood on the little porch. 'There you are,' he said, pointing down the street. 'I moored it there so you could see it and if I asked you to come on board for the day on Christmas Day you could see where you'd be and that it'd be quite all right. I thought if I asked you to spend Christmas Day on my boat and you couldn't see it you might think it was some kind of sardine tin and that it might sink,' he said, 'or whatever.'

'Good heavens.' Evelyn took a deep breath. He was pointing towards the yacht with turquoise sails. 'Is that yours?'

'Oddly enough, it is. I always wanted a yacht but I could never afford one and then I won Lotto just after my wife died so I thought I'd buy something I really wanted. I liked my house so I didn't feel I wanted to change that, and I liked my job so I just bought the business and stayed on, and I always wanted a Rolls-Royce so I bought one of those too. It's parked around the corner. I didn't want to block your street.'

'Good gracious,' said Evelyn. 'Actually I intended to hide in my back garden all day tomorrow so a hideous non-friend I've got — I don't even like her any more — couldn't find me and yell at me about things I didn't want to do. And then there was the awful business of the busker with no teeth and the Robinsons, whom I don't even know, and the City Mission having a waiting list for four years of people offering to help, and another friend I've got who's quite nice but mad and she has to spend Christmas with a relative who's a recluse living in a house full of cats and empty tin cans but,' she said, 'you don't want to be bored by all that. You won't even know what I'm talking about. Of course, I'd love to have a picnic tomorrow. I'd absolutely love to, really, but how will I get on board?'

'I'll row ashore and collect you. Just come out onto your upstairs balcony sometime late in the morning, perhaps about eleven, and wave something — maybe a red scarf or something bright — and I'll be watching through the binoculars. I'll row ashore immediately and get you. You can just wander down to the end of the street and I'll be there. Bring a nice sunhat and some sun cream and something to read if you think you might get bored and that's all you'll need.'

'Good heavens,' said Evelyn again. I am becoming repetitive, she thought. And probably boring, but never mind. 'Thank you very much. But I don't really even know your name.'

'Bill. Bill Thomson. I haven't ever had it put up on the building. The business still trades under the old name.'

'I see,' she said. 'Okay, then. Thank you. I don't really know what to say.'

'There's no need to say anything. Yes is quite enough.' He grinned at her suddenly. 'Perhaps you could give me another one of those sandwiches and another half glass of your excellent battery water.'

Early in the morning on Christmas Day the telephone rang again. Dawn was breaking and the sea had a silvery sheen as if to promise beautiful weather and a lovely day.

'Mother? Is that you?' It was Teddy again.

'Hello, darling. Twice in one week — this is marvellous.'

'It's Christmas morning there, is that right? I just thought I'd ring again and say Happy Christmas, and the coat probably won't come for ages but it's on its way and it'll be there sometime so you're definitely getting a parcel but I just don't know when. I wouldn't ever forget you. You know that.'

'Oh, lovely,' said Evelyn. 'Of course I do. But how are you, darling? And what on earth are you going to do for Christmas?'

Afterwards she sank back on the pillows in the big brass bed and thought about Christmas in Mongolia. Someone had had a hamper sent from London with a tin of turkey and a tin of ham and a pudding and a couple of bottles of bubbly that wasn't too bad, Teddy had said. And there was always the fermented mares' milk, which was fine when you got used to it. They were going to listen to the week's recordings and then have a kind of party and a dinner. He would be all right, she thought. The boy, as Frederick always called him, would be all right.

And she would be all right too. It was just a matter of doing a few pretty chores like picking a bunch of flowers to put on the kitchen table and rearranging the pink roses and getting dressed and packing a little bag with some sun cream and a book and her sunglasses and a hat. Maybe the black sunhat with the roses sewn under the brim, she thought, even though it might not be exactly suitable for a yacht, but she felt sure the tall man called Bill would sail quietly somewhere that was suitable for someone wearing a black hat with roses.

At that moment the telephone rang again.

'Evelyn? Is that you?' It was Marky, speaking in a peculiarly strangulated voice. 'Evelyn?'

'Hello, Marky — what's the matter?' From his tense tone she deduced that something must be wrong. Perhaps Jennifer had broken a fingernail, or the roof had fallen in.

'Evelyn, Jennifer's been taken off to hospital in the night and as I speak she'll be in theatre having emergency surgery. It's been just dreadful. You couldn't imagine the night I've spent. I know it's terribly early, but I thought you'd want to know. We had to come home early from the Robinsons' cocktail party last night and she hasn't even opened her parcels or given me mine and I can't find them.'

'I don't know what to say,' said Evelyn.

'I suppose she hasn't told you where she hid them? No? Oh, well.' He sighed deeply. 'I'll just have to wait, I suppose. Poor old Jennifer's having the most dreadful operation, Evelyn — haemorrhoids. I simply do not know how we're going to come to terms with it, Evelyn, I don't really. I mean — we've always tried to make our lives perfect, to be exquisite, Evelyn. And now — this. I can't even begin to imagine how many stitches she might have.'

'Haemorrhoids? Jennifer?'

'Haemorrhoids, Evelyn.'

'Oh dear.' This, thought Evelyn, would explain all those sudden dashes for the bathroom, the curious absences, the distracted tone and so on. Poor old Jennifer, all manicured and made up to hell, had been rushing off, in 'difficulties', to the loo.

'I'm not sure "Oh dear" is a very adequate remark, Evelyn.'

'I don't know what else to say, Marky. I'm most fearfully sorry about it all but I don't know what else to say.'

'You could ask me to Christmas dinner for starters. Whatever am I going to do now with Jen in hospital? It's the least you could do after all our years of friendship. There's no one to get a meal for me or give me a decent sort of a day. What I thought was, "Good old Evelyn won't be doing anything — I'll take the turkey over to her place if the poor old girl hasn't got one of her own and she can bash about and whip me up my Christmas dinner." You can have some too, of course. I have to be at the hospital at five to see Jennifer and there could be some washing I can bring back for you to do and meanwhile you can put the turkey in the oven and do the vegetables. I'll bring over a couple of bottles of Moët and you can get them chilled ready for when I come back. And, Evelyn' — his voice lowered to a conspiratorial depth — 'I may even stay over.' He chuckled richly. 'Don't think I haven't noticed that you've got wonderful legs and a really neat waist and beautiful boobs. So I might very well stay over and give you a bit of a thrill, but we must never tell Jennifer and it can only be the once. It can be a memory to treasure all your life.'

'I beg your pardon?'

'Don't be coy, Evelyn. You know what I mean.'

'It's impossible. To start with I don't even like you, Mark. And I'm doing something else today. I'm going to be away all day sailing around the harbour on a beautiful yacht with turquoise sails that's owned by a man who's also got a Rolls-Royce.' These were the sort of statistics that would wound Mark the most.

'Don't tell such stupid lies, Evelyn. You're being very silly.'

'No, I'm not. And I'll have to go now because I've got to pick some flowers and choose my sunhat and pack a little bag with sun cream and a book, so I'll have to say goodbye, Mark.' I must take a cheerful book too, she thought — not the one about that sergeant.

'Who on earth would believe such a load of nonsense, Evelyn? Don't be so silly. I hope you know, Evelyn, that if you don't have me to dinner and offer some help to your poor, poor old friend Jennifer, who's remained loyal to you no matter what, I feel this is the end of our friendship.' He spoke heavily.

'I do know that, Mark. Goodbye.'

'Evelyn, I haven't said a word to anyone about this, even Jennifer,' — his voice became deeper, and the tone heavier than ever — 'but I'm in deep, deep shit with that development of mine over on the point. I just happened to use quite a bit of kiln-dried timber over there and all those townhouses are rotting, Evelyn, after only six months. Some of the balconies have already fallen off. Come New Year and I'm going to be taken to the cleaners over it, Evelyn. I'm going to go belly-up. And that bloody awful son of Jen's is also in deep shit over shonky motor deals. You've got no idea what trouble we're in. I need sympathy and kindness, Evelyn. I need oblivion. And I need someone to break all this news to Jennifer because I just can't bring myself to tell her. You'll have to do it, Evelyn.'

'I'm sorry, Mark. I can't help you. I'm going on the yacht with turquoise sails for the day.'

'But who'll do Jennifer's washing? And how will I cope when she comes out of hospital? And what will I say to her when I have to take her Christmas diamond bracelet back to the shop and get a refund? I'm going to need every cent I can raise.'

'I don't know. Maybe you'll have to do the washing yourself and Jennifer will just have to get herself and her arse sorted out and she'll have to manage without the bracelet. Cheerio.'

'This is the end, Evelyn. I'm shattered that you're so disloyal.'

'I know. I am, aren't I? Goodbye.'

Frederick's old binoculars were in the bottom drawer of the desk so she went downstairs in her white night-gown to find them. Such feelings of despair, rejection and horror had come upon her slowly and relentlessly in the past few years that she suddenly wondered if the yacht might have gone, and Bill Thomson an apparition she had conjured up out of nowhere.

The air outside on her balcony was crisp and beautiful and scented lightly with flowers. She sank down carefully onto her knees and crawled slowly out one of the French doors, which she had opened just wide enough to allow her to squeeze through. Poised beneath the level of the top bar of the balcony railing and thus hidden, she raised the binoculars and stared out secretly through the trellis and all the leaves and flowers from vines that had clambered up there. On the deck of the yacht, sitting in one of the turquoise canvas chairs, was the tall figure of a man reading a newspaper. Bill Thomson. So he was still there, oblivious to her uncertain and illicit inspection. The yacht was still there. Everything existed just as it had done the day before. Christmas Day would indeed occur as arranged. When she waved a red towel about eleven in the morning he would see her, and would row ashore to get her.

The old clock in the kitchen struck nine so she had a couple of hours at least to sew another rose on her sunhat, lie in the bath looking at the stencils of leaves and vines with no idea of abandonment or loneliness, and choose what to wear. How delicious, she thought. How charming. And she went off swiftly through the little house to begin it all.